D1586044

INTOXICATED

Terrey McCormack

ISBN 978-1-78222-881-3

Book design, layout and production management by Into Print
www.intoprint.net
+44 (0)1604 832149

When you combine natural narcissism
with the basic need for self-esteem,
you create a creature who has to feel
himself an object of primary value:
first in the universe, representing in
himself all of life.

ERNEST BECKER,
THE DENIAL OF DEATH

There is no such thing as the essence
of woman because woman averts, she is
averted of herself.

JACQUES DERRIDA,
SPURS: NIETZSCHE'S STYLES

Reality no longer has the time to take on the appearance of reality. It no longer even surpasses fiction: it captures every dream even before it takes on the appearance of a dream.

JEAN BAUDRILLARD,
THE ORDERS OF SIMULACRA

PART 1

1

SHE WOKE EARLY, to find her father's severed head on the white pillow next to her...

There it was, staring up, all wretched and torn in a ghoulish smirk. She remembered being cold – at home in her flat at London's Chelsea Harbour. No, she was hot, and at her apartment on Gran Canaria – Puerto Mogan – under a glossy, silent sunshine. Francine Coy, naked on the bed, became momentarily iridescent. She'd been floating in a big dream, in an enormous light: that of the island's dawn. Magically, she attempted to focus on what appeared to be a visible silence in the luminous room, then gave a brief shriek, which caused her to feel outside of herself, she felt. *Somehow drifting. Somehow not-here.* Somehow, detached from the creature she'd believed she'd become in her 32-years on the planet, she opened her eyes fully to see that it was her American boyfriend, Joel Maize, who was beside her in this light, and not her father's head. She blinked in mild astonishment.

Small mercies. Joel didn't stir. He was dealing privately with the remains of his own ultra-bad dream, of which his unconscious mind had grown tragically, if not comically, accustomed to...

It was a terrible, deep-cutting dream, which caused him to groan in his sleep. Indeed, Joel regularly had dreams that altered the way he actually woke up. He had dreams that were still in animation, as he woke! *Burning breasts flopped with a chunk of tattooed, naked buttock all around him,* yet still he didn't stir – even though Francine squirmed a little next to him. She gave a little-girl stretch while coming to. As a response to this, in the sticky, hot morning light, Joel gave a conscious shudder as his dream grew paler, its movements becoming slower. For he'd recently murdered someone

6

in New York, though Francine didn't know this – would never know this. Hence, perhaps, the dream he was having. Already vague.

It was a bum in the back-streets who'd approached him for money while he was coming down from some heavy drugs. An unfortunate move. It was before he left for London, before they all came out to Gran Canaria in search of what should have been the ultimate paradise. "I'll cut your goddamn heart out!" he had screamed. And he did, too. The bum stood little chance. Joel didn't mess around when he was coming down. He was shit-hot with a blade when it came to it. And it came to it then, in the New York dark, inside the Big Apple – blood spattering his killer's face. Over in seconds. No one looked into the incident. No one *would* be looking into the incident. Joel Maize, the bum's killer, would get away with his lowly deed. Bums in New York, it seemed, were killed almost every day anyway – or died under mysterious circumstances. Who freaking cared? Joel thought. Inadvertently, then, it was wise of Francine not to wake her lover, as she at first wanted to, who used drugs like some use drink, and tended not to be in a good mood when woken early. Joel boozed drugs, in fact. He lowered them by the tankard. By the frantic mug-full. Francine, somewhat delicately, only ever did cocaine, of which Joel would use as an aperitif…

Paradise, was the first word that settled in her privileged and protected brain, as it came to on that hot day, in that eventful year – all those years ago. Joel, coma-rising, let out a weighty fart in this paradise, which turned this pristine air blue. It turned it sour. It was a hot, twisting, stream-of-consciousness type of fart, borne from a bowel that could have been, well, not privileged. Rancid from all the shit it had surmounted over the years, a bowel fart-squeezed-in

7

for ages; farts held at the director's side on set, next to the camera, where Joel normally worked, and where, over recent years, he'd held these terrible farts in (he needed to see someone about his bowels, man). While grinning like the idiot the holding-in of them was making him look, Joel became luminous in unconscious distortion: his vague but waking mind felt it was outdoors with a plastic cup of coffee, shivering on the job: fuck it! He let it rip. And out it came in reality, in the room. No probs.

When Joel Maize met Francine Coy way back when he told her he was a gofor to get her sympathies – and ultimately her body. To say nothing of her money. But that's for later. However, he was actually an assistant-director to a small indi-crew of under-funded film-makers – if such a role existed in such a small outfit. But it did here. And they'd made three films in two years about moody loners crossing America in five days. True, none of them reached the box-office as they should have done – (hence Joel's pathological frustration, perhaps) but they were good movies. They should have reached the box-office. Joel and his crew had something – were good at something, once.

CRASH! came Francine's silent vision of a mythical paradise made semi-excellent from never once having to worry about money. Yes, Joel's smell grounded her. It hit her where she lived.

In a single reactionary second to this, she whacked him on his bare buttocks – which were riding up in the air in a mound of ape-haired fuzz – and the fizz of pain his brain sleepily registered became part of the fading horror-dream the same organ was unconsciously giving to the screen of his mind. Golden brown. Aw, man! So, from sipping coffee while farting luxuriously outdoors, Joel now, on this screen, visualized a distant summer back in New York State where he grew up. He was a little boy, and he'd just killed his sister's kitten by strangling it in front of her. (This was actually the beginning of Joel's on/off killing-career). Consequently, his father took him outside in the yard and, not to put too fine a point on it, beat the crap out of him. He beat him up in a very big way – having no other response: fists and all. Joel was left for dead with broken ribs, a fractured jaw, internal bruising, concussion and folded kidneys. (What was that about violence begetting violence?) The sister was screaming. The father was screaming. The mother was screaming. He woke up… screaming! 'Ahhhhhigh! What the fucking hell are you doing!' Francine was still slapping him hard when he snatched at her wrist… psychopathically.

'You've stunk the room out, you slob!' she bawled.

'Ahhhhhhigh! Where am I? I'll fucking kill you!' He gave a spit-slobbering shake of the head, then a dead-eye, crazy glare as he squeezed Francine's wrist vice-like from his somnolent cataclysm.

Francine cavorted, no, cascaded out of bed as she slipped his firm hold and stood before him in the bright room, most nakedly. She was a woman with a lot on her mind these days. There was, after all, much to do. But nobody, oh, nobody, had ever attempted to grip her like that before!

The light brought out blondish hairs, Joel observed, and longish curves. It had brought out fleshy shapes and manicured grooves – sparklingly. Her grinning, roundish, somewhat sinister face – that ultra-wide, sensuous mouth of hers – was being dazzled in a director's harsh light. Pan back, boy. Joel was now at work. He'd been woken, sure. But hey, now he was creating. For it was a vision of heterosexual heaven had his mind been working in, for him, the correct order. (Violence too being a part of that integral arrangement). Home in on the snatch. His dream-time fart

9

had made Francine angry, and, in turn, the slapping had made him consider punching her in a big way. Really. In a big, American Misogynist's way, of which his father had been the perfect example. Wha? Chill, bro. Sex lay dormant for at least a minute now. Joel was still, he kind of reckoned in this minute, only semi-conscious anyway.

'How dare you speak to me like that! Daddy was right. You're a no-good yank!' And with that Francine comically stormed to the en-suite for a swift pee, most indignant.

Wondering what the fuck he was doing here, Joel sleepily rubbed his tiny ass in her manic absence, then scowled at this absence enormously. He glanced at the brightness throughout the room brought on by this absence as though glancing at a snorting pig, itself glancing at brightness while suddenly becoming mysteriously conscious via the sudden appearance of a cerebral cortex, and appeared shocked at this brightness – which indeed he was, looking disconcerted momentarily – which indeed he was too. He now felt rightly pissed-off. Ahh. Shame. So he farted again with malice and terrible soft noise, then nestled back into the white-hot pillow for more ultra-cool shut-eye, smiling an assassin's smile. He immediately spun in a glib darkness to the sound of a strangled cat's mewing, vaguely wondering what the hell he was doing in goddamn mother-fucking Gran Canaria!

A vision of Francine came crashing back into the bedroom like some crazed pantomime character, talking in what appeared to be a gift-of-tongues babble to Joel's howling dark. *O no it isn't!* Her voice, Joel figured, now that she was up and ready to get this trip under way, intermingled with the dream-time sobs of his little sister echoing from 20-odd years previously. Weirdly, it could have been argued, if anything was to be said, which engendered an

10

eerie, after-life sort of sound that could only be described as haunting – which it was beginning to do – as Joel broke surface once more. 'Shit,' he gasped in terrible being-led-to-the-gas-chamber displeasure.

'Yes, shit. Exactly!' She stood over him, hands on hips, long hair aflow, occasionally swished back. 'Get up, you lazy pig! Remember, we've got things to do here. This isn't just a holiday, you know! You can't stay in bed til lunchtime like you normally do!' And with that the purposeful Francine pulled the single blue sheet from Joel's half-tanned, almost-effeminate body, who, while squinting upwards as though viewing the same world from the awesome eye of a cramped spacecraft, was still convinced that he was dreaming. He had to be, man, he calmly reasoned.

The moment seemed to hit him right in the chest.

Whump! His unexercised heart gave a sudden, unexercised shudder, which made *him* shudder. But it was only a dream. His heart shuddered only in his mind. Yet he was still dreaming as he came to, when his father stamped heavily on his face "Why, I oughta…" A raised hand as well.

Jesus. And why did his skin sting so? 'Dad?' he said, then said no more. The heart-shudder made him dizzy. Or was it the drugs? He couldn't tell. Whichever, it silenced him anyhow, anyway, good and proper – as street-gangs used to silence him through threats when he was a kid. But then, focusing on Francine slipping her G-string over those long, taut, brown-lovely thighs of hers, and covering that lovely bulb of bliss with it, and then, searching for a T-shirt with the thing firmly in place – all the bending down, all the opening of drawers – he felt suddenly fabulous as her voice definitely calmed. Ah yes. A sexual-promise kind of fabulous, this. A mind-blowing fabulous in the mysterious land of sexual-promises. This, he reasoned, was why he was

11

on vacation! Yiiisss!

Unfortunately for him, it was short-lived. 'Daddy didn't come home last night!' Francine then manically mangled in the light of Joel's swelling loins.

He rubbed his short dyed hair painfully, which made a fuzzy bristling sound. He then rubbed his long and weary 31-year-old face with the same early-morning palm, and sighed. Oh, for God's sake! Johnny didn't come home last night? He stayed out? Shit. How fucking terrible can it get! 'He's a big boy, Fran. Chill the fuck out. Like, big D. He'll be okay.' Joel's loins, wherever they were, had become hard. Yes, a hard-on, he was pleased to discover, yawning terribly. Laying there on the bed like a vacant walrus fondling the thing in full view of his lover, who never once glanced its debauched way, he popped the question. No, not that one. He asked for a tit-fuck, astonishingly.

On fierce rejection, he glanced outside and pulled it himself. Yikes! The home-boy American abroad! This wasn't supposed to be the deal, though. He hadn't flown all this fucking way just to put one over his own wrist!

12

2

THE PORT OF Mogan was a slightly strange and mysterious out-of-the-way little place on Gran Canaria. It lay beneath even more mysteriously vast mountains, which gave it the appearance of a dramatic location. Comically, that's why Francine's father, Johnny, (59 – age being relevant to our story) of whom more in a moment, had bought this traditional green and white apartment many years ago because he fancied himself as a slightly strange and mysterious little man: it suited his character.

Indeed Johnny had, at one stage, used the apartment as nothing more than a sex-den for his myriad – though inexplicably willing – female fans. This lasted until he was 49/50, which was the age when sex suddenly became too much for Johnny to handle. Now he, along with Francine, Joel, and Francine's two gay friends, Stevie (39) and Bernie (29), were here to rendezvous with a certain man with a certain injection – of which a lot more later. Promises, promises.

For it had become Francine's dream in recent years (an immortality-dream of old) to experience immense longevity with those she felt closest to: namely, for reasons unknown, the above four. And by immense longevity she imagined herself living for hundreds of years. Hundreds and hundreds of years. This had been promised to her (and a handful of other ultra-rich, naive people who could pay the price) by a rogue scientist, of which, from the mid 20th-century onwards, there appeared to always be a glut.

Now then, Johnny, Johnny Coy, the ex-has-been pop-star from the band The Wallbeats, who were famous in the late 1960s, (he played bass moodily in this drab outfit) was a multi-millionaire thanks to careful investments. He had been that way since those days: decades of living as

13

a millionaire – of having just what you want and when – not to mention *how!* This had also (paradoxically) prevented him from being aware what effects his words could have on others, as we'll see. Indeed Johnny had become totally oblivious to words. Francine, on the other hand, the apple of his drugged eye, a fickle lady certainly, indulged-in and vastly privileged nonetheless, *was* aware to a degree of the effects her words had on others, and had begun to name, during recent times, what she truly wanted. What she really-really wanted. (Hadn't she always?). She'd been twisting Johnny's bony arm – even though she was hugely wealthy herself because of his investments for her – to come along for the ride: this naming of the impossible which she'd read about. She wanted the ultimate. She wanted the best thing a girl could ever have: semi-friends, millions in the bank, and a few hundred years on the planet, thank you very much. Yes. That was perfect to her – as long as you didn't age along with it. That'd do nicely. That was what she was now naming, what she really-really wanted. The Nano-injection!

She'd begun to pursue it, and, in the consequence, it had become her heart's golden desire. After all, she had everything else; now, at 32-going-on-33, before it all started to go wrong, she wanted the ultimate everything. She wanted to live for virtually ever – with all the money, the beauty, the opulence – but as she was then, intact, and with those she, ah, loved. Yes, she wanted time to stand still for her as it zoomed off for the rest of the silly world! Brilliant! And Johnny, the oblivious father, who would do all in his considerable power to get it for her, was going to oblige yet again. No problem, doll. And for himself as well, of course! For it was true what Francine had said: he would need to be there to look after her. He would need to be there to take care of her.

14

But how to acquire this fabulous dream?

Francine had developed a superficial interest in science. A pseudo-interest, it could have been said, if even that. But she took it very seriously. She'd acquired a pretend sense-of-importance towards the subject. Or, to be more precise, nanotechnology. Somewhere along the way Francine had accidentally read (possibly in a magazine at her gynaecologist's waiting-room) that nanotechnology was being engineered to prolong life by creating submicroscopic robots which could be injected into the bloodstream and actually live off the blood for three centuries or so. They would thereby devote themselves to maintaining the entire system that sustained them, by cutting away things like tumours and clot-formations – prolonging the host's life-span almost indefinitely. It was a you-scratch-my-back-robotic deal. That's what she'd read, anyway.

She had then, after further investigations, been informed that an ultra-expensive injection would be available shortly – in the first years of the new century – this being the summer of 1999. Thank God for rogue scientists, she had thought.

The price, indeed, wouldn't even come into it. Daddy was worth millions, and so was she. Millions, she knew, grew out of millions. For obvious reasons, though, the injection would have to be kept a secret. (Would it? And was it obvious? Was anything ever obvious?) Well, yes, to Francine, who had read this, and, curiously, believed it. Why shouldn't she? She believed it like nothing else she had believed before. In fact she believed *in it*. The ideology of rich and poor appealed to her immensely too, on the quiet. She was rich, which meant, somehow in the privacy of her mind, that she was better. Best. Superior. She deserved to live forever. But what appealed to her most, perhaps, was

15

that, according to the somewhat fanciful article, the participants would never age. Yes. That's what really did it, what really-really did it. They would remain forever young. *She*, to be more exact, would remain FOREVER YOUNG. FOR-EVER, *YOUNG*! Imagine it. Queen Francine! These nano-robots would apparently destroy whatever it was that turned your skin all wrinkly, your bones to powder, your eyesight into haze, your blood into water, your bowels into thin, torn-pockets, your skin to a transparent, vein-showing covering, and your hair into grain, to nothingness, or just sun-glare white.

'Fucking hell…' Francine had whispered in the quiet waiting-room, her eyes all dusty. 'Imagine it?' She had since discovered, or perhaps imagined, that a man had already prepared these very nano-robots and was surreptitiously selling an injection of them for the price of a Formula-1 racing car. That is, for a lot of money. One shot. He gets rich. You live for an awful long time. Deal? But it must have been a reality because Johnny had made contact, and it had been arranged that they'd meet on Gran Canaria, of all places – as that was convenient for both parties at the time. Somewhere out-of-the-way. Johnny had also said that there would be two injections required (still a lot of money) and not five as Francine had wished for and believed. The other three would be given a harmless liquid, at Johnny's request. No way was Johnny paying for Francine's jerk-off friends to live forever. No way. They'd never know anyway. It wouldn't begin to show for years. By that time Francine would have come to her senses, Johnny reasoned. She'd have met other people as well. She'd have moved on.

She had met Stevie and Bernie, for example, one night in Soho. They had, in their time, been her moving-on. She had drunkenly intervened on an argument they were having and had histrionically arrested them. Francine then invited them both back to her lavish flat for some expensive, pure cocaine. Wow, twice over! Bernie was originally from Wolverhampton, but had lost his devastating accent in London while trying hard for many years to do such a thing – to disguise it. In the end he didn't have to try any more. The vowels simply rounded. However, two situations would tiresomely drag it back with unmitigated avengeance from wherever it had taken refuge: (a) when Bernie was instantly excited, where a kind of high-pitched, *Look at all them chimneys* would burst forth, and, *We havn't got any monay?* Or (b) when he was desperately and hornily drunk, and his tall lover, Stevie, (himself from London with the accent Bernie had always longed for) had his long prick so far up his arse that Bernie could feel his eyes actually bursting out onto his split cheekbones like someone roasting in the Electric Chair: *Yaw splitting me in two! Stop!*

Neither Bernie nor Stevie did coke that night: they were much too agog at being in a fabulous flat in The Tower at Chelsea Harbour. Wow! Oh, my dear! But, jokingly, (and what humour it was) Francine leapt from a huge chair and began kissing Stevie on the mouth as a jealous lover, to which the latter had immediate, if not mixed (no erection) emotions. While Bernie, limp-wristed and cognitive, simply watched in an appalled air. Later she would say that she did this to stop Stevie pontificating about the post-horrors of Margaret Thatcher – a dame Daddy admired only too well in his musings. But in truth it was done as confirmation to Francine that Stevie was actually gay and not just pretending in order to appear initially cool and interesting for Bernie to fall in love with – thereby fucking with his mind as some straight men had done with gays, Francine knew. She found him devastatingly, instantly, spectacularly attractive! Indeed

17

Stevie could turn the sternest female head in any restaurant, bar, art-gallery, hair-dressers, road. His entire demeanour was a provocative come-on to any heterosexual woman. To all women. But he only had eyes for his own sex. And the kiss in Francine's apartment confirmed this. For Stevie, in a mad moment, quickly wiped his mouth, pushed her away melodramatically, felt crazed, squatted, jumped upwards, said Ugh with intense malice, felt ill, spat like a little boy tasting something bitter, shuddered extravagantly, sighed thespianically. Francine laughed so much that she actually pissed herself. Possibly out of disappointment. She peed her pricey knickers where she stood, then fell back onto her crazily expensive ultra-soft sofa. But a semi-loyal friendship was seemingly born... one that could last for, well, hundreds of years.

3

JOHNNY COY LAY snoring in the third and smallest bedroom to the apartment. It was the one he used as a masturbatorial den when two of his nameless female fans had, on firm request, got down to it together in the main bedroom as the man himself voyeured through a spyhole – which was still there, somewhere. And why shouldn't he? He had often told himself, in a kind of guilt-ridden suppression, that it was the pop-star's duty to do such things – especially when the law had on occasion felt his little collar. Why shouldn't he gape through a gap at two girls licking the shit out of each other? He could afford it, was his usual classic reply. It was a bloody good turn-on. It made for a bloody good wank. And so Johnny, a bloody good wanker, lay dreaming of all the young girls and boys he'd watched fucking over the years – all their sucking, their licking, their private entering of every fuckable orifice – watched without ever knowing they were watched, without ever knowing they were being used – giving pleasure to where it wasn't strictly intended…

Johnny twitched as, in the bright, morning dream, someone ominous came into the room he was wanking in, and, in full eye-squinting view, gazed upon him in monstrous awe. In shocking terror. Gulp, went Johnny's subconscious little throat. In reality it was Francine entering the room to see if he'd returned home from last night. To see if he'd finally gone to bed. He had, but only just. For Johnny had sat moodily drinking (the intense bass player still) in a dark, seedy bar until the radiant early hours, thinking only of how he could get people to listen to him once again as they had done when he was a young and hip rocker.

For the group The Wallbeats actually survived into the early 1970s. They became, for a period, a glam-rock band

– *glam-rock* being a terminology conceived many years after the event, Johnny was only too happy to remind the odd stray journalist who, for some reason, still wanted to interview him. And who could forget them? Who could forget The Wallbeats? Famous for songs like, *Didn't He Want You?* and *Who Says You Can't?* and *Why Say No When You Can Say Yes?* and *If Only I'd Met You Yesterday?* and *Why Are You A Bad Girl?* and *Isn't It Time We Broke Up Susie?* They regarded themselves as intellectually interesting – interestingly. No. No one would/could forget them. The Wallbeats would be remembered in musical history just as importantly as Arnold Schoenberg.

"Who?" Johnny would seriously ask if ever that was said to him. "Was he a solo-artist?" But everyone had forgotten them. Everyone had forgotten The Wallbeats. What had gone wrong? That wasn't part of the plan. No one knew who The Wallbeats were any more, even though they'd had many number-1s. This pissed Johnny off to the very core of the very quarks in his very atoms. But it was Johnny, not the other members, who had become a multi-millionaire because of sound investments at the time. He wasn't rich through fame alone. He happened to have a friend who knew a clever accountant. It was the clever accountant who, in turn, advised Johnny to invest his hundreds-of-thousands wisely, in the long-term. Johnny did. He never looked back. But how come he'd always get desperate when booze-wrecked and (aggressively, but without the physicality to ever carry violence off) feel the overwhelming urge to run round telling people who he was and even hitting them if they didn't remember? For Johnny didn't quite surmount that glam-page in glam-history. *He wanted the fame!* It was still with him in 1999: why didn't anyone know who he was? Consequently voyeurism (along with simplistic right-wingism – the given debaucheries documented therein) remained to date his ultimate sexual undertaking, and, needless to say, he'd been secretly watching his own daughter coupling with the panting American Psycho – which was, seemingly, the ultimate-ultimate turn-on for him. Ouch! Yes. To watch, ah, one's own daughter, ah – but that could never be said. It could never be spoken about. Johnny would never allow the words of this sentiment to actually form in his half-crazed mind. But he nonetheless felt its abstraction very deeply. He felt it like a lump. For he'd known about it since Francine was six, this sexual-love for her. He'd had this lump for 26-years! The words, though, could never be heard. Could never be said. That would be sacrilege in his misplaced ideology. The lump was a silent covenant between himself and what Johnny would regard as his soul. It was between himself and himself, he'd say to himself. But the desire of it? Oh. The desire! That was a burning one all right. That set him on fire! Indeed the words, had they been spoken, would only kill the craving. Would only put water on the sizzling lust. (Was there a song there?) Fortunately words and Johnny had never really been the best of mates. They'd never been in bed together. Johnny was, after all, a musician. Others wrote the lyrics…

However, the manner in which he acted and spoke whenever his opinion was sought concerning musical, or, more terrifyingly, political, matters possibly went beyond an exalted image of himself. Indeed exalted didn't really do it justice. But he could be amusing. For Johnny would give much credence to his opinions – his head would bow solemnly as he spoke them. It would then get stuck up his fetid arsehole. People would laugh: Johnny would take the credit for being funny, when he was trying to be intelligent…

And so it was, as the hateful clock ticked away that

21

sparkling morning, with Johnny Coy now surrealistically dreaming of laying the law down to people who, in his view, needed it, and his daughter entering to see if he was really there, to see if he was alive, that he opened his eyes and said, 'What the fuck do you want?' hyper-groggily, hyper-unpleasantly.

Francine had murmured something about *If only, daddy.* Or, *Tell me, daddy.* Or something like that. And, after two and a half hours of sleep and three bottles of white wine Johnny simply sat up in bed and rubbed his rubbery-wrinkly face. Yes, the world needed to hear his words of wisdom yet again, it seemed. Also, a 30-year-ingestion of pure amphetamine saw to it that Johnny no longer needed a full night's sleep anyway. Two, three hours? That did it. And food. Oh, don't mention food!

'Has he phoned or something? What do you want, Francine? It's very, ah, very early!' Still with his leather trousers on – a bared, barrelled, minuscule chest – he reached under the single silken bed-sheet and rubbed his aching, world-weary knees. But again, the sense of unimaginable freedom that big money brings settled naturally into his psyche like a summer breeze across glinting wheatfields, and his mind actually smiled – even though his face didn't register the mandate.

'I thought you were going to get an early night, daddy?'

'Hey? What for? Oh yes. You're right. I was. Well, I didn't, did I. But it doesn't matter. Look, we're fine. Everything's fine.' He waved her away, then sleepily removed the sheet and slid to the corner of the naked bed. He unconsciously showed Francine his ancient leathers – which didn't disconcert her in the least – as perhaps they should have done. (Leather trousers? In Gran Canaria?) He was in pain, somewhere. That little worn-out body of his was definitely

22

hurting. But he didn't want to show that. No fucking way. Not to the only female he'd ever truly, truly loved. It was his tiny bones, he reckoned. They throbbed. No. They ached. That's what it was. But no matter. The old Nano-injection would take care of that. Yes. That would sort Johnny's hate-world joints out all right. (It was a philosophical question never asked: why were millionaires always filled with so much hatred?) Odd, for at this particular period in history not many people alive could recall the powerful sense of optimism felt by many during the early to mid 1970s, as could Johnny. Even though he kept it to himself. Anything could have happened, then, it seemed. There was a tangible sense at that period that anything was seemingly possible in the futuristic human condition. Things were taken more seriously. Was this why Johnny hated so? Because all that optimism had gone? No. He wasn't that deep.

But it was only for some that the 1970s was a fulfillment of what the 1960s was about. The 1980s would, for the same *some*, crush all that optimism for all but the greedy as opposed to the hungry, it could be argued. And yes, Johnny Coy was once hungry. He had been hungry. Not hungry like a struggling boxer, say, from some shit-hole estate. But hungry. Hungry for fame? Love? Money? He was once genuinely optimistic. Now, though, Johnny only believed in his adorable daughter and his idea of a nanotechnological ideal! He knew, in his icy heart, that it'd be a panacea for the rich. It had to be. Hence more hatred, as it mightn't work. (Johnny had seriously needed therapy). But no, nano-technology, via his daughter, was the thing that had been designed to come into Johnny's very important life: the time was right for it. *It fucking would work!* And so, without being aware of it, greed and abomination had gloomily descended on Johnny's weak spirit. His 70s-optimism had been transmogrified into something quite the opposite. And it is in this state, this condition, that we first find him, that we first meet him.

Select, was the word that now settled in Johnny's under-used, money-elite, empty brain, as he came to on that distant, shining morning. Paradise? No way. Too wishy-washy. Too girly. He'd had all that shit anyway. Yeah. Fuck paradise, he vaguely thought. He'd lived the paradise ideal all his adult life! 'Get me his number,' he then growled. 'I'll call the cunt…' Yes, Johnny Coy falsely believed that he was a great musician. This greatness, he knew, had to continue. It had to go on. Johnny Coy believed that, as a great musician, his greatness was there for a purpose – that of informing the world *of* his greatness – and he wanted buildings for superficial music studies to be named after him. That's what also had been brewing, somewhere.

24

CAN MOLECULES BE built by pushing atoms together?

Francine pondered this profundity, bereft of any knowledge concerning either molecules or atoms, as she calmly ate her lunch some hours later on the sunny patio. Can they? she mentally pursued, without even knowing what *they* were. The harbour's salted air drifted hotly over the apartment in the searing sun, while she sat baking her already-tanned back. She was wearing a brief green bikini and sunglasses, with a pale-blue baseball cap turned back-to-front. Not, it has to be said, as a fashion-accessory – cognizant as Francine was of fashion. But simply to keep the sun from burning her paler, easily-burnt petite neck. Bernie had camply rustled up the food and organized the lunch: local fish, salad, bread, champagne-glinting cutlery, a separate dressing for the greens, a sparkling table-cloth over the worn-out sunburnt furniture – cut glass shimmering in the intense blue light. He was the perfect housewife, naturally. Or, at least he was for Stevie, who sat watching his pussy bend as he brought things out onto the private patio from the kitchen and arrange them neatly on the large wooden table. Yes, he would fuck that pussy later, he darkly mused. Solidly. Imperially. He'd pour champagne over it.

The boiling air appeared to visibly rise from the quiet harbour as Bernie moved this pussy. It rose as though ribbed in deeper grooves of heat that had even larger waves of salt in them. This then added to what looked like an actual salt-haze billowing up over the brown mountains behind, turning, curling, then back out again across the stinging Atlantic Ocean in a kind of illusory shimmer. It somehow engendered the notion of silence everywhere. It was as though the mountains were in confession. Or to at least

25

speak in a whisper. It was odd. There wasn't a sound. And Johnny spoke in a whisper. He said, 'What have you done with my mobile, you fucking turd-burglar?' It was the hard-done-to Bernie he was addressing, who simply ignored him in sullen hauteur.

'Daddy…'

'D'yer know,' pondered Stevie in some sort of protection, 'I haven't heard a phrase like that since I was 12. Well said, Johnny, you illiterate dunce!' He shook his head in slow dismay.

Johnny glanced at him swiftly, angrily. 'My mobile's gone missing, and I reckon he's a thief!' He pointed with lowly derision at busy Bernie, who, no thief, was now about to sit down.

'Here it is,' sighed Joel casually. 'Is this it?' He pulled a sleek slim mobile out from under a pressed napkin and held it up in the shining air, shining. It was Johnny's all right.

'So it was you, was it!' Johnny snatched the thing from him mightily nastily. 'Fucking yank. You lot'd steal anything given the fucking chance! You're all bandits. A robbing lot. You stole… Canada!' He added that sparkling notion without much conviction.

'Yeah, right.' Joel laughed at him. He'd already taken a handful of amphetamine pills to counteract the effect of being woken and virtually dragged out of bed at dawn – a deed he still wasn't sure of – and these were making him distinctly, if not warmly, happy. Oh. Lovely. All sparkley. All filled with an understanding for one's fellow man. Although Johnny did push this induced-axiom to the edge. But why dawn, huh? Aw, who cared anyway. Only Francine knew, and, as she was paying for this long-life injection-deal, well, Joel was fucked if he was going to like argue over it, as indeed he would have done had he not taken speed. Had

26

it been any other mother-fucking situation with any other mother-fucking dude? Yikes! But the drugs, man! Hmmm! Such a lovely feeling, so early in the goddamn day. Ooh. Chill, bro! thought Joel, chilling…

'Daddy, please. No one wanted to steal your mobile. You simply misplaced it, that's all. Oh, for God's sake! Why are you always so angry!' Francine said all that with a full mouth of oily fish and salad. She then turned away into the beaming sunshine to swallow this load, and moodily took a sip of spicy champagne to wash it all down. Bubbles enhanced the strong taste of fish like an internal firework. So, pop! went her sunbaked skull. And then she added, 'Daddy, you look terrible, by the way,' as though she subconsciously loathed the idea that her father's head wasn't on the pillow next to her when she woke up, but, as with her father and her father's ultimate fetish, the words of wanting him dead would never actually form on her sweet tongue. Indeed the notion which engendered them was too vague anyway. For daddy would always be there: he'd always be around. Death wasn't an option for him. He was one of the *undead*.

'Yeah,' Joel ganged up. 'Are you all right, huh? You look like shit, man.' And he laughed again, but more out of how the stolen pills were making him feel than anything else…

Johnny ceased all movement. 'What? What is it?' Slowly he drew a cold hand to his sickly cheek and tremulously touched it. Three bottles of vodka a day had taken their toll on his skin all right. Not to mention his green and wooden liver. The vodka had been required in order to give him the semblance of normality. Now, Johnny's skin probably looked more like the abnormal liver, which had ever-so-slightly extended either side of his tiny ribcage to give his little body the peculiar and misshapen appearance of having a gut.

27

'You look like a corpse, I think they mean,' Bernie added, now tentatively eating himself as he'd finished his voluntary waiting-on routine. He gave a wry, sly, shrinking grin at Stevie, who popped out his tongue and pointedly ran it round the air seductively. Bernie smiled most coyly, down at his bright salad there. A glow-red smile.

The patio backed onto the sheltered harbour, which was surrounded by fat palm trees and, as has been said, curtained by huge burnt mountains. They kind of augmented the port's setting, giving it the appearance, in another light, more of a south-seas location than dramatic. Stevie always commented on their strange beauty whenever he'd been to stay – their curious, other-worldly stillness – whenever he sat to eat on this patio. He always commented on the port's setting as well, in the handful of times he'd been there as a guest. And he was about to do the same then, in a prosaic manner, but the set-to with Johnny, as Stevie was, despite it all, easily-affected, halted the twee preamble.

'Look,' sighed Francine firmly, placing her silver knife and fork down flatly, 'we're here to meet someone who is going to give us long life. Saturday will be the first day of the next three-hundred years, hopefully! We should be jubilant. Be happy! It's absolutely fantastic!' She raised her hands as she said that in fickle staginess. 'I can't believe you're all arguing…'

'I'm not arguing,' said Bernie, eating.

Johnny sneered in the knowledge of deceiving the others. Only he and Francine would be doing the living, he darkly mused. The rest were as fucked as everybody else, hee-hee-hee! Falsely he said, 'You're right, darling. I'm going to turn over a new leaf from today. It is fantastic. I'm sorry. Lads, I spoke to our man earlier. Everything's on for, as Francine says, Saturday.' Then he added, 'Do you know,

28

you're the best looking chick I've ever seen! I adore you, my darling. Give us a kiss.' And with that he actually leant over somewhat lecherously to hold his reluctant daughter's head and kiss it with a dry mouth, as the other three gazed on in a type of shocked awe.

What a creep, thought Joel, his eyes as wide as Saturn's rings. 'Any olives left?' he then asked Bernie, who went to stand and get him some but thought better of it.

'He can get them himself,' protested Stevie, fancying Joel also. Then. 'Johnny, darling, please don't lick your daughter's shoulder like that. Can't you see she doesn't like it. It's putting me off my food! Oh, really!' He looked to Joel, who only saw the good in it. A mild breeze caused cables on the masts of boats to rattle a little menacingly, breaking the silence, and Johnny, for Francine's sake only, tried his best to ignore Stevie's comments. But he nonetheless released her from his fiendish clasp, then scowled. He then added, while picking at some salad uninterestedly, 'You'll be glad to know that we'll be meeting our professor on time.' Johnny felt the need to lie once again through his yellow and gold teeth, as liars often do. 'I spoke to him this morning, and he has our five injections all ready for us in his metal suitcase. I can tell you that he himself had a tumour, and the little robots removed it. This, my friends, is true.'

'I don't like injections,' moaned Bernie innocuously, still eating.

Francine suddenly became strangely anxious at her father's convincing story-telling, though she said nothing. Instead she frowned a little as she thought about it, then thought: You haven't spoken to him at all! She then carried on eating, now unhappily. And Johnny, with the body of an old-looking teenager, the body of a jockey, living off something like 400 calories a day for the past 25-years or so

29

for fear of putting on any weight and losing his pop-image, was quietly disgusted, as only a superficial moralist can be, by everyone filling their fat mouths with rotten food. Everybody was too fucking fat, he had often contemplated in tut-tut skinny revulsion. Tall Stevie and medium Bernie were both sitting in sexy long-legged swimming trunks. Not fat. Not thin. Possibly even turning Johnny on. In no need at all of being judged. But Johnny had judged them, would judge them, needed to judge them until the end of time. Or for at least 300-years. Long after they were dead, in fact, he would fucking judge them. Yes, it was the old DNA deal as well with him. The old genetic-inheritance. The lower-orders, of which, of course, whoever uses that term regards themselves as quite the opposite, would be slowly eradicated through gene-therapy, Johnny guessed yet again. But with this nanotechnology he was now the one in charge, the one who would deem life-spans. Oh yes. He would say who could live or die. Johnny was fucking king all right.

'So, these nano-robots definitely do the trick, huh?' Joel then investigated with speed-time sincerity. Honestly, he then commented, 'I don't know, man. I smell a goddamn rat somewhere. And like what the fuck are we gonna do for 300-years, huh? I mean, I get bored real easy, baby. I'd have to like keep on the move and shit. D'yer know what I'm saying?' He gave a broad but disingenuous smile to Stevie. 'Nah. Something ain't right here. I reckon it's a trick.' Without being aware of it his speeding brain had put him onto something, but he said no more as that was what the drug dictated. Instead Joel simply wanted to hug everyone and maybe say what a great life it was, too.

Johnny was disconcerted by this. 'I for one intend to educate the world,' he then astonishingly remarked – perhaps to throw people off Joel's unsound track.

30

Stevie looked at him. 'What? Oh my dear! Oh my sad dear! And who has educated you? It would take 300-years to penetrate that-' He was about to say skull, but Francine stopped him.

'Daddy, don't be silly. The world can educate itself. Just enjoy the long life. We will be the first human beings to live beyond 120-years or whatever the longest life has been. We should be ecstatic. We can do many things in 300-years – and with our money as well! It's absolutely fantastic. I can't believe you want to bicker like this. I just can't believe it...'

'I can,' commented Stevie.

After an afternoon's quiet sunbathing (and why did Francine want them up so early?) they ate locally. They ambled to a tiny restaurant just around the dusty corner from the apartment and sat like burnt cowboys around a well-used, greasy table – Johnny smoking tactically, silently, slyly. Stevie and Bernie were holding hands. Francine and Joel were blowing kisses to each other, the latter beginning to feel the horrors of a downer coming on, which he would counteract by lowering vats of local wine followed by, possibly, whatever shorts were available.

The air in the village seemed to embellish the ambience (if not create it) as it threw a fluorescent red over the approaching dark, which, almost antagonistically, seemed to want to take over the entire world and subdue it with its horny blackness. Johnny's blackness.

It was a warm red sky, whose distant, veiny shades only enhanced the great gleaming mountains behind like a global lightshow. But it was a powerful red, and the creeping dark couldn't quite surmount its glowing force. And so it was that our seething gang sat outdoors, in this red, in this fading light, where the owner of the restaurant came to

31

greet his 'famous' but, to him, familiar, guests… extravagantly – arrant locals, in fact, they were here so much. 'Oh! The Johnny Coy! Oh! His beautiful daughter! Kiss-kiss-kiss! Mmm-mmmm-mmm.' But did he sense that an argument was bubbling with the on-set of this darkness? It seemed unlikely.

For there they all where, together at such loveable close-quarters, Francine and 'The Johnny Coy.' They had other holiday-homes as well: an eight-roomed New York apartment, for example, as well as Johnny's modest 10-bedroom Berkshire mansion set in 11-acres where he mostly resided and where he would dictate to the world, their spectacular little villa in Grand Cayman overlooking the sea with its own private cove, (Johnny could escape there if things got too heavy as he laid the law down over the next 300-years), as well as their sprawling, exclusive apartment in downtown Cannes. And of course this cute little place here – the first holiday-home Johnny bought abroad in his days of yore. And as with here, in Gran Canaria, whenever Francine awoke on her first day in one of these homes she always believed that she was at home in her flat at The Tower. It was most odd. It always affected her that way. She'd have to look into that, she mused. Yes. Over the next century or so…

'Sad dago,' Johnny sniped as the restaurant-owner, Marco, a nightly-coloured, world-weary, moralistic man with a frantic twitch, who was not much larger in the body than Johnny himself, hugged and kissed Francine in a grand, happy manner. He kept squeezing her as a lost girlfriend whom he'd always been in love with even after she'd dumped him for the man who'd earlier made her pregnant. I, ah, forgive you! 'Nice to see you again, Marco,' phoney Johnny went on. 'Yes. We did. We arrived yesterday. No.

32

I had a drink in the other place over the road there. No. Nothing to eat. That's right. Just…' Johnny mimicked drinking from a glass… 'el booze. El drinko, Marco. Oh, ci. El booze. Yes, that's correct. Now fuck off, there's a good dago. Yes, Marco. We *took off* from Stansted yesterday. Ci. Took… off! Fly. In the air. El first-class-o, el plane-o and all that. Zoom! Straight up in the sky-0, you stupid spick. No, Marco. El booze, that's right. El Booze, you silly cunt. Ha-ha-ha. No, Marco. It was blunt. Blunt. Yes, blunt. Not sharp. You know? Blunt-o? Cunt-o? Blunt-o? You plonker. Ci, Marco. Cheers. Thanks a lot. We will. We always enjoy our meal here. Yeah, great. *Cunt*…'

'Marco,' said Francine, totally ignoring her father's mirthful scorn, 'have you seen anything of Susan?' She gazed up at him semi-urgently.

Marco gazed down at his red and white polka dotted plastic tablecloth in a serious, solemn air and rubbed his hairy, mottled chin for a very long time. Folding his arms as if about to stand talking for an hour or so, he, now without twitching, nodded as though divulging something enormously secretive. 'Oh ci,' he said painfully, almost in a grave awe. 'I seen Susan. I seen him…' he paused to gaze aloft, 'two days ago? Oh ci. Yes. Two days ago I seen him…' Alas, Marco stank to high heaven of ancient sweat; as he stood there in front of the listening table, now twitching again, this pungency floating through the hot air as a helium-balloon across a fairground, could almost be seen.

'Fancy…' said Johnny, contemplating knifing Marco if he didn't fuck off with his smell and bring the free bottle of wine he'd promised. He actually stared at a knife on the table. 'El stinko, old boy,' he added with a phoney smile, glancing upwards, showing gold teeth.

Francine, trying hard not to embarrass Marco with the

33

slightest facial expression that showed him he stank, was fairly fluent in Canary Island Spanish (all the mainland lisps expunged) and wanted to discover if her friend Susan – a man – was still around. She felt the need to continue the conversation with Marco in Spanish, as she didn't want any of the others to hear. 'Is he still around? I needed to speak to him, Marco. I wanted to ask him about something very important.'

'Hark at her…' said Johnny sarcastically.

'Yeah, well, you know Susan,' Marco waxed. 'He owns Gran Canaria, I reckon. He owes me money. He owes me a boat. I need to speak to him as well. He wouldn't stop to talk the other day, the big ape. If I see him again I'll tell him you were asking. He may have gone to Lanzarote. I don't know. I'll speak to you later about it. Oh, and by the way, tell your dad I know the difference between blunt and cunt will you.' He then reverted to broken English and said, 'Okay The Johnny Coy!' as antagonistically as possible. 'You have lovely daughter. She very blondy, very nice. Very…' And just to wind Johnny up even further Marco did a shapely slope of the hands down and over his little wiggly hips, then took off with a wild, magical laugh.

Johnny took the bait. He went to stand in Marco's fading presence in the possible hope that Marco wouldn't quite hear him. 'Hey, get the cunting wine, you fucking dago!' And he pointed to Marco's kitchen – where Marco presently entered – like a bad-tempered lackey to the Royals, and, as with this type, without blinking once. He then got comfortable again with a livid mouth.

'Daddy, you're such a pig sometimes. Marco is a really sweet guy. He's been good to us over the years. If you speak to him like that again I'm leaving the table and going back to the apartment. I mean it.' Francine then took one of

34

Johnny's cigarettes and lit it with half-lidded eyes.

'I don't think he heard him,' said Bernie diplomatically.

'It's the privilege of genius to be obnoxious!' Johnny then magically declared.

'What...?' gasped Stevie, half choking.

'Genius. I am an artist! But you already know this...' He was serious.

'No shit,' said Joel.

'*Artiste*, perhaps,' Stevie instantly commented. 'You played bass-guitar in a very lucky 1960s pop-group, to use that old term. How does that make you an artist?' He frowned in anticipation.

'What took place in the 60s *was* genius,' said a haughty Johnny. 'And I was a part of that. Ergo, I too am a genius. I am an artist. What's wrong with that? Huh. You're just jealous...' And Johnny waved him away.

'Jealous?' said Stevie, getting slightly exasperated. 'Of You? You can't be serious. Look, you silly little man, I'm afraid, like all your breed, you have believed your own propaganda! You have fallen for your own ridiculous image! Musicians are not artists. They're musicians. That's it. Full stop. Why has it always got to be more with you people? Why do you always imagine yourself as greater than the sum of your parts? Pop-music, to use that outdated phrase, is entertainment. But that's fine. That's adequate. Entertainment has its place. But do not dull thy palm with entertainment, Johnny. I've had it with entertainment. I've done entertainment to death! It goes nowhere. It gets you nowhere. Some of us want more.' Then he got all pretentious and said, 'How did you defamiliarize the familiar with your work? What questions did you ask by doing so? None. You provided, as l say, entertainment – like any good jester. The questions are asked in art through the defamiliarization

35

of what we are already familiar with, and that is acquired by using the tools of your art – be it acting, dancing, painting, writing. That's what Art is! That's how it asks its questions! Do soap-operas do that? Does pop music do that? NO! They simply endorse what we already know! And yet, for some reason, these days they all insist that they're artists in their particular field of entertainment! Why is that, I ask myself? What the fuck is it with entertainers calling themselves artists all the time? I just don't get it.' And Stevie shook his melodramatic head, melodramatically.

'Oh, don't get so heated, dear,' said Bernie, calming his lover.

'Okay, okay, I know,' Stevie calmed, holding his pale brow. 'I'm sorry.' He then gave a great gasp while quivering from the unnecessary use of un-called-for brain-power.

Johnny actually forced himself not to spit bile. It took a while, but he did it. He looked at his daughter, who was waiting for it there on his right, but it did not come out as it should have done. He did not spit bile. Instead he took a deep, hit-man type of breath, and quietly said, in profound educative seriousness, 'I'm not a silly little man. Please don't call me that again. If you do the injection's off. It's as simple as that. I can assure you of what I say. Now then, the 1960s, if you must know, saw the true beginning of the pop-group, to say nothing of the teenager. We changed it all. You lot are just jealous because you weren't there. Remember The Beatles? What a great time we had then. What was so familiar about them, eh, go on?'

'Everything,' sighed Stevie. 'That's what made them. It was the boy-next-door philosophy. They were as familiar as bread and cheese, but they sang about it. Big deal…'

'Fair point, man,' said Joel, astonished. 'He does have a point.'

'Yeah,' laughed a flippant Johnny. 'And he uses it on the other one here. The other pig's ear.' But Johnny didn't really care. No. Not really. He didn't *really* know what an artist was. Not way down inside he didn't. He'd had no need to know! Like any child, he'd just expressed himself…

'Look, I couldn't care less about this stupid nano-injection of yours anyway,' Stevie then affirmed. 'It's probably a con, like Joel says.' (Joel said nothing). 'I'm sorry Francine, but it probably is. It's a joke.' Then he said, 'Yes. I remember the moronic Beatles. We are never allowed to forget them! Another bunch of unlikely lucky idiots. Remember their management? It was Brian Epstein who made them. He was the artist, in my view. Epstein invented them, if you like. And, like you, they have never worked, have never been part of the work-place, never been to a job-interview or anything like that – all the anxiety. You pop-stars are actually quite psychotic, when we look into it. You're psychotic entertainers!' Stevie tapped the side of his crazed head as he emphasized that newly-discovered proclamation.

'Oh, don't be so precious,' moaned Francine at him.

Snap. 'That's it! You're fucked!' Johnny hit the table. 'He's out, love! I'm not paying for him to live forever! I'll be fucked if I am! He can piss off right now, as far as I'm concerned!' And Johnny suddenly smiled inwardly at what he felt he'd – perhaps accidentally – achieved with the discourse. Fuck it, he thought: Stevie had played into his dastardly hands. He had unwittingly gone along with Johnny's little agenda, for Johnny always had an agenda. Stevie had fucked himself in his own gay arse. Consequently, Johnny felt vindicated. He felt pleased. Tough shit, he thought…

37

5

MARCO HAD BROUGHT the wine, along with three dishes of Gran Canarian potatoes as starters – on the house. 'Enjoy your-ahh meal!'

People had been picking at them without much interest. They'd been dipping into their garlicky salaciousness somewhat blankly, chewing as aloof camels.

But it nonetheless struck Stevie that, again, while picking at cold potatoes quite fopishly and feeling even more judgemental than usual, he guessed, even eating Johnny took himself very seriously. Just look at him! Those smirking black eyes! Stevie couldn't bring himself to say anything about it, though. It really wasn't worth it, he told himself. No. Not any more. There was just too much grief with the guy. "It wasn't worth it," he whispered under his breath. He was on too much of his own juice. Too much to prove. Johnny made everyone around him visualize the world as he visualized it, which was superficially moral and always black, then tut-tut at those who rejected this, ah, vision. Stevie knew this. So why did he come on the trip? "Just keep it closed, old boy."

It really wasn't worth it.

For Johnny had that kind of power, Stevie reasoned, trying his best *to* keep it closed. He could bring about a horrible heartache with his horrible shit to those, like Stevie, who were susceptible to it. He shouldn't have been susceptible to it, but he was. He was susceptible. Try to toughen up, he told himself! No. It never worked, that kind of childhood-psychology. That line didn't do the job at all. It had no place in Stevie's fairly adult, complex head.

For Johnny was a dabhand at heartache. That was that. He had heartache cold. Full stop. He knew how to work the

38

desolation-deal. Johnny purposeully kept the emotional dial depressed. He was brilliant at it. No, he was bad at it – bad being the way he wanted people to always feel.

And Stevie was finding that he'd had it with the desolation-deal these days – he'd finished with grief, as he had with entertainment. Grief was proving too much for Stevie to handle, as sex was for Johnny. So Stevie was secretly asking himself the following question: What the fucking hell am I doing here with these philistines – people I don't truly care for – and with this grief-giving, shit-eating berk?

'That's right, Daddy,' Francine was saying somewhat sensibly. 'Take it all back. If Stevie doesn't get the injection then I'm not bothering as well. Seriously. We're all in this together. So, Stevie, stop hassling Daddy. You know he's no match for you. Give him a break. Tell him he is an artist! He is, you know. You're wrong, Stevie. Daddy was an original. Daddy, say you're sorry to Stevie. Come on. Kiss and make up. I mean it. Do you want to have this nano-injection on your own?' Francine glared at him. 'Daddy…?'

Johnny gave this earnest consideration.

Yes, okay, he almost said. 'No, of course not,' he did say, phoney in his make-nice drivel. 'I want to be with you for centuries, sweetheart. That's the whole bloody idea!' Then, enormously sheepishly, he said to Stevie, 'Okay. You're back on board. You can have the bleeding injection.' You can have your clear liquid, he nearly added, thinking, as if, mate. You're so fucked you wouldn't believe it! Smiling, no, grinning, he sipped cold white wine with a chilling underlying leer, and added, 'But I am an artist. I won't have it any other way. I *feel* like an artist!' He raised a fist.

'Yeah, great,' Stevie remarked, desperately sarcastically, now slightly drunk. 'But the thing is, you see, and I hate to go on, not many people are actual *artists*. An artist is an

39

extremely rare phenomenon. It's a term that's been well-over-used these days. Maybe philosophers are artists? I don't know. Perhaps it is, after all, subjective what an artist is. It's vague, really. Exceptionally unique. You see, it's all about making strange what we already know, making it alien, thereby viewing it from another, hopefully objective, discovery angle. As I say, defamiliarizing the-'

'Stevie, you promised,' sighed Francine.

'Am I still okay?' Bernie seriously asked Johnny, fairly drunk too.

'I get it!' Joel then burst forth, hitting his brow with a slap of the palm as though hitting his downer and attempting to banish it. 'Of course! It's all so clear when it spelt out to you! Shit, man. Why didn't I see it like that before! Holy mother-fucking cow.' He looked to Stevie and shook his head in the final throws of his speeding, of his on-coming downer. A learning-admiration still remained, though. But it was now acutely tentative. 'You're saying that, like, The Beatles and shit didn't – what was that word you used, defamiliarize? They only like sang songs about what like we all already know anyway.' He had to concentrate to say that bit. 'Yeah. I get it. It was nothing new, right? Only a confirmation of what we like already knew? We could do something on those lines in a movie, man. We could. We could do a real good story with shit like that…' Joel became intensely thoughtful.

'Another one!' snarled Johnny. 'Any more mutineers?'

'Will you two stop it? Joel, pack it in now!' snapped Francine. 'Get off my father's back! Just drop this artist-crap, yeah. It's pathetic. It's really pissing me off!'

'It's cool, man. I'm learning here. Hey, I'm done already. It's over. No more artist-crap. I'm done. Hey, I'm just talking. What is this, huh?' Joel was now feeling suddenly very bad. He began to experience the first deep waves of shuddering

40

throughout his system, followed by awful feelings of intense misery and tangible depression. A depression that could actually be seen, he reckoned. This fucking whizz! But, no biggy. He had uppers. Yes, Joel was expert, no, *master* at smuggling drugs through customs. He'd done it for years. He'd even made money from it. Joel could hide drugs where X-rays couldn't locate them. So, in ghastly silence, he lurched to the restaurant's unclean lavatory to remove some flesh-coloured tabs that he had strapped to the underneath of his scrotum via see-through band-aid and gobbled them down like chocolates. He then craned his head backwards and felt very dizzy. He felt whacko. 'Eeeyow!' he screamed. His penis had shrivelled drastically, too. Consequently, he couldn't piss. Hard as he tried, not a drop would breach the slit in his moistened bell-end. Or, as his sister called it when they were kids, *Jap's Eye*. So he remained with a full bladder.

'That's not all,' said Stevie in Joel's absence, cutting through the on-going conversation that he himself had perpetuated with rebellious disregard. 'There's more to art than just asking questions! There's-' Catching a glare from a fuming Francine, he cautiously added, 'But I'm not really in the mood for explanations just now…'

'You're becoming a pain-in-the-arse,' Francine suddenly said to him. 'You know Daddy doesn't like being undermined. You're being facetious, Stevie. You're winding my father up. Stop it now! Final warning…' She waited for a response as some kind of out-of-date schoolmam.

'I'm great,' said Joel honestly as he returned to the table most brightly. 'Yeah. I'm fine now. Wow! It's cool. Ooh, man.' Then to Stevie, 'Oh, what else is there, huh?' He rubbed his hands together and grinned. 'Tell me more, oh master. You can wind me up all you fucking like! I don't care.'

41

'There's lots,' said Stevie.

'Oh yeah?' Joel all earnest.

'Consider me wound up!' said Johnny.

'I'm warning you,' said Francine, warning them. 'This whole thing is beginning to seriously bug me. You know what I'm like when I'm bugged. I've given you your last chance…'

'Cunts,' said Johnny. 'All cunts.' *Dead cunts*, he also thought, reiterating the word Permanence in his mind regarding his own little existence. Yes. Permanence. To last forever. Intact now. (To believe that the whole of existence exists just for you?) Terrifying Johnny smouldered in this belief as his own long-lasting millionaire's hatred boiled within him.

Two other smirking waiters arrived at the table with the five main courses.

They both glared at Francine, bereft of any hatred, at close quarters, almost drooling. Needless to say Marco had done something extra to Johnny's dish. He'd added his very own separate flavouring. Something… special for my famous, ah, guest! He'd sprinkled a finger in the fraudulent air as he did it, too. For Marco, the great chef, put some spit, a dash of piss, a flick of snot, a flake of skin, a touch of dandruff, a smear of hair-oil, a pinch of ear-wax, (preferably congealed) a modicum of helmet-cheese, (preferably old) a tease of arse-hair, a slime of arse-grease, a slip of nail-dirt, a tincture of runny eye, a hammering of throat-phlegm deep from tainted lungs, a smattering of toe-sand. He'd mixed it all up with a finger directly out of his hot and fetid unwashed bumhole and used it as part of the sauce over Johnny's steak. Blunt-o? Cunt-o? We'll see. Oh, ci, The Johnny Coy. He then tore himself in two with raucous laughter in the kitchen as he secretly watched Johnny obliviously digging in, licking this sauce from his fork in a matter-of-fact meagre-appetite manner. And for the lovely Francine too – as he'd never get his dick anyway close to her – he ran the thing around the rim of her plate before his two hysterical waiters shakingly took it out. 'Compliments of Marco, eh?' It excited him to think that the aroma of his rank cock rose into the very beautiful nostrils of sparkling Francine (two holes in one? Oh, ci) as the plate sat steaming in front of her – touching those, ah, English nipples. Marco, eh? He was a killer with-a de ladies. A respectful chef's bow.

Wasn't ignorance the most wonderful bliss?

Speaking of which, Francine's mother, Tina, Johnny's first gullible wife, had died in a boating accident while staying at the apartment in Cannes back when Francine was about 11. At the time Johnny was already seeing his future second wife, Monica, whom he'd bring but to Gran Canaria to see the nude beach at Maspalomas at the drop of a hat, and was not at all disconcerted over the casualty. For Monica, too, would never get her hands on Johnny's millions – even after the eventual divorce. Casualty? Tina's death? You jest, of course. These special sauces of Marco's, however, began around then, some twenty years ago. Ergo Johnny had, by now, without being aware of it, consumed an enormous amount of Marco's well-scratched body-parts with innocent, if not bland, relish. (If Johnny ever found out, if he ever, ever, found out). Was this why he was so thin? And as Marco had begun rubbing his helmet around the maturing Francine's plate every time they ate at his seedy little restaurant, Johnny, it seemed, went just a little bit madder, a little bit nastier. So, chances were, possibly, that it had been the infected oil from Marco's body-parts which had affected Johnny's already-affected brain, and maybe, just maybe, had given him the notion of being Henry the

43

fucking VIII, or at least paying for people to be done-away with as a king. That is, if he had done that. It could never be proved, of course. (Can any contract-killing, truly?)

Johnny never gave blood or anything like that. Whenever he visited his doctor, he insisted that he couldn't care what was wrong with him as long as it could be cured without ever giving a blood-sample. (He had this thing about not being traced. Yes, the man who believed he was king was mad, as was the king who believed he was king). Would Marco's sauces show up in a blood-test anyway? Doubtful. King Johnny was mad, and that was that. Even his doctor knew it. He was certainly mad enough to pay for a contract-killing: he was Henry the fucking VIII after all. Well, a thin version of that crackpot. Madness and violence were definitely hand in glove. And Marco's moralizing, like lots of waiters, was as legendary as his many faces. Almost as legendary as Johnny's. It was the moralizing, actually, in a roundabout way, which subconsciously drove him to spike food, which he did a lot, and the spiked food had traces of his DNA in it, which, in turn, possibly tipped Johnny's balance. It was the moralizing – all the huhs and the ha-haas – which made Marco into a 24-hour snob…

Content with the meal and, one, two, three… how many, ten bottles of wine on the table? Johnny then began to darkly muse on all the deaths he'd engendered over the years. It was good sometimes to muse on these things, these secret killings which could never be proved. Seedy bars were normally the places. Something about their lowness being conducive to, as far as Johnny could take it, deep thought. Or something like that. And noisy bars, too. Johnny could always think clearly in noisy bars. Especially when the musing-mood descended upon him. Were people really killed by hit-men, paid for by the alleged respectable?

44

Johnny knew the answer. It took many bottles of wine for the mood to descend, but Johnny knew the answer. YES! No, they did not *all* die naturally at, usually, a young age. Not at all. These thoughts would ring around his mind like an unexciting ride at a theme-park. But did Marco's sauces engender this evil in his brain? That was the question. And it was a hell of a question. For only a moralist and a snob could reek such havoc, could reek such horror. And those who spit and do things to other people's food without them knowing? Aren't they themselves deeply moral vulgarians who should not be in the service-sector but should instead be in a dungeon somewhere drinking their own piss? Maybe. But only a moralist can say that, really.

'Daddy, I was dreaming of mummy last night...'

Gulp. 'Which, er, mummy? Oh, Tina! Were you, darling. Fancy.'

'Yes. In the dream she was asking me for help. It was really weird. I can't get her out of my mind.' With that whatever it was that Francine couldn't get out of her mind went out of her mind. It just slipped away. 'Hmmm,' she then drivelled. 'This salad is lovely. More wine anyone?'

Bernie looked at her as though he didn't quite comprehend, which indeed he didn't. He then, hearing Marco's distant hysteria – this faint roar – wondered about the aroma of penises.

6

'DO YOU REMEMBER what your mother looked like?' asked Johnny tentatively, some moments later.

Francine thought for a second. 'I think so. She had short, black hair, didn't she? A little nose. Nice ears. No, not really. But she was real in the dream. In the dream she looked… frightened, daddy. I think she was scared. It was quite horrid. Poor mummy. Who's for more garlic bread? Marco darling!' click of the fingers.

'Yes, poor mummy,' Johnny added guiltily.

'You see, the thing is,' a drunken Stevie felt the need to heroically interject, 'it's okay for you two. You two are stinking fucking rich! But what the fucking hell are we going to do for money for 300-fucking-years? I'm certainly not going to work. I mean, really! Work only demeans, my dear. So are you going to make us rich as well? Hm? I mean, darlings, how else are we going to live forever?' He looked at an intoxicated Francine, who clearly hadn't properly heard him – never mind thinking about what he'd just said, and felt quite fierce towards her all of a sudden. Work for 300-years? No thank you, for Stevie, who had dropped out of university after his second year as an undergraduate philosophy student for that very reason: work. Live like a millionaire for that length of time? Yes please. It would be the only way, he philosophically reasoned, eating something. London's Birkbeck didn't know how lucky it was not to have him for a third. Its noble intimacies were impossible, but a display of those intimacies were harshly shown to Stevie in his two glum years there, through its reserve and empty severity, thereby engendering a shrinking of intimacy in him, itself nothing but a contrived notion of shame where the concept of trust within this intimacy

46

could never have been shown. For that would have only displayed one's humaness, which could never, sin of sins, be allowed. What! That's how Stevie saw it, anyway – via the passionate Neitzsche. These kind of phrases occasionally broke surface in his mind. That was the way he used to talk.

'Make you three rich?' Johnny unphilosophically began.

'What I thought, hic, was that we could set up a kind of, hic, trust-fund for you,' Francine kindly improvised. 'Daddy and I could invest a, hic, token-amount to begin with. Hic. Pardon. We could let it build, then we could-'

'How much?' Joel criminally wondered, who was by now in another time-slot wormhole dimension beyond human understanding. He actually didn't know where he was, who he was talking to, who he was, what he had to say, who he'd been, nothing. But he somehow knew what money was, what it sounded like, what it smelt like – especially when being offered to him... whoever *him* was.

'Enough,' said Francine firmly, business-like, drunkenly, meaning money. 'We'd place it in a, hic, long-term high -interest account in Switzerland where, hic, it could accumulate until you were, hic, about 110, 120, say. Then, you could, burp, live off the interest happily for two, burp, more centuries and we could all like have, hic, fun, hic, like we normally do!' She smiled a romantic, utopian smile and resumed eating somewhat mindlessly. It was true, Francine had, up until her mid twenties, and like a dutiful wife, been primed for every situation and occasion by her possessive father. If someone says this, then she responds with that. If someone says that, then she responds with this. Primed ready. Yes. The priming of a bourgeois face-value background. But by her thirties this priming had begun to wain, to falter, to alter, until she got very drunk; then, because her own mind fell silent as it drifted backwards, the priming,

47

which was, after all, a very powerful, contrived instillation, came forth. 'But look, hic, daddy and I can't have any messing around, okay? Hic. Hear me? Hic.'

Hear her? Joel was as high as a rocket launched from another galaxy en-route for the planet Earth with no knowledge of what it'd find there. Wow! No way could he eat anything any more, too. No way. 'Shit…' he gasped. 'So, like, it's really going to happen, huh? Like we're all going to live for like 300-years and shit, be rich? Wow. Yahoo, man. Yahoo. Hot damn! Un-be-fucking-lievable! I could speed for like a whole century and never come down! Gee-suss! These probes, man, or goddamn robots and shit in our bodies, would see to it that like I'd be okay, yo? I'd be like, cool anyways and everything? I could like speed all I wanted?' Joel laughed his cowboy's laugh, which always entailed slapping the goddamn motherfucking table. But the question was: was he really worth perpetuating for that long? Even he had his doubts on that score.

'It won't work,' gasped sensible Stevie. 'The probes will turn on their host. That's what'll happen. Just you wait and see. The probes will turn on their host!' The huge span and tension between envy and friendship, Stevie thought. (He was taught this at Birkbeck). Envy and friendship. You liked them, but you also envied them. Could that be maintained for long? That lingering-feeling? And what about self-hatred and whacko pride? That's where it all is, Stevie reckoned to himself. One in one, one in the other. O yes. That's where it all is, all right. Stevie dreamed this. I hate me, but I also admire me. Yes. That's where it all is, all right. That's where I'm fucking coming from…

For had Francine actually thought through what she'd proposed? If the nano-injection was for real, then why should she bring semi-strangers with her for the enormous ride? After all, Joel Maize was Francine's 100th boyfriend. He wasn't that special. Stevie and Bernie? Well, maybe daddy was right. Maybe they were just, well, sad gays. 'It will work,' she then weakly commented, with the priming-notion in the brim of her mind. 'Living off interest is the best way to live! Daddy and I have always done it, haven't we daddy…?'

Whoops. A devil-glare from found-out daddy. Done what?

'Just the idea of it,' said a dreamy Stevie. 'It won't, hic, work.'

Perhaps. Perhaps not. Maybe Francine was scheming. Maybe she was just an overgrown child. Who could say? Maybe Stevie, with all his philosophical training – all the logic, all the Derridian-questioning of the alleged reality of dualities – just didn't know himself. Anyway, can they? Can molecules be built by pushing atoms together? And did it matter to our group, ultimately? The drunker Francine got that night the more the answer to this question, in her ignorant haze, was a definite and powerful Yes, they bloody can. Nano-probes w/could do that! They'd make new molecules by forcing atoms together, somehow, thereby making good whatever was, well, bloody bad! Holy shit, she perceived in ignorance-of-the-subject exultation. And in the witchy dark of the quiet port she smiled as her father blew her a lewd kiss, as he himself slowly picked at his shit-strewn meal and drank an awful lot of piss-sweet wine. They were going to make it. It was all going to happen. Longevity was a reality. What a great feeling! They were the long-lived! WHAT A GREAT FEELING! Francine was going to get something she'd thought about for ages: to spend 10-years in every major city of the world!

'What dreadful feelings cheap wine can induce,' commented a drunken, dreadful Stevie, thinking also of

49

how tormented his poor soul was, has been, could be. The torment, of course, being inflicted upon it by others, always. For he was fine on his own, he had often deduced.

Bizarrely, Francine then went on to ramble about the science of the nano-probes. And a ramble it was, because it was mostly made up. The wine had enabled her to wax imaginatively on whatever bits she'd read about and picked-up on. Like someone writing a novel, say. An imaginative wander in a voyage of discovery. The hiccuping and the burping had now been replaced with 'What you'd need, yah, is an AFM-type cantilever arm, yah, which would make you a diamondoid, a diamondoid, yah, carbon ring, by, yah, actually pushing, okay, atoms together, yah, using, yah, an unknown synthesis called, okay, Piezochemical, yah...' She play-acted pushing two ends together with her fingers, but they missed each other.

'How come you know about it if it's unknown?' asked the philosopher Stevie Cook.

'Leave her be,' said Bernie.

'Who's on the throne?' asked Joel.

'I am...' said Johnny.

'Fucking shut up, you. Fucking... shut up.' Francine pushed a long finger to her lips as she said that. 'Okay. This carbon ring, yah, once made, yah, would fashion a type of sleeve in its own image, yah, and that would go towards like making what they like call a molecule-train, hic! Yah. Both structures, okay, would then like need to be, yah, coated with fluorine-atoms, I read, for like perfect lubrication and shit?' She said that last bit as in a question. 'Isn't that incredible? Because, yah, if molecule-trains need anything, yah, it's like perfect lubrication. Ha-ha. No. I'm not joking. Really. They do. Whapp! Just like that, yah! nice, yah, slide. A sex slide. Then, and this is the, ah, clever bit – this is

50

what we've all been like waiting to hear, yah, because, yah, it's what we'll have in our like bodies and shit by Saturday – the train would like dock like mechanically at like various like stations around the like body to make like repairs, hic, having, hic, listen, listen, *set-up*, yah, the stations in the first place! Do you understand?' She burst out laughing. 'Great, eh? Brilliant, yah!' It was what was known as a ratchet-mechanism, created by a few hundred atoms, that would apparently do the trick – but Francine was too drunk to add this. Instead she said, 'The robots, yah, would arrive at like a growing tumour… on… yah… a… yah… fucking train!' And she burst out laughing again at the idea of of it all.

'You're nuts!' Her father mournfully noted.

'We don't know what you're talking about,' said Bernie.

'No. No. No. No. No.' Francine went on, sighing from the outburst, 'Don't you get it? These little probes, yah, would like arrive, okay, unload themselves like little workers, okay, wave bye-bye to like the driver, okay, then get to work, yah, like bloody miners! It's hysterical! They'd be hacking away at the tumour-face, yah! It's true. Daddy, tell them! You know. That's what would happen, isn't it! You've read about it too!' She laughed again, holding a hand to her white, shaking teeth – appearing, it was true, nuts. She'd lost the plot.

'Don't drag me into it,' moaned Johnny. 'I haven't got a clue what you're talking about, girl.' He said all that in a very London 60s brogue – a kind of 'gowl' pronunciation of *girl*. Who, it must be added, wore just a vest tucked into shorts which were, wouldn't you know it, skin-coloured and skin-tight; and, in the candle-dark as she rambled, these appeared to mutate into an outer-covering of sheen-gleaming shifting electronic skin, yah, which gave Francine, yah, the appearance of, yah, at a swift glance, yah, being naked. Naked and nuts. Perhaps, Joel mused in other-wordly

51

projection into the stars, it was nano-skin? Perhaps, he further seriously considered, I could tear it off and eat it! Eat it as I fucked it! But Francine just continued to laugh. Like a robot. She laughed and laughed and laughed, laughed at the moon.

'Fuck…' gasped Bernie, somewhat concerned.

'Calm down girl,' said her father.

7

SIR CLIFF. SIR Paul. Sir Elton. *Sir Johnny!* Sir Johnny Coy, knight of the fucking realm! Yas! And not before time, too, Johnny furiously mused at the table! Bastards. Ignore my achievements, would you? What I've done for queen and fucking country? (*To say nothing of being well paid for it*). *SIR JOHNNY COY!* BOW YOUR HEADS, LESSER BEINGS! Johnny felt angry again. Knighted? Benighted? Terribly close to each other. Too close for comfort, really. And, to further exacerbate the situation, as the 1990s wore on Johnny had never, ever, been on the A-1-Celeb list. Not once. How could he? Who was he? He'd never even been an A-2 or 3. This also angered him. This also made him want to run round hitting people and telling them who he was. Don't you know who I am! (Which sane and intelligent person, though, in reality, would have anything to do with, let alone sanction, an A-1-Celeb list?) Johnny and reality? Well, they didn't quite make it, did they. Johnny and sanity? 'Hey, Marco!' And Johnny actually contemplated telling him to bow his dago head.

We would need some kind of invisible powerhouse, dreamed Joel fantastically, a powerhouse that no doubt lies out there somewhere in our beautiful, vast, expansive galaxy. But invisible. Yes. An invisible powerhouse. That's the deal. And there it is, waiting to be discovered and used. *Out there*. It's probably smouldering right now. Fuel, my little friend, he thought to his imaginary goblin, is a no-go area where the speed of light is concerned. Just don't go there with fuel, man. Fuel who? Smuel? No way. Fuel and light-speed don't go together. They don't mix. Aw, shut the fuck up!

Joel drank deeply on a big bitter short.

53

His eyes saw not the table, Francine, Bernie, Stevie, Johnny, the restaurant – only outer-space. His eyes saw outer-space. The strong drink plus the peculiar uppers (were they uppers? Couldn't they have been side-winders?) had heightened the red rings around these eyes, heightening also his sense of the universe, of dark-matter, of event-horizons, of crazy singularites, of wormholes. It seemed to make his thin lips even thinner, too, and the red rings to augment like a big cosmic firework. Joel's eyes were now bright fireworks, burning away at the warm night star-spangled sky. And he began to pronounce words very slowly, very precisely, very mythically – under the stars – in this firework haven. For he had become an angel of the stars. Joel had now left his earthly body and was soaring in the galaxy-heavens in search of this invisible powerhouse that could drive a spaceship at the speed of light – *his* spaceship! 'My… spaceship,' he slowly choked. 'Others. Could. With me…'

'Your spaceship?' said Stevie in nodding agreement.

'The glowing heavens, man…'

'Can anyone detect my Wolverhampton accent?' asked a brave Bernie, bravely – without a trace of the aforesaid execrated modulation.

'Everyone, darling,' said Stevie, slurping wine, disgusted.

'Accents,' said Joel in a New York up-state one, and never once attempting to disguise it. 'Out there. Accents and juice. Power and space-flight. Never… ending…' Astonishingly, he then leapt to his feet and ran away from the table, screaming. All in a split second. He'd apparently seen an approaching asteroid, it would transpire – its trajectory dead-on for New York. Minutes to world's end. It would hit, and no one knew about its approach – except perhaps, the powers that be, and they, the scum-fucks, were saying fuck-all! AAYYYEEEE!

54

'Junky…' sneered Johnny, listening to him scream, but pondering still his knight(ed)hood (benighted) and what it would do for him over the on-coming centuries. The opening of doors? The contacts? The birds? The hiring of even better hit-men? Well yes. What else were knight-hoods for? No, Johnny did not see that pop-music came about to be anti-establishment, really. He'd never known that. Hence a knighthood, for a pop-star, was anti what pop-music stood for, it could have been argued by someone like Stevie. It was the antithesis of pop-music, really, Stevie might have said. But he didn't, because Johnny never spoke. Yet he would have done. For most of them went for it – when offered. *Knighthoods*, that is. Most of them wanted to be conventional and respected by a bourgeois public in the long run. Suppression and power? Suppression *through* power, subconsciously? Yes. Johnny was going to have Joel bumped off. No question. He'd just decided on it. Suppression? Yeah, okay. Why not. That'd do him. That'd be fine. It was, as Stevie previously alluded, the endorsing of the familiar through soaps and conventional pop-music that mollified the populous and made them easier to manipulate en-masse: hence suppression. It made their emotions more easy to dictate, more easy to believe in tabloid ideology. And that was right up Johnny's street: dictatorship. Johnny wanted not only to suppress people who had latched onto his empty phoniness and therefore needed to be silenced because they'd sussed it, but he also wanted to tell them how they should be feeling amid all this restraint, this conquering, this ultimate extinction of what they could've been. He wanted to be, it was true, a dictator. A despot. A little Hitler, as the saying used to go. Johnny wanted to rule the world right down at his worthless standards!

Motherfucker. 'The breadwinner, you see,' slurred a

55

horrible Stevie across the table, 'is usually an oppressor, too. You know, daddy and all that? Daddy earns the fucking money, so daddy says what fucking goes in the household!' He burst out laughing, then fell into his own folded arms.

Bernie, hearing this, and knowing also that Stevie's own father beat him, felt the subconscious pain/pleasure of being both oppressed and redressed by Stevie – the bread-winner in *their* little household. Yes, it was suppression-time all round now: Bernie felt he was being put in his place. No, he felt he was being told where his place was: namely the home, waiting for Stevie's glib and promiscuous return. For Bernie was, as Bernie knew, the perfect petty-bourgeois housewife. He'd wait for Stevie no matter what, no matter how, albeit sometimes begrudgingly, as long as it looked good to their imaginary neighbours, who could become good friends. Yikes! Yes, Bernie, who not only knew where his place was – he also wanted to be told where his place was in a very domineering fashion – had been secretly watching too many damn soaps, in between being told where his place was. Yet Bernie loved his little place in the world. He loved it a lot.

Joel, on the other hand, was still at the other table, in another world. He'd been contemplating the speed of light, and what it would do to a human being on its unimaginable approach. For it seemed to Joel that you would need a gas-tank the size of the planet Earth to fuel a craft at that speed for any length of time. Conventional gas, that is. But of course a spacecraft that could travel at the speed of light would be fuelled by something else, Joel surmised, and this also gave him further problems: what, man? What could fuel a craft at the speed of light? There he was with his head in his hands, worrying, worried, worries.

Nothing. Johnny's head. Empty. Forever dull. However,

56

in all the boozy mayhem, he had deduced that, dare he admit it, Stevie did have nice gobbling lips. Yes, Johnny could imagine those suckers around his little cheesy pecker gobbling away. Ouch! He could see Stevie's reluctant eyes gazing up at him from down there in that airless, once crabby, crotch. Stay down, boy. One more glass of wine and, ah, yes. Slurp, slurp. Johnny now had a Roman face – all glowy and pointed and hornily homosexual. For the lovely Stevie wore a large, somewhat tasteless earring in his left ear, which Johnny now found himself staring at totally obliviously. For Stevie had sucked lots of cock in his time. Enough to form a bar-rail around the Isle of Man. In fact Stevie had gobbled so much cock in his time that he constantly had the taste of it on his tongue and had begun to believe in his darkest moments that his surname was actually Cock, instead of what it really was, which was Cook. To be numerical about it, Stevie had, to my knowledge, looking back now, sucked around two-thousand different penises – mainly in the London area. Not that it matters. Well, it did to me. Hence, perhaps, how come he could be so brutal towards Bernie, who had only ever had around ten different lovers and didn't particularly like sucking cock – except Stevie's, which was different. For it had often seemed to Bernie in those long-ago days, not that he was much of a brooder, that sexual promiscuity was a form of self-abuse, a form of self-destruction. In turn, he felt, it transformed the soul/mind into a bestial horror show. But he wasn't sure, and he could never prove it. It was just an educated, thoughtful hunch he had. Educated, as in seen it at first hand via Stevie, who'd never stopped fucking other men throughout their somewhat lengthy relationship and had definitely become more brutal as time wore on. Ergo Bernie put it down to promiscuity. My Stevie was never as brutal as this, Bernie

57

had pondered, who, in silence, would never actually speak those words for fear of, well, more verbal brutality. Although Stevie could also be very kind and gentle. Bernie was loyal to this, ultimately. He was loyal to the gentleness.

And it seemed to Francine, too, that, way down deep inside, Stevie actually hated himself. But, like Bernie, she wasn't sure, and she could never prove it. It was just an educated, thoughtful hunch she had. Educated, as in seen it all before with her father, who, ultimately, truly loathed himself too – way down deep inside. Somewhere in those darkest reaches of that shallow mind, Johnny loathed himself. So much, really, that he'd invented the facade of one who adores himself. And Johnny did love himself – in the darkest reaches of his self-detestation. He loved the phoniness of it all – the con of him being a great bloke. This facade had stood him in good stead. It could therefore never be confronted: the facade of one who adores himself? 'Prick…' Johnny snarled quietly in the candlelit murk at Marco, who'd been waiting on tables all night and, a man of 56, no longer wished to any more. It was just too painful. My, ah, legs! And the other waiters, too, dressed in pirate's outfits? What was that all about? What the fuck were they on? Johnny shook his weary head.

At that moment Stevie glanced up into the darkness of the Port of Mogan and saw himself riding on horseback on the surface of the moon.

8

SUDDENLY, IN THE dead of night, in the mysterious dark of the silent universe which seemed to actually be bearing down, there was a huge presence lurking at the entrance to the outdoor section of the restaurant. This presence could, in turn, be felt within the terraced area where everyone was. It was a presence that Marco, now with his feet up on one of the tables inside the restaurant and smoking a slim cigar sleepily, instantly recognized. For the presence was, to him, as he awakened in a kind of alarm, and as always, an ominous one. The presence was prophetic. It may even have been glorious…

It was past midnight. All other customers had long since departed the now forlorn restaurant. Even the island seemed quiet from the point of view of the Port of Mogan. And our gang, too, hadn't talked for some time, mercifully. There was a full, silent, sparkling green moon. The stars were glinting in a dilation of hushed eternal light-speed whiteness. The mountains appeared luminous, almost phosphorus under this infinite gleam. Luminous and still. And the presence entered. It was that of a huge bear-like cat, a cat the size of a man. The presence was that of *Susan*…

…Two-metres tall with a chest-width to match!

Gulp. He appeared out of the night, looking, at first glance, like a giant, biblical figure of some sort. For Susan was as black as any human being could possibly be. Blacker than the night itself, which he always used to his advantage. He was like a cat the size of a bear. Huge, infinite, starlike Susan, stroking his whiskers gently, ponderously. The night had rendered him invisible.

And Susan was cosmic.

He'd been known to block out the sun up in his village

59

there if the mood took him. And it often did. If Francine was bordering on the matriarchal, then Susan was fully embroiled in the universal with his sheer physicality. To gaze up at him caused a wonder in people. Not fear, just a wonder. A phenomenon-gaze wonder. Because it was great to look at Susan. Consequently the silence as he entered seemed to deepen. It seemed to chill. Then there was noise again as Francine broke the silence. She stood up slowly, drunkenly, grinning ludicrously like a dunce, and showing a red-wine sloshed set of red teeth, when, in her vertigo-sensation, she said, Whoooooo, as though falling from something. Susan edged in. The candles appeared to heighten their flames as he passed them. Booze-grinning, the rest of the table gazed up in abject wonderment. But Susan was used to having this effect; he'd used that to his advantage, too. 'Susan!' Francine shrieked as though shocked. Then she squealed. People winced: it was a shrill, tweaky squeal that was high-pitched enough to bring Marco eventually out, looking superficially concerned. For it was a kind of fluorescent sound.

She attempted a hug, but big Susan was too big. He big-hugged her instead.

'How are you, my pretty friend?' the big man barked. The voice was spectacularly deep, as deep as it was dark, dark like his gravity-collapsed black-hole skin. Susan spoke in a broken, pidgin English most loudly, which seemed parodied from a daft old film made about deep voices and pidgin English. It even caused the spotty tablecloth to vibrate in a minuscule quiver. Truly. If you put your hand on it you could feel it. 'It am been a while!' he boomed on. Then he edged over to the table like a glacier slipping and let Francine go; to drop her; he'd actually lifted her off her feet. His shadow flew across the table as a great cumulus cloud over a field: Susan always brought his own special darkness with him. A shiver also flashed across the table – after the vibration – as the candles dimmed. It was an eerie shiver. For it wasn't that the night had taken Susan, it was as though Susan had taken the night, the whole night, and nothing but the night. He'd taken all of the night into his body and lived with it in him. Consequently his gargantuan hug in his night-embrace to Francine appeared to actually squeeze the soul out of her. It wasn't a deep, over-the-top hug; it seemed as though his enormous strength could hold back light, so even a mild embrace appeared violent.

He wore a hanging black garment that went right down to his massive sandled feet. It was circled in gold braiding at the neck, with a baggy hood, which flopped behind on his wide shoulders. There was a section that came up and covered his nose and mouth, which he would remove to speak. But the eyes. Those staring, yellow-white eyes! Susan was a Spanish negro. His nose was flat fat and very splayed – his lips, (naturally) very thick. He had a scar under his chin where someone had once tried to murder him with a knife. For this attack Susan not only ate his attacker, but he ate all his brothers and sisters as well, leaving his parents alive to ponder on what terrible children they'd raised.

This was in Susan's bloodlust-hungry days. No one reported them missing. (No one dared).

Joel had never seen anyone like him anywhere, including New York.

Susan's black garment, Francine knew, in the daylight appeared as diamond blue. It was most odd. Bright, diamond blue. There was no trace of blue in it at night. None. As when candlelight magically reflected upon it, as now, this black-night garment – a form of kaftan – seemed to wrap around him like the dark itself and make him even darker, even blacker. For it was a garment *of the dark*.

Stevie, sitting slightly girlishly now in Susan's overwhelming presence, a limp tremble, melancholically intoxicated too, gulped into the abyss on the big man's approach. Yes. A total abyssal swallow. It was as though he was watching a great sea-monster awesomely rise in the harbour next to him as he sat sipping Pernod in wonderful, contented holiday isolation: he was motionless to act. 'My god,' he whispered in a type of blissful fear. He then drew in a hot breath.

Susan had been smoking a joint. Had been, still was. Was always. But it wasn't just your everyday kind of joint. Oh no. Susan had been smoking a peacepipe joint, and was holding it by his side as a dagger: his great eyes were gazing orbs because of it. For pot and Susan were inseparable. They were lovers. Marijuana was a solid part of his mysterious life. Had been since he was six.

'Ask him what he's selling,' bawled a joking, quaking Johnny, 'then tell him to be on his sooty's way!' As he said that he thought of a myriad more wild racist comments, all of which have no need of being written here.

Stevie contemplated what Susan could possibly have underneath his shroud.

Joel lit a cigarette somewhere, somehow. His eyes, not his brain, watched through the smoke. His skin appeared to actually steam. Then his face, not his brain, smiled. His brain, not his mind, was happy to see this big fuck-off Susan guy, Francine's big fuck-off friend. Yup. And yep. For he sure was one big mother. Don't get any bigger. Look at the size of those feet! A regular Green-Mile giant! Then Susan stood next to where tiny Johnny sat, well, hell, he was a moving, shit-stomping mountain, man, thought Joel's brain and mind, whose eyes simply gazed upon this mountain in brainless fascination.

62

And Johnny was dwarfed even more. Johnny was magnetically sucked downwards. Johnny and magnanimity, though, even as a dwarf, had long since parted ways. They'd been divorced for years. He did not/could not feel pleasure at other people's happiness, including his daughters'. So, as he lapped his old tongue around his expensively-capped teeth, seeking and finding food-debris, he gave a weak scowl up at this 10-times-his-size behemoth, as it glowed and gleamed towards his giggly daughter. And what did he want anyway, this big fucking black piece of shit? Jesus, Johnny. Shut the fuck up. Stop speaking through me decades after your death! The world's not like that any more. Johnny felt a deep urge somewhere inside himself to take up arms. It was a jealous urge. Why had God, though, that comedian, made him like a useless little jockey! (Johnny had always hated horses).

'I heard you were looking for me…' boomed Susan with telepathic pidgin niceness. 'Yes. It am so good you am here like this. So good.' And Susan again kissed Francine on the cheek and gave her a manly, or perhaps a bearly, hug. To which Johnny, under different circumstances maybe, might have paid, there and then, to have him de-balled. What, with the money he had? A fucking big egg-and-spoon like this licking his lovely white daughter's face? No way. A swift nick. All over. But who, or what, could hold Susan down long enough to inflict such a wound? There weren't many.

Francine then finally turned to the table – looking disconcertedly for Joel – and announced that, 'Everybody, this is Susan. Susan, this is, ah, everybody. Hic.' Francine was no female manikin. But standing there next to the big guy, well, dwarf or vertically-challenged person might have been close. She gaggingly went on, 'This is my gang!' Francine was by now elegantly drunk – drunk with flowing, long arms – but her hint of mascara had ever-so-slightly run. So

63

she now looked somewhat clownish as well as diminished. 'Susan, darling, come and, hic, join us. Pull up a, hic, chair. Sit, you big lump! Hee-hee. Hic. Hic. Hic. Hic. Fuck…'

Susan sat heavily down, and wind rose gently around the table. He wasn't fat, but his girth was thick. Treetrunk thick. He scanned the gang beadily, with big floating eyes. Francine yelled to night-weary Marco for five more bottles of, yah, wine, and she almost called him a smelly dago too. Daddy's, yah, priming still. Then she herself sat down next to Johnny and laughed. Whether at the situation or the sheer appearance of Susan, she didn't know. Who would? She didn't care. Why analyse what's funny? Susan then took it upon himself to shake everybody's hand – Johnny's last of all – who gave him the limp dead-fish-in-the-bowl hold. Susan's hands, unfortunately for Johnny, were as big as feet. Johnny's? Well, a ten-year-old's?

'Nice to meet you, ah, Susan,' gasped Bernie as limply as possible.

Susan drew in breath. 'It am far from England to here?' he asked.

'Oh, yar!' belched Francine. 'It am very far!' She laughed again.

Stevie laughed too, visualizing Susan's, he imagined, elephantine cock – what it would do to his pussy. My God. Too big. Just… too big. No. Take it away from me! Focus it away! 'Whereabouts do you live?' he managed to ask the big man, almost adding, because I'd like to go back there and blow you. An insect landed on his shoulder as he spoke, but he didn't care.

An insect of the night, thought Susan in Spanish, gazing at it. Then, in the same language, he said to Francine, 'What did he say? I didn't get a word of that.'

'There weren't many words used,' Francine cleverly

64

replied. 'He asked where you lived. I think he's got the hots for you. Say nothing. Play him along. Him and the other one are lovers. No. Not him over there. That's Joel, my boyfriend. This one here, hic. The little one, burp. The stupid one. Play the tall one along. It could be fireworks. It'll be a laugh...' And Francine laughed.

'Your Spanish is good, my beautiful lady.' Susan then put his cover up and scanned more beadily than before – eyes over the top of it. He looked, to Bernie, fucking freaky. No, scary. A scary creature. For only two white bloodshot balls floated in the blue-dark of night. Like insects. The insect on Stevie's shoulder, which suddenly flew away. Probably because it believed Susan's eyes were after it. Then Susan said in English, 'Up in dem mountains der. Up in dat village. That am where I live. Up in dat, valley, you call it? Yum. Dat Valley.' He said all that through his cloth. Curiously enough Susan had once done hang-gliding. He hang-glided from *up in dat valley*, and had landed *out in dat ocean*. Way out. Unfortunately, the instructor hadn't told him how to land properly, how to nose-dive. Susan simply glided on like a great seabird from another planet. He believed he'd developed wings. Big wings for big Susan...

'Why is he hiding his face, darling?' Johnny asked ultra-sarcastically.

'It am my religion,' Susan said for her. 'I am in der religion.'

'Yeah?' Johnny said. 'Which one? The towelheads or something?'

'Not heard of dat one...'

Joel appeared. 'Hey, dude, like what's that smoke, man? It's like gotta be good shit, and shit! Yahoo, brother.' Marco flashed in behind him with more wine. His eyes were like mad dog's bollocks. They were all veined and bloodshot and

65

swollen. The vision caused Joel to leap back. Yikes! And then Susan's penetrating eyes from over his veil, or mask – yyyyikessss! He lowered the veil periodically to smoke his potpipe, which gave off an intensely aromatic smoke to the arena.

'Hey,' scowled Marco in Spanish to him as he laid down the bottles, 'where's my fucking boat? You said I'd have it by April. Where is it, you big freak? You've wrecked it, haven't you? You're dead. The boys'll get you. That's the last time I do you a favour, pigdog!' And Marco left the table-ambience, moaning, to Susan's deeply phlegmatic gaze.

'Spick-chat…' whispered Johnny derisively. Then he said with more volume and perhaps venom, 'He's a fucking-towelhead, Marco, what do expect! That's what he is: a fucking towelhead wiv a hard-on!' He laughed terribly at that East-End hilarity, even though he didn't know what was said between them. 'You,' gasped Susan at him, 'am de silly little fuckey! I have de power! I have de power over you, silly fuckey! I have de power over him out der!' He meant Marco, who was ready to close up no matter what and could now be found staring at a candle-flame in the kitchen most dejectedly. 'Me am big Susan! You am little English fuckey prick!' And Susan smoked some more, phlegmatically.

Well, that was it. Johnny wasn't going to take that. No chance. A good old Cockney boy like him? Queen and country and all that? Whoo! Because, when it came to it, and, like the illiterate comedian who suddenly gets reverential about his country, Johnny Coy would stand up and be counted. However, before he could either stand up or say anything in return to Susan's comments, the big man rose from the table like a tidal wave on approach and made for the exit wizard-like. He flashed under the brick archway, which was covered in old fairy lights – one or two either

66

going out or flashing – and seemed to vanish. (Fairy lights encircled the entire outdoor area of the restaurant in fact). The candles went out (puff) as Susan stood, which half-shocked everyone – booze preventing full-shock from ever triumphing – and then he was gone. He'd disappeared. And it was incredible the way he rose. It was almost beautiful, Francine thought. It was Susan's party-trick, after all. That's all it was. Susan's party-trick. For Susan was, it has to be said, a magician – of sorts. That's what he did: tricks. Rising from tables awesomely and causing candles to go out then vanish was one of them. Susan: the wizard of Gran Canaria. Susan the sorcerer, the enchanter. Lord Susan of the Canaray Islands.

'The candles have gone out,' noted a glib Bernie in unmistakable Wolverhampton, but with considerable surprise too, which seemingly negated the droll tones with a shocking sparkle.

And then, as Susan actually left the premises invisibly, somehow gliding, the remaining candles went out along with the antiquated fairy-lights. Who was this man? Johnny went to stand in the darkness, but fell, drunker than fat Winston Churchill. A towelhead wiv a hard-on? I think not. He even looked like Winston Churchill, writhing around on the floor there, holding out a desperate hand to whomever might accept it. Nobody did. Instead, Francine gave a loudish giggle. It was that of a child's in the presence of Father Christmas, say. For the sudden darkness, under the shadow of the great mountains, was rather spooky, it seemed to her: it made her cower a little. Then Johnny grabbed at something, a chair (the drowning man) and, in an attempt at standing, fell onto the table with enough force to up-end it. Crunch! Oh, you Cockney spiv! Ten-zillion empty bottles fell to the floor and bounced – two or three breaking. The

67

five glasses fell and smashed, and the noise, rising in the blackness, was horrendous. Marco came dancing in, then manically tripped. He fell, cutting his hand deeply. Blood appeared as black. Crazed Joel recalled Letterman years ago back home. The Munsters were on it. It was like this. No question. Fuck, man. It was vaudeville. The Munsters had come to town! And then, after the mayhem, in another type of void, there was a silent vibe. It lasted seconds. Then there were odd vibes. Vibes that were conducive to scanning the skies for UFOs. And yes, there was one there! A big dude. No. It was a satellite. Aw, Joel couldn't be, hic, fucked any more…

Then Susan seemed to come floating back across the table.

It wasn't a hallucination.

It could have been Susan, or it could have been something just as big only from the animal kingdom, with the power of flight. Now, Joel and everyone else looked up. No. It was Susan. Jesus. Susan hovered over the table, gazing down at the awestruck five, gazing up at him. The whys and hows didn't even come into it. Susan the magician just hung in the quiet air over the table!

A silence fell that not only could have been cut with a knife but was powerful enough to surface a nuclear submarine. A nuclear silence. An aftermath kind of silence. Stevie actually choked at the vision, in this silence, then wanted to touch it. Artists? Piss-artists? Yeah, right. That stopped him. For his swallow was a luminous gulp in a malign smog of overwhelming shadows, he thought.

Then. 'It's a con – a trick!' little Johnny began yelling, on his back on the floor. But no. Susan was flying. He could do that. He could fly. And just to check it out Joel very bravely reached up into the cold air – to, to, touch. And that's when

68

he did it. That's when it happened. That's when Joel for the first time in his life screamed like a terrified woman and fell backwards into Johnny's reluctant arms, who, in turn, fell further into the floor under the relative weight. For Joel touched Susan in flight. He touched him, and he shouldn't have done that. Susan wasn't to be touched while hovering. That was an unwritten rule at the Port of Mogan. For Susan wasn't really there. What Joel felt was air. That's all. Joel felt Susan's projected image from out of the infinite darkness which surrounded it.

'Get a doctor!' he then screamed from on top of squashed Johnny.

'There's a light in the kitchen!' Bernie squawked mysteriously.

But they were silenced again. Susan (or his projected image) moved as a probe from a vessel across an alien landscape, and everyone saw it. Even his massive sandles floated by. They all watched, pointing – as one might watch a total eclipse of the sun: a slight squint, wholly awed. Then Marco threw the switch to a couple of spotlights which were situated at certain angles for this very purpose it seemed and with the instant brightness everyone made an "ah" sound as big Susan vanished. Poof! And, crash! No, Susan's image didn't vanish, his actual body was there and it smashed right down onto the table like a boulder falling from a small cliff. Whenever he'd done this before people usually ran away and invariably either left the island or moved to somewhere in the north of it. But not our gang. Shocked, certainly, they moved back on their chairs and simply allowed it to transpire...

Marco came screaming out of the shadows, and, in mad Spanish remonstration, yelped wildly at his own kitchen-gesticulations as though he wasn't expecting this or his

69

kitchen-gesticulations, which were more agitated than usual and were quite unique in themselves. But it was definite. Susan's great body had crashed onto the table from a height of 2-metres! It had dropped… very mightily. Marco called him all the arsehole shitbergs he could put his brain to at that moment, which, as it was Marco, was no mean task. Susan then climbed to his big feet and stood rock-still in a white-eyed trance. The famous drunken five watched him closely, in a kind of drunken fear. This wasn't right! This shouldn't be happening! The trance was that of a child seconds away from being stampeded to death by a thousand wildebeest. It seemed it was an African trance of old.

Johnny, on the floor still, wondering also what had happened to the vision, wiped his tight-lipped mouth in hungry anticipation. There wasn't much going on inside this mouth. It was a theatre not very often used. He then got to his feet while emitting a hairbrained, lowly moan, and attempted to run away from the scene. He pushed past his daughter, (save me! save me!) then knocked little Bernie from his chair like a bowling ball to a skittle. Bernie, in turn, almost summersaulted backwards, as he'd done sexually many times before, while Johnny simply tore off into the darkness like the shitfaced coward he truly was. Thankfully Stevie caught Bernie's chair. "There, dear."

A broken table. Two broken chairs. Marco made a feeble endeavour at dancing, (was it dancing?) then sparred up at Susan. It was vaudevillian attack. But then, whack! He smacked a fist onto the underside of Susan's broad chin. Susan did not move a single fraction. It was a stoneage trance he was in now. He held his arms out and began to mumble something rapidly.

9

THE VILLAGE OF Mogan, as opposed to the Port of Mogan, was way up in the brown mountains. It was where the great Susan resided, and was a very old village. Indeed Susan himself lived in a large old stone house just outside the perimeter, where the road goes up before forking off to somewhere else. There's a lower lane then a higher one. That's where Susan lives. That's his house. He lived with his three wives and ten children. Everyone knew that. Everyone knew him. Susan was a very well-known sorcerer, resplendent in his myriad black kaftans. He also had pigs and chickens on his land, as well as a tame white wolf named Mallibenny…

Mallibenny was tamed when fully grown. He was a very nice wolf.

The following evening after the gang had had breakfast, they decided to check out Susan's place in Francine's Suzuki jeep, which she kept parked in a garage close to the airport at La Palma. The reasons for checking out Susan's place were unknown; they all seemed to simultaneously feel them, though. And so, feeling slightly ill, if not decidedly delicate, they trundled up to the village of Mogan in a half-dead hungover heat-haze. It wasn't difficult to locate Susan's big stone house. In fact it was like a landmark for the village it was so prominent. Stevie, standing in the rear of the jeep, holding onto the roll-bar in a ghoulish purple-haze pallor, wizard in his burping, howled out blind directions with his eyes closed. Francine's sudden swerving made him feel seasick, as well as hungover. Those instant burst of acceleration? Stevie held onto his jaw as he belched bile.

And Susan was waiting for them, expectant.

The whole village knew they were coming, seemingly.

71

For many of them were out, gazing at the jeep as it went by. And then, there was Susan, standing in the warm breeze from the ocean far below, his half-covered face, the great head tilting upwards, the arms out under the billowing gown. Mallibenny the wolf began howling with the onset of a magical dusk…

Joel, in the front with his lover, suddenly felt hysterical at the vision. Which period was this guy from? Intoxicated still from last night's deluge, he suddenly had bad feelings about coming up here. The house, to him, seemed ominous, as they bounced and trundled towards it, and Susan, who simply stood before it blocking the fine aspect, seemed prophetic also. And again, thought Johnny, in the rear with Stevie who was in the middle, look at the size of him! A huge fuck-off towelhead! Christ. But Joel had other thoughts in his wretched mind. Thoughts of… thunder. Thoughts of… ghosts. Thoughts, dare he visit them, of this Susan guy with his massive scaly pecker stuck all the way up his girl's box. Oh my. Was that sexy? Yes it was, to him suddenly. Ouch. He'd never felt that before. No. Not that one. Not that before. Never. Murder, yes. But intense voyeurism?

Fucking A. Then the jeep gave a front-wheel spin and the rear seemed to lurch to one side. Francine stalled the engine, but they were close enough anyway. Yes, very close. Indeed Susan, as an elephant, edged over to the jeep to inspect it, awesomely. Mallibenny appeared from behind his master's shadow. Awwwwoooooohhhhh! he said. Meaning welcome, Joel surmised as they all climbed stiffly out. Then he growled when he sniffed Johnny. Susan pushed him away with a hulking foot. 'Welcome, my friends,' he boomed, with Francine smiling at him.

'You knew we were coming?' she asked. He did. It had all been arranged.

72

'How?' said Stevie.

But Susan had already got to work on the jeep – as an opener. He caused it to move of its own free will, seemingly. From where Francine had stalled it, its engine started up and the vehicle actually moved in first gear for two-metres. Then it stalled again with a cough. They all looked around. Somehow the jeep had transmogrified from white to pale-green too in the darkening light. It was fucking weird. It was fucking fucked! Susan cleared his wide throat, then mysteriously said this: 'If the jeep had talent, then its talent would be am hiding place. Its talent would be what it am could do. And what it am could do would be to throw people from itself. That would be how it am talent would work. That would be how it am would be am hiding place. The people who it might throw would be am hidden by the jeep's am talent, you see. So if the jeep had am talent the people riding in it would be thrown into am hiding place. Its talent would be am hiding place, which would be to throw people into this am bushes!' And Susan waved his curious hands at the jeep again.

'Have you been on the pot?' Francine asked him with sisterly familiarity. Mist was descending from the cool mountains as they walked towards the darkened entrance.

'This guy is one serious wacko!' coughed Joel surreptitiously.

Then Susan picked up Francine with one hand and raised her into the air as one might do a rag-doll. It was something to behold. Francine gagged as she couldn't breathe for a second where Susan gripped under her arm. Then he removed his grip and she hovered there, motionless. He turned to his guests/audience and held out his arms as if pleased. Joel dashed in to help break her imminent fall, as he saw it. But she didn't. She didn't fall. She didn't

73

move. She just hovered. Floated. All gazed on in shocking astonishment...

Then this. Susan also possessed a genuine flying-carpet.

It arrived on the scene from inside the house as if by, well, magic. Susan had summoned it. Whoosh! It came in directly under a frozen Francine Coy, who somehow, in her sense of magic realism, dropped gently onto it. It then drifted off with her on its back and took her directly into the house via the first-floor balcony. Agog, was not the word for it. Johnny shuddered in his spellbinding agogness. Again he was terrified. (When was he not?) Again he wanted to shit himself. Speaking of which, occasionally tourists had seen this flying-carpet, flying. Usually their hotel-reps recommended a little less sangria. Occasionally too, Susan's flying-carpet flew by its own dark means. And so Johnny, then, felt like he imagined a tourist might feel who happened to witness this flying-carpet flying. He felt helpless in his lose-bowel quiver. He'd never felt like that before. No. He'd never felt like a tourist in Gran Canaria – *his* holiday-resort. What, with his money? With his fucking money? To feel helpless? Hapless, yes, with the sullen prospect of never being knighted. But helpless? No, not Johnny. To make matters worse for him – a man afraid of the dark as he was – Susan only used his flying-carpet in the dark, in the night, where the pilot-lights of jets would soar overhead. It was not for tourists' eyes, Susan's flying-carpet. It was not really for Johnny's eyes, either, who only wanted to be lead and said to then. *Take me!* No. Susan's flying-carpet was his most secret of all his secret magic-things!

And Stevie, wearing a flowery T-shirt, now believed in ghosts.

Was there anyone else around who felt the same way?

Inside the big cool house Susan's three wives and ten

children were getting ready for bed. No mean task. Indeed the ambience was that of many dogs trying to find hidden bones somewhere in a small forest. Their shrieks and screams bounced off the internal bare stone walls atonally. Wooden floorboards to the upstairs were visible, and these too echoed the hypnotically demented, now polyphonic, screams. Yes, it was a tiny medieval castle Susan had. A dark castle of many sounds and shapes. A forest of bones. A work of art one could live in. It was illuminated by candle-light alone. Even during the day candles were alight – an ambience conducive to hours of dreaming. The three Wives, in an antithesis to this ambience perhaps, gave witchy giggles as they got the children ready. Indeed, in this light, this yellow, evening flicker, their faces appeared as demonic…

Then Francine came clattering down the wooden stairs in hysteria. Children scattered before her as rats. She'd never flown on a magic-carpet before. 'Did you all see that? Was it just me? Did anyone else see that? I flew on a magic carpet! Oh, tell me you all saw it!'

'We all saw it,' said Joel ultra-calmly.

'It's… incredible!' sighed Johnny, looking round and still with the need to shit himself. Then he himself felt that he was swimming. Magic again, surely. Because he wasn't. But he was – in his senses. He was swimming around the darkened room as in an ocean. Susan was in control of his environment. Even the dimensions of it. Dark-matter entered Susan's abode at his will. No, Susan's abode was built on a dark-matter mound. Yes, that was it. Somehow it was a hole in space. A dark-matter hole. A black hole. Susan's hole?

Ouch! Johnny bumped into something.

Suddenly the three wives and ten children weren't

there. All looked at Johnny, who sort of felt himself being dragged down to the ground, even though he wasn't actually swimming in the air – although he was. It was like, while swimming in this magical ocean, an undertow was pulling him to the bottom. It was pulling *at* him. Bernie, watching Johnny with intense interest, did not see anything else in the world and, like the others, did not see the wives and children leave. He did not see them go upstairs. Johnny then fell to the stone floor. To the others it looked like he'd just fallen over drunk. But to Johnny, he was being dragged to the seabed! He gasped for air, as he struggled on the floor. Francine went to him. Seaweed pulled at his ankles. There was a stingray hovering around somewhere. Then Stevie, suddenly compos mentis, and watching Francine in bizarre equanimity, uttered this to her: *You actually flew on a flying-carpet!* He rubbed his chin.

'What is this place, man?' asked Joel, now feeling violent.

It was as though, really, they were all still intoxicated from last night. Because, after taking cold water from a large jug with ice in it, they were all, well, intoxicated again. Yes. A top-up, as it were. And looking at Johnny you could believe it! The guy was now doing breast-stroke with a red and panic-struck face! He was making for the surface! Francine stood back and watched him, perplexed. *Daddy!* What a jerk! Joel began laughing uncontrollably at him as he did before a kill. Bernie wanted to be held by Stevie for comfort. Then Susan stopped it all with a wave of the arm. Whoosh! Johnny was now washed up on a beach. He was all right. He was going to be okay. Oh, great.

76

10

THEY ALL SAT happily down. Kids could be heard giggling and running round upstairs like tiny animals. Then Susan's mind began doing something to Stevie's as they sat on a massive green sofa which was situated in front of a huge stone fireplace, where flames had never burned.

Stevie didn't know what it was, but it was nice. Kind of. Kind of sexy, too, being Stevie. But no. Because what was really happening was this: Susan was doing something to Bernie's mind, and Stevie was somehow finding out about it. Huh! Stevie was finding out (telepathically) that his little loyal lover was blowing the big man in a molten daydream, snorts and all. And, like Joel with Francine a moment ago, Stevie was furtively enjoying the sensation. It was rotten, yes, but lovely. Fucking lovely. They all sat looking at each other sipping water, waiting for the promised jugs of sangria. For Stevie, Bernie was sexy because he was untouched, unused, unsullied by life, it had seemed to him, yes, unviolated. Stevie could only love the pure, he had often told himself and even felt. Hence, paradoxically, how he came to love nothing, including himself. Because nothing or no one, ultimately, was pure. But what was going on here? Bernie the slag, the slut. Bernie the little fuck! So Bernie, sensing many things, all of them infinitely dangerous, edged in close to Stevie for a kind of child-like comfort, which never came. Because Stevie then gasped: 'Get off me! Get thee away from me!' rather horribly, as he was suddenly revolted by the idea of the pure, for reasons inexplicable…

Innocent Bernie was left alone.

Francine, on the other hand, unpure and content about it, in her continuing drunken state, had somehow believed (had she spoken about it?) that the real reason they'd come

77

up here to Susan's mini castle was to make contact with the rogue scientist, that cad, and his electric box of tricks. But make contact *mentally. Telepathically!* Why or how she knew this nobody knew, including her, because it was all done, well, telepathically. But what was wrong with the old mobile? It didn't seem appropriate, somehow. Mobile phones and Susan just didn't connect. They didn't work. She couldn't get a signal anyway. She'd even made Johnny bring his cheque-book!

Then Susan stood and walked across to a big old oak chair that had red velvet padding on it and a gold motif in Latin. He sat lordily on this chair, then scanned his guests like a gouty magistrate. Francine wondered if the professor, the nano-guy they were meeting, should he come to the house with the injections, would take payment in jewellery? She'd paid for cocaine in the past with this method. But no. She didn't have that much with her anyway. Just a few gold rings, a necklace, or two, one or three diamond studs like the itchy one she had there in her belly-button. Susan, she was then told telepathically, was going to live for 300-years anyway! He would be in no need of this nano-injection, these nano-probes. And at that moment Mallibenny the tame wolf came skulking into the main boom-room and began growling at everybody. Seriously. He meant it! Gouty Susan scanned him, too. For it was a terrible growl he gave. A sickening, kind of I'm-going-to-eat-your-flesh-because-I'm-an-empty-headed-animal growl. It seemed he wasn't tame any more, Mallibenny. Johnny, deliriously disoriented from his mental swim, and not tame either, gazed at it in fearful soap-opera-star anticipation. *Is my contract to be renewed? I'm so talented!* Susan wagged a big black finger solemnly. Mallibenny swallowed his tongue with a quiet squeal, then sat. He also stank. Animals did. They stank to

78

high heaven. Even when they were clean, they still stank like cooked flesh. Did wolves wag their tails? This one did. Mallibenny wagged his big bushy white tail as he sat bolt upright, stinking-staring at Susan through ice-blue deadly eyes.

There was also a parrot – Cervantes, of course. Well, obviously.

Cervantes spoke perfect Spanish. He'd been part of a circus on the Spanish mainland and would take questions from the audience. Cervantes the parrot had been around. He'd seen it all. But what a shit-stirrer! You couldn't divulge anything to Cervantes because he'd twist it and use it against you to suit his own warped agenda, a bit like Johnny. As a parrot, though, he was a right prick. Cervantes was a prick of a parrot. But Susan's children loved him, and so Cervantes the con-parrot stayed. But he had the run of things, much to Susan's chagrin. No confinement on a pole for him! Cervantes was a whore of a parrot. A woman in Madrid was beaten to death because of him, actually. The old Iago-to-Othello-situation. It was someone attached to the circus. Her boyfriend had been believing Cervantes' propaganda. *She's at it again! She's at it again! The sword-swallower this time! She's at it again!* Snap! One night while drunk the guy beat his innocent girlfriend's head against a wall until it opened up and her shocked brain fell out into the cool air for the first and only time. Cervantes got his sinister wish. And here, too, at Susan's, the damn parrot had tried to cause trouble between the big man and his three wives! It never materialized, but there had been rows between the children because of him…

'Look at him!' said Cervantes in Spanish, meaning Johnny. 'Who's he then? Who's he?'

'Hark at this bird!' gasped Johnny on a similar wavelength

79

– Mallibenny, glancing sheepishly up at his master in the king's chair, swallowing another growl as Johnny spoke. And then, in a circus atmosphere, Susan banged a bronze gong fairly loudly. The gong had inscribed on it To wake the dead in Spanish. Cervantes made some glib remark about its tones, then said:

'He's after the children! He's after the children! Sit on his knee! Sit on his knee!'

But the gong woke the dead. Well, it disturbed Susan's wives (purposefully) who came dancing down the stairs like ghosts, then scurried through the archway into the dining room and kitchen beyond. They each giggled and laughed as they ran. Oddly, they were wearing some kind of sack outfit. Yes, clothes made of sack! Francine blinked heavily at the sight. Was this simply routine for Susan? She didn't know. It was a fucking madhouse, she knew that. But whatever. She was hungry. Cervantes, watching Mallibenny through horrible parrot-eyes, said this in his mainland-lisp voice: *Here they come! Here they come! Slaves to the master! He'll have them all in the pot…*

Susan went to belt the parrot from behind. But the bird, in anticipation of this, hopped up onto a wooden curtain rail and squawked out of the way while doing a couple of shit-drops. Then he nodded with a big smile, and said in English, 'It am de man you want to speak to. De man with am de injections. He come. He come. I know. I see him on plane. De man am come with am de injections!'

'Yes but how do you know?' asked Francine.

'No matter! Now we eat! Am food am de ready!' And Susan stood with a frantic gush of wind, then clapped his hands whose sound echoed around the stone walls.

'Have you done food for us, man?' said Joel. 'Cool.'

'Yes! Am de wives have it ready!' Susan then gave two

80

swift hand-claps and all activity appeared to cease in the dining room, which was just out of sight of the lounge.

'But you see, er, Susan,' Joel went on, 'we are so fucked-up, man! Aw, hey. Like, you would not believe it, dude. I mean, we are really messed!' He gave a whistle as if to emphasize this assertion.

'Messed?' asked Johnny, as he began leering at Susan's wives in his usual, phantasmagorically corny manner. 'That's a new one on me.' Free from real angst at all times – that is, the angst borne from an examined life – Johnny Coy simply took this whole house-thing in his expectant stride. He just wandered into the dining room like some kind of unaware religious goon, sat at a place around the great oak table, grinned through his tight-lipped, leathery mouth, eased his tight leather trousers up a bit, farted silently inside them as he sat, then helped himself to a mug of sangria. No prob. Then he added, 'Messed?' again, laughingly, as he openly leered. Susan's (half naked) wives began bringing out the dishes, and Johnny's eyes were big and bright – big, bright and yellow, then.

'Yeah, man. Messed. As in messed-up?' Joel gazed at him.

Fortunately for Johnny, Susan never got either jealous or disconcerted at any flirting towards his wives by others – even though it happened a lot. Jealousy just wasn't on his agenda. But magic was. Lots of it. Only in magic did a kind of paradoxical jealousy transpire, curiously enough. Yes. In magic Susan got jealous of his wives. Susan had raged over his wives – in magic. And then, when the magic subsided, the rages would vanish. Just like that. In the dining room was a big 16-seater table. It was a banqueting table, clearly. Magic apart, food was miraculous…

Stevie thought this then. *Miraculous food*. When Stevie

81

was a young gay lad he went out with an older gay Indian gentleman, who, in turn, was initiated by an older Indian gentleman himself. This older man used to say to the younger one, the one who took Stevie, in a thick Bengali whine while rocking his head and chuckling: *You are ready for the anal-fucking!* At the sight of this huge table, Stevie, now well and truly anally-fucked, gave a brief snigger, because, one of his first excursions was on a long wooden table by his Indian gentleman lover, who, by a weird twist of fate, also believed in magic, and used to insist upon Stevie gorging himself on Indian food afterwards. Hence Stevie, then and there, related being buggered to lovely, miraculous food – until he put too much weight on and felt the urge to *bugger* others with the weight behind him. That is, to deliver rather than to receive, as Stevie preferred. But it was all down to historical perspective, really. Yeah. That's where it was, he thought. Historical perspective. You couldn't appraise something without it! No, not really you couldn't. And so, historically, Stevie thought this as he saw Susan's table: *You are ready for the anal-fucking!* He gently rocked his head from side to side too, smiling.

11

'I WOULDN'T MIND gevvin' stuck between that!' declared Johnny to one of the wives. Serena, who spoke no English, at 24 remained in the house under Susan's enormous will. She remained there magically – unlike the other two – Moya and Moon – who remained there because they gave birth to four each of the ten kids (two to Serena) and Susan, whom they actually loved but whose age could have been 60 or it could have been 40, would think nothing of having sex with the three of them simultaneously while controlling some magic trick in another room, which, in turn, controlled Serena! Johnny, of course, couldn't have handled even one of them. But the fading rock-star could never approach that psychological bridge – Viagra and all.

Francine sipped tangy sangria, listening to Joel suddenly ramble on about his crack-days. Aw, man, the dens we used! Joel had actually grown out of crack. This wasn't thought possible at the time, but Joel had somehow managed it. The crack no longer had an effect on him! Yes, Joel had needed something stronger. And so it was that he began inventing his own drugs, usually a combination of many already-used ones. To mellow he'd used a mixture of heroin, Diazepam, brandy and laudanum, all blended together in a milky drink – applied every ten minutes for 36-hours. To fly he'd used cocaine (pure) prescription-amphetamines in tablet-form, asprin, rotten cheese, rotten mushrooms and vinegar, all mixed up with a bottle of Bud, and taken intravenously. Two days and nights later he'd go out and murder someone, while smiling. What a high, man! But what a dive. He'd even got Francine on this once out at Staten Island. She was on the point of serious delirium, when Joel ate a live pigeon in front of her, feathers and all. He made animal sounds, as he

83

coughed violently. Francine then collapsed. She dreamt of a black sky full of stars. The sound of surf. The sound of birds in a quiet wood. Joel raped her while she was unconscious. Anally. He'd raped her severely. Francine never found out. She never knew. Yes, she was sore. Even cut. But she'd simply put this down to either all the sex she'd had over the years, constipation, or a mild infection. Ultimately, though, her soul laughed at her for going out with someone like Joel Maize, someone as crap as him. I mean, who was this fucking shithead hanger-on prick-with-ears? He had LOSER stamped on his brow in neons the moment Francine first saw him. He was a lower-class bum, really, to her, had she been thinking clearly like she used to. A nothing. A shit-eater. A no-mark. All the importance felt when making a movie was completely contrived, she had subconsciously verbalized when first they went out and he was waxing about himself. Movies were nothing, ultimately. Like middle-of-the-road pop-songs they were forgotten almost as soon as they were released! Even indi-movies, Joel. Forgotten. (Forget it). Of no importance, dude. Like you. Fuck-all. But the subconscious verbalization never made it to the waterfront of Francine's mouth. It never made the big time. Sad, because Joel would have thought about it. He would have thought about what she said. Then maybe killed her. Indeed Joel thought he thought about lots of things, once. He thought he thought about what Francine said too regarding nano-probes and the insignificance of poor people, but perhaps he only thought he thought about that and didn't actually think about it until he had the time to think about it, which may well be never, he thought, thinking about it then. There. In Susan's great dining-room, he thought. I think, therefore I don't know anything. Joel was definitely in his own world…

84

Francine lit a cigarette. She thought about Joel, who was sitting next to her, thinking. She thought about finally verbalizing her subconscious articulation – which, incidentally, and to the horror of all Hegalians, was much more dexterous and lateral than actual words spoken – but she found that she couldn't bring the sentences to life because of booze, not emptiness, and instead tried hard to forget about what she thought about Joel, because she knew, somewhere, that he was a bum, ultimately, and she couldn't ever conceive of herself actually being involved with such a burn-out. In trying hard also to make her mouth function subconsciously, this inaccurate concept called *Speech* just wouldn't work. So she forgot about it. (Forget it). She waved a smoky hand.

'It's forgotten,' said Joel for some reason, rocking his head slightly in the now darkly-lit room. His lips creaked and slobbered at the same time. Only air came from in between them. Air – no sound. For Joel now had been rendered dumb, sealed and frozen, and it was all Susan's fault. (Time passes. Time had past). Time was passing, then, in time, and Joel, in a trancelike, frozen haze, farted as though wanting to do so for hours – in time – after he'd eaten boiled sprouts. 'It's remembered,' he then whispered, and time passed again. But where did it pass to? Joel reckoned he had the answer.

'What are we here for?' little Bernie suddenly asked in sound logicality, gazing around at the massive table, at massive Susan, at the parrot and the massive fucking wolf.

'I have no idea, darling,' said Stevie. The wolf also seemed to shrug in agreement with this. What were you all doing in my house anyway? he seemed to wolfishly ask. Tonight was for everything and nothing, Mallibenny then seemed to telepathically tell Stevie. It was all very mysterious. As every night can be. All or nothing. That's what nights were for, for

85

everything and nothing. Oh, shit. Stevie looked to Francine to see if she heard these wolf-words. She hadn't, the floozy. Shaken, he then looked to Mallibenny. Had he really spoken them? The wolf gazed back at him, head tilting slightly in curious animal wonderment. The wolf was a philosopher! *Turd burglar*, Stevie then heard spoken in his brain.

Johnny downed a whole glass of sangria in one. His eighth. He burped loudly. At that moment the three wives came marching into the dining-room carrying a roasted pig on a shoulder-high platter. Susan applauded them sarcastically. Long, slow slaps. But Johnny had only just eaten breakfast. Susan was playing magic on him still. Well, at 6.30 p.m. That was about right for a rock-star. Wasn't it? Sir Johnny, the great late-breakfast eater?

Then, from somehow regaining his alleged equilibrium from the gross effort of speech-intoxication, Joel, taking it all in his stride, pointed at the roasted pig as though only mildly perplexed. 'That's, like, where time goes, man!' he declared. He looked a bit like Stan Laurel, looking then at Francine, flummoxed. A whole Pig? A whole time-void? He took a sip of the sweat juice of sangria and grinned a crazy, wild-boy, idiot's grin, then blinked very slowly. The pig had had an apple stuffed in its mouth which had been glazed in toffee, or something. No, on second glancing, the entire pig had been glazed in aspic, or something. What was that? It was a glazed, roasted pig, still steaming, that'd do. Appetizing? Well. It was true, alcohol moved in mysterious ways. Alcohol had moved Joel in mysterious ways, many times. It had taken him to places no sober person would ever dream of going. For booze could alter the perception and cause you to believe almost anything, as is known, including what you believed and the way you felt. But could it make a fucking cooked pig look appetizing? Well, yes, it

86

could. Especially if time had gone into it. The whole gang's perception had been altered by sangria, and the whole gang now collectively believed that it was ready to eat a roasted pig. So the whole gang would do that, it'd eat Susan's pig. (It had been the pet of Moon's eldest daughter until yesterday, Susan's pig, pun and all). Suddenly everybody was salivating, including Susan. Francine, now incredibly drunk all of a sudden, looked at Joel, who, to her, did not appear as either a bum or intoxicated. For alcohol had moved her in mysterious ways, too: she was now roaringly drunk. So drunk in fact that she wanted to scream with a wild laughter and fall over backwards off her chair, laughing. Did nanotechnology really exist? She burst out laughing, slapping the table, almost falling. She didn't care. She looked at Susan, who appeared disconcerted. Nope, she just didn't care. She snorted, then a vague notion came over her. Richard Feynman had once asked back in the 1950s: What would happen if we were able to arrange atoms one by one in the way we want them? Francine had read that, without even knowing what it meant – what atoms did – before booze had moved her in mysterious ways, causing her to temporarily disbelieve everything, including nanotechnology. Richard who? She laughed uproariously again, crazed in her own surreal world…

It was a case of indulging in microscopic graffiti. That's what had been happening in the world of nanotechnology during her adult life. People had been carving their initials in nano-probes for all posterity to view. (Was this the future of writing?) But again Francine didn't know that either, even though she'd actually read it. And like many, the more she thought she knew, the less she actually did. But of course, she was moneyed. This meant that knowing things and being intelligent (to say nothing of talent) had little value.

87

(Value being whatever it was, to whomever, however). All things could be bought, including talent. For in Francine Coy's world value had to glitter, of course. At the dining table in a strange world, what could the implications of rich people living for 300-years be? Was that of value? It was a glittering, terrible concept, really, not to mention a limiting one. But Richard Feynman was a far-thinking scientist, it seemed, though Francine had been loathed to read this. He knew, unlike her, what the implications of giving rich people a triple life-span could entail. There would be over-crowding of the one type of person on a scale beyond the call of nature. Thus, nature would no doubt bite back, as was nature's wont, Feynman guessed.

Chomp! Therefore Richard Feynman wanted a fairer share of his micro nano-robots, one of which he himself, it is said, carved his initials on. He would put in place a system of health-care delivery. That is, the probes would be available to all, or they'd be available to none. But Francine didn't want to hear that, even though these thoughts and voices entered her head then. All, who? She shook them away. To none but the rich, she wanted, and I'd heard her say it. She was going to have her own initials carved on a nano-robot and have it as team-leader in her belly!

Chomp! Susan ate a pig's ear before Stevie's watery eyes.

12

COULD SUSAN EAT? Could wolves fly?

Only the few, was Francine thought as she too ate roasted, steaming pig most hungrily. Maybe a small colony? That'd do it. A small colony of very rich people with nano-probes in their blood. That'd do nicely. Oh, if only Lady Di was still alive! Francine wished at Susan's extravagant table in Gran Canaria. Her and me. Best mates. Two cool sloans, yah! And then, Francine darkly mused even further, as she later told me. Once we, the rich, the few, the beautiful few, have the technology in our systems, all traces of it would be destroyed. Nano-technology would be rendered void. But wasn't this just alcohol talking? Surely Francine was a nice person? Now, all these decades later, I honestly couldn't say whether she was or wasn't. I just don't have an opinion any more...

'My friends,' Susan then said during a ravenous, slobbering pause, 'this am de early-morning feast!' (He'd surely got that wrong). 'You will need am de strength if you am to trek over to am de other islands in search of your am de bad man.' He then held out his great arms as if in greeting. 'Dis pig, whose name was am de Drake, is de feast for you all! Eat!' In he dived once more.

A pig called Drake? Hmmm. Susan dropped his big robe with one single flick, and was, Bernie was astonished to behold, totally naked where he sat. A great subconscious gulp echoed around the table. For Susan was huge – in every way. Then he rose to his feet and snatched at a carving knife while still masticating. It was a very long knife, and he used it fairly violently to hack off great chunks of hot pork (poor Drake) for himself and, perhaps, others too. But no one could keep up with him. He ate as he carved – he ate with a passion. He even devoured the glassy apple in one unholy crunch – seeds and all. Terrifyingly, his black penis was as long as a donkey's – ee-orr – as it swayed and flopped before Bernie's rounded eyes. Exclusively for him, it seemed. In fact Bernie became mesmerized with it, as a child watching a roaring bonfire. Spellbound, he was. And Johnny, too, seemingly. For the little man gave an awesome gasp at its humongous horror.

'I'm as drunk as a brown dog!' Stevie then declared, somewhat inexplicably.

Francine, ignoring Susan's great nakedness, tucked into smouldering white meat as though under a famished spell. In fact they all ate as though compelled to. Even Johnny, who hadn't properly eaten since he was a teenager, snaffled and tore like a starved hyena. Indeed the more they actually did eat, the more they appeared to gather speed with it and turn bestial. Poor old Porky. Then the wives brought vegetables and more plates into the room, giggling in Spanish and bowing to Susan's protracted, jumping pecker. Johnny, of course, gorging himself heavily, enjoyed their subserviency. To him it was right: that's what women were for: he gorged on nonetheless. However, the appearance of the wives did engender another sarcastic comment from Cervantes the parrot. Something to do with being tamed and ready. Or cocked and ready. Indeed Susan did seem to grow as he ate, and not just in the middle. He seemed to swell all over. Susan's great black body seemed to enlarge in a kind of tyrannical smothering. For if arrogance gave rise to mediocrity, then bigness gave birth to a type of superfluity. A needless encompassing of people. And that's what Susan was doing now. It seemed he would grow all over his guests, as well as his dumbed-down wives. His gargantuan nakedness at the head of the table appeared so outlandish

90

that it begged explanation. It just wasn't required. He was a black, hairless bull without anything to do. A manatee on heat somewhere. He was a fucked-up hippopotamus lounging in a rotten swamp.

And Susan had large thoughts.

Bernie, also eating as though the sun's light depended on it, was beginning to feel strangely fearful in his slopping-gulping of food. The hot pork in his belly gave him a healthy paranoia concerning his host's possible plans. For Susan had been watching him. O yes. Like a hawk. Bernie's ass twitched a little as he noticed this. It could have been the thought of Susan's massive pecker in it – the mind thrusting that image downwards. He wasn't sure. It just twitched. He sensed Susan was up to something. He moved his buttocks on the chair in order to alleviate the sensation. It was a big thought Bernie was thinking: Susan's cock deep in his ass? Sweet Jesus. It twitched again. It was a damn big penis. And Bernie only now realized that he'd not taken his eyes from it since Susan de-robed. He gulped, burping pig. He tried to remove his stupid gaze. He could see the thick dark stem over the thick dark table, as Susan sat back. He could see the space-black pubic hairs, all matted and glistening in the candlelight. No, he couldn't take his eyes from the thing. But surely it was an inhospitable place? (There was a poem there somewhere). The face? The place? The snake? Nice assonance. He didn't care. Bernie now visualized Susan entering him. So he ate more hot pork, and brazenly, steamingly, kept his eyes on Susan's dick. Grease surrounded his trembling mouth, as indeed it did everybody else. But Bernie shrank as he sensed what might be coming to his pockmarked lower-bowel. He shat himself metaphorically: *Susan was circumcised!*

The head was like a head – a human head! Stevie had already seen it. He was sure it winked at him, too. This pecker

91

should have been in the Guinness Book of Records. It was certainly, Stevie knew, one of the biggest in the world. How many holes must a thing like that have entered? Stevie was sure that a monster like that would stay hard for hours. Days even. It would be in its nature. But then, looking sheepishly at Bernie all of a sudden, and sensing the now mediaeval atmosphere intensely, Stevie said, 'What are we doing here, darling? How did we arrive at such a location?' all meekly and coyly. For he too was visualizing Susan's brontosaurus penis in his cowering pussy…

Francine finally lost her balance. While snatching at some vegetables, she gave a great big burp and fell backwards off her chair. Moon went to help her, but Susan waved the wives away. Francine was by then laughing her head off on the floor. She couldn't get up, and food and grease and sangria were all over her expensive clothes. So she just continued to eat while flat on her back, laddishly giggling, choking, coughing, burping. Susan farted. It blew Bernie away. Joel jumped at the great rasp of it. For Susan's farts sounded like some kind of high-powered tool at work. But then Johnny informed him that he was going to pay to have him bumped off. Joel shrugged. Aw, man! Quit bustin' my balls! From the floor Francine kept saying, "Here's to the injection!" as though a toast.

Two hours later and they were still eating. Even Johnny, who now probably would never stop eating: something was compelling them. Chomp, chomp. Gorge, gorge. Burp, fart, scream. Hee-hee.

They ate without being aware they were eating.

Camels chomping, with the exception of Susan, who was aware he was eating, and loved it. But the whole pig had gone. Ribs were sucked, bones were licked, bellies swollen.

92

It was true, for wasn't it life which killed us in the end? Breathing, eating, walking, being? It killed you. Life would end your life one day. Just like that. It was life's job. That's what life had been designed to do: end life in the long run. But nano-technology would put a stop to that. It'd stop life ending life.

Johnny had been telling Joel how *his* life would end by one of his loyal hit-men, then, in the same breath, was telling Susan, in ear-bending annoyance, what it was like being on stage, being adored by fans. It killed him. "It's great. I miss it. It's fab. To be up on vat, stage! Brilliant. I knew Gary Glitter you know. O yes. Him and me? O yes. Mates, yer see. Drinking-partners and shit. Gary and me? Like vat we were. Two fucking peas. Mates, mate. Both of us recognized in our own time, of course. Great, we were. Fucking great. Changed the world. Me and Bowie, too. Changed the world, we did. Changed the fucking world…" Johnny's eyejob, like every male eyejob, now looked even more burns-orientated, Joel was loathed to observe, hearing Johnny prattle. Like every male eyejob, it aged him awfully and made him appear deathly, it had seemed to Joel. It made them appear waxy. (The nano-bots would sort all that out in the long-run, yeah. No probs. They'd de-eyejob him if needs be! Put the character back which had been sliced away, they would! My words, imaging Johnny, not Johnny's imagining himself. And did Susan know who Gary Glitter was? Certainly today, some two centuries later, no one younger than me has heard of him. But that's for later).

Lots of lolley equalled more sophistication. Francine, believing that, now standing with her back against the stone wall as in a club, believed also that she'd earned her money, and believed that she'd worked hard for it. She believed it. Lots of lolly, she had. All earned. Challenge this notion at

93

your peril. Yes, it was a fierce Francine who used her many boyfriends as royalty used the Courtiers. Well, Joel Maize, no Courtier, but a part-time killer certainly and the most current in a long list of lackies, was now being asked to get rid of Stevie and Bernie. What Francine actually meant was for the night only, for some hazy reason. Get rid of them from here! We'll see them tomorrow. But, as with royalty, the hints were often vague and dangerously ambiguous...

'Joel, get rid of the fruits!' In one single mad second he lunged at Stevie like a dog from hell across the table, and attempted to slit his throat with the blunt knife he'd been using to eat the pig. In one single mad second also Susan's magic raised him from his victim, only to throw him to one side of the room as from a catapult. Joel was so out-of-it that he neither knew what he was doing nor what'd happened to him. Susan then laughed at him attempting to get to his feet. Stevie, on the other hand, holding his throat and red with fear, drunkenly slurred abuse, then shook at the incident. He wanted to know what the problem was. Francine then beckoned him to come closer for a kiss from mummy. Bernie watched in intoxicated trepidation. His dismay and nervousness, not to mention his abhorrence at Francine's obvious dark change of heart towards them both, caused his spinal-column to quiver. He quaked as his lover did actually sit on Francine's treacherous knee to be cuddled. 'Mummy didn't mean it. There, there.' Stevie wanted Joel to be put in jail for that. He pointed.

The lackey previous to Joel, Sam Lovejoy, a tall rich silly person from Berkshire whom everybody overestimated, had fallen under her charms as well. He'd actually paid for three thugs (he couldn't do it himself) to 'hurt' a man whom Francine felt was stalking her. She felt the man was a kidnapper. It turned out that he was a private detective

94

watching a married woman come and go from The Tower in a divorce proceeding. The man, while in hospital, spoke to the cops. The three thugs were easily arrested, and they blabbed. Sam Lovejoy got four years along with them, and was still, in 1999, inside. God alone knew what state his arsehole was in. Joel, however, was different, in that he was crazy enough to carry out the deeds himself. Francine knew that. She knew he was up for it. Consequently – and this wasn't the first time – she would wind Joel up for action all for her own entertainment. As was life. Life was for entertainment, for Francine. So imagine 300-years of it? All the changes? the entertainment? Only for the rich, though. Only for the few. Joel's head was cut from the crash, but he wasn't aware of it. He had often thought that the American establishment didn't give a stuff for his (poor) existence, even though it constantly ran with the ideal of *The Individual*. Yet he was a psychopath, which possibly made him a proper individual in the truest sense of the term. His face, now his head, bore the scars as proof. But what Joel wanted to hear more than anything else then was the click of high-heels on a stone floor: Susan's three wives dressed to kill! Yahoo! Joel wanted to get malignly desolate with the sexual frustration of it. In his now ghosted condition, his now luminous intoxication, it wasn't so bad that sobriety was awesome, it was that it was hornily awesome. Sobriety was horny in a biblical sense, and only Joel could know this because only Joel could never achieve it. A proper hard-on, that is, along with total sobriety. Hence frustration. But in his desolation, in his insobriety, distantly hurt from being flung against a wall by forces unseen, Joel had convinced himself that he was in a drunken club someplace, and had begun dancing seriously to the guitar music which was playing somewhere else in the fuzzy background through Susan's antiquated

95

stereo. Johnny, still waxing about Gary and David's genius, suddenly saw that no one was listening to him, and saw also Joel's madness rise in the room like a lifting-bag from the seabed. His head jolted back as he glimpsed Joel dance. It was... remarkable!

And Stevie too, still wanting Joel imprisoned for ten years – held in chains in a dungeon – with a full belly gawped full-on at his American comrade. For Joel moved as though an eagle escaping a great downdraught in a hot canyon. He moved as though approaching the speed of light: his body appeared to rise...

It wasn't a pretty sight. And then, as Joel danced – or perhaps transmogrified – Susan engineered one of his mammoth tricks. The food had gone, the sangria had spilled. All were over-the-top with everything and were lounging-looking at mad Joel, when Susan transported them back in time three days. It was to the day *before* they arrived on the island, yet they were all somehow there, at Francine's. They shouldn't have been, because they were in reality still in London. But they were. And it was as real as you now glancing up from these pages to check out your surroundings. They're real, aren't they. Well, you hope they are. You hope your surroundings exist. You believe your surroundings exist, don't you, and not just a great big trick played on you by Susan who's been watching you since you began this book! A very different Johnny Coy was cooking breakfast inside. Stevie, Bernie, Joel and Francine were outside on the sunny patio, talking. They were sober and very much all right. Somehow it was a different atmosphere, because they all liked each other. Johnny was an obliging, nice, modest, retired rock-star happy with his lot. Francine was reading a novel, perfectly naturally. (The only novel Francine had ever read in her other life was something by Jilly Silly or somebody). Yet here she was, reading The Naked And The Dead by Norman Mailer. She'd been glancing up from out of her sunglasses too to add to the pleasant conversation. Bernie, Stevie and Joel were wearing identical army shorts. Johnny *did not* have leather trousers on.

'I'll go and help your dad with the breakfast,' Joel magnanimously suggested.

But before he could do that Johnny appeared with two plates and gestured to everyone that it was ready. The brilliant sunshine enhanced the colours in the food. Scrambled eggs sparkled, smoky bacon glistened. Hot toast and orange juice shimmered under the glossy ultra-white gleaming. Happy, Johnny then commented on the beauty of the day. He was glad to be alive. Francine sat her book down and, raising her sunglasses, thanked her father for making such a lovely breakfast. The novel she'd been reading before the Mailer was V by Thomas Pynchon, which she felt was quite unsurpassed and felt the need to say so. A total masterpiece, in fact. She began comparing the Mailer somewhat intellectually with Stevie, who, of course, had read both.

'I find with Mailer that the characters merge into an endless portrayal of eccentric reality.'

'Have you read Gravity's Rainbow?' Stevie then asked her in loving admiration. 'It's incredible. A bit long, but incredible. It's a one-off. It cannot be categorized in my opinion, which is one of the reasons I like it.' He sipped chilled orange juice in the warm sunlight. It was cold. The toast was still hot. The bacon, crisp. Ooh. He sucked his lips.

'Just like my love for you!' Bernie then said to Stevie. 'It too cannot be categorized!'

'Ahhh,' said Francine. 'That's sweet. Oh, he's lovely, isn't he!'

'Reading is a pleasure which can't be got elsewhere,'

97

Johnny then declared, sitting. 'It's a demanding-pleasure, sure, but then the best pleasures are! I don't like my pleasures to be reassuring. It bores me. Being reassured only makes me feel old. No. Give me the demanding-pleasures of a novel any day!' And the pleasant Johnny tucked into his own morning cuisine with relish.

'I agree,' agreed Francine. 'This book here is very good. I feel as though I've gone through the Second World War with this platoon, in the Pacific. It's unnerving.' She glanced at Joel next to her at the table, who didn't appear to be fully under Susan's spell. 'Joel? Are you okay?'

'Get me home!' he then roared. 'Aigh! I'm floating! Aigh! Fucking hell! What's happening!' With that he stood, turned, and flung himself in the harbour with a great other-worldly splash.

Francine let out a swift scream. She didn't know what the problem was: Joel, in this ghostly reverie, did not do drugs or even drink. So what was the matter with him? Why was her loyal handsome man behaving so oddly, behaving so badly? She stood while Stevie rushed to the wall's edge which surrounded the apartments to see what he could do. Joel never surfaced. Stevie contemplated diving in, Johnny beat him to it. From behind the little man came, a successful jockey leaping from his great horse at the winner's enclosure. Sp-lush! White sea-foam engulfed his small figure as he leapt into ocean-blue. Now Francine came to the water's edge, holding her middle in mild concern. Bernie, perhaps diplomatically, remained seated while masticating crispy bacon. It tasted too good to leave. Johnny surfaced, spluttering, treading-water, gulping. No Joel. The water wasn't deep. It was clear. No one could see his figure. There was no sign of him anywhere.

Then they were all together, including Joel, standing on

the jetty. It was 1875.

Francine was attired in a suitable outfit, as were the others. They gazed around. It was a lot quieter and a lot hotter. All the yachts had gone, and so had the apartments. The mountains were the same, though. Yes. There were still up there, all red and huge and silent in their timelessness. It was a different jetty. No, it was the same, only newer. Johnny edged towards it in the heat. Joel wanted to say something about being careful. It was a good scene for a movie, but he didn't really know what a movie was. He had to frown to think about the concept. An ashen-faced Bernie tried to remain calm. Even the air tasted different. Stevie was smoking a pipe very naturally. He had long sideburns and long, wavy hair. His jacket, which had broad lapels over a fluffy white shirt, was a bright green velvet and had brass buttons on. Bernie blinked hard to take it in. Although, he had to admit, the pipe suited Stevie. But what on earth was going on? Then, splash! A reversed splash. A kind of sucking-splash. Susan emerged from the harbour waters like an energetic leaping walrus…

The gang turned on their heels and ran. No question. Shrieks echoed around the silent domain. But Susan was in front of them, calming them through gestures. 'My friends, it am all right. It am good. This is mine am de party-piece. I am de sorcerer! You know dis already!' And he vanished.

'My God,' commented Stevie, sucking his pipe as he slowed then calmed. 'I've never seen anything like it. My friends back at Oxford would be utterly amazed. I am utterly amazed!' He sucked on, an interested 19th Century scientist.

Then, to Bernie's total amazement, it was 2270, and he was alone. All alone. And strange. Yes, it was his 300-birthday, that's how he knew the year. That's why he'd

99

come back to Gran Canaria. He'd be 300 on 5th June 2270 and he'd promised himself the trip. He'd marked it in his century-almanac exactly 100-years ago. He'd been looking forward to it ever since. But the Port of Mogan was now completely different. Crafts hovered over synthetic flooring. People, dressed in silver and gold, flew on hired anti-gravity belts slowly over the mountains, which were still there, red and brown as always. Bernie recognized where he was, yet he didn't. He didn't know where he was psychologically, because he hadn't grown to it through time. But that was okay. He'd get used to it. He had a sense of where he was – where for art thou? There'd be a lot to discover. 2270? It was a wonderful, terrifying sensation. He was in the future! And there, just along from where he stood, was where Francine's apartment-house stood. So much. So… much. So few knew of so much.

He walked to the edge of the jetty as Johnny had done in 1875. It was very much decayed and faded now, sections replaced with new materials. A holiday-maker droaned overhead on an anti-gravity belt, waving at someone in the sunshine. Bernie glanced up at him, then, glancing back down, he was sitting around Susan's table again in 1999. He could still hear the soft hum of that anti-gravity belt as he turned his head quickly and vomited quietly on the floor. He didn't mean to, but he just couldn't help himself. Susan had spiked the sangria with his own special brand of hallucinogenic potions.

100

13

'TOKYO,' SOMEBODY SAID in the meniscus stillness.

'I've seen the future,' Bernie gasped in an idiosyncratic composure. And that was that. Illusions were made to be destroyed. After all the food and the tripping, they simply drove back down the mountain in the jeep, in the dark, in the cool Gran Canarian night, and never crashed once. Well, Francine caught the wheel-arches on a few rocks, but it was nothing serious.

Susan had released them, in the knowledge that they'd be returning very shortly. He was good at things like that. He'd released a policeman once in the days when he only had two wives and Spanish television had no gameshows. The policeman, it has to be said, accidentally killed himself the following week by releasing the handbrake on his car as he had sex with an unnamed girl, unarmed. Turning to look, the horrified man showed his bare arse to the ravine his car tipped into, before it lunged downwards into the screaming fireball that it became. The policeman entered night with vodka and a girl he'd only just met, he entered light. As then, Susan was also exhausted after his control, but no one could ever know that. For Susan was very secretive when it came to his own physical set-up. As secretive as a black hole. He'd once been aware of his father, a mystical taciturn mountain man who had been a Muslim before Susan was born and who lived to be 122, looming over him as he masturbated watching his mother bathe in a tin bath in the kitchen. The father did nothing. He simply watched. Terrifyingly, Susan, not being able to stop, (the vinegar-strokes) was on the point of orgasm as he noticed his father. He couldn't prevent the white sticky stuff from spilling onto his wrist. The father turned,

101

changed, then walked away. This incident altered Susan too. From then on he wanted to become a magician. He wanted to transmogrify his surroundings. Tokyo flourished because it transformed by the month. People had said that it was the greatest city on earth because of this, because it transformed. Nothing stayed the same in Tokyo, nothing stayed still. It therefore lived forever in an infinite possibility of what it could be, of what it will be. While Susan slept in a vast bed with his three wives that night, secretly concealing how tired he felt, every cell in his body became new and transformed. They thrived from what their supernatural predecessors had effected – almost consciously. Susan's cells mutated like things evolving. They metamorphosed. Consequently he shat ectoplasm. This happened twice monthly – an unusual body-phenomenon. For Susan had invisible power-lines that stretched all the way to the African mainland...

Gzzzzzz! It may have been a week later, or it may have been the following afternoon. But Joel and Francine were alone on a quiet plateau up in the mountains and Joel had been praising her as well as telling her how much he loved her, in his permanently ghosted condition. He'd wanted to find the time and the place to kind of extend his feelings all over her, he said. 'I... really do love you!'

'Crap, Joel. Men will say anything for sex.'

'Yeah. Maybe. But hey, I feel it. I do love you!' There was a remarkable view from where they'd parked up; now they were sitting on rocks looking at it. The Atlantic Ocean glinted all around the southern end of the island, which was spread out below them in a vaporizing haze. It was as though they were higher than they actually were, almost like viewing it from space. For there was a silky dryness in the air which seemed to allow them to completely take in the vast amount of area. They kissed inside this space. They sucked faces like snails entwining on a branch. Minutes later Joel had the same tongue deep inside Francine's vagina and was licking the internal walls to it hungrily, as she gazed upwards at seabirds hovering on the wind. The sensation tickled her mind. It also soothed her body: feelings of daydreamy sensual mental masturbation. An intimate feeling of being pleasantly disembodied. But then, Joel pulled his shorts down and had entered her before she'd had time to fully enjoy his tongue's delight, before she'd had time to realize the tickling of her mind. Complexly, it was as though Francine then absorbed him. The afternoon heat was drying things as usual, and his knees dug into scorched gravel as his motion lifted him to the edge of the mountain's aura. But Francine's body seemed to involuntarily draw Joel's through it as if by osmosis, and he adored the sensation beyond words. She was the only woman he'd ever had sex with who could do that. Sexually, everyone had their own little tricks. But Francine's vaginal-sucking, or whatever it was, womb-sucking, left nothing to be desired. It was something that, all men, whenever they'd ever experienced it, never tired. Once tasted, never forgotten. Absorbing Joel in a helpless pant, her nails suddenly tore at his sunburnt shoulders, too. Ooh, a bit of pain. He growled a little and shook his grovelling head. She spat upwards into his mouth, causing him to fuck in the gorgeous anger of it. The taste of Francine's genitalia on his tongue, the lovely metallic squalor of it, was, to him, the actual taste of sex; he knew he could never fully live without it – but combined with spit? That taste? No. He knew he could never survive in a world where cunt-juice had dried up – the actual taste of sex.

Outdoor Sexual Intercourse. A possible working-title for a

103

movie. They moved together as regular lovers – outdoors screwers. Joel, by no means well-hung, often disastrous in the cot with drug-droop, seemed to use half his lower body which had been taken into Francine's, engendering, to both parties, the illusion of bigness. He might even drown in there! For he found himself actually wanting to *step inside*. He wanted to walk into Francine's vagina and call out her name. SHE'D MADE HIM LARGE! Susan was standing there, watching them. 20-minutes in, Joel was about to come. Dust and sweat now covered his prickly skin. Francine saw Susan as she squinted in the strong light, but did not stop Joel, who then exploded lustfully with his shoulders cut and bleeding. He burst open, he burst out, like a crashing meteorite. Then Francine, now watching Susan intently, whose big black head blocked out the sun, creamed in the enormous vacuum of her womb's pulsation. She shuddered in spasmodic modulations of her vein's creations. Streaming sunlight filtered into her swollen, wobbling brain, as a little mouth inside her body arched forward and pecked at a puddle of Joel's drug-packed semen. The harmony of it and her orgasm seemed to isolate all her emotions and pinpoint them directly in her navel. For Francine cried a little as her molten fluids flamed. She flared her eyes as her taut body curved. She was a crescent moon gleaming in the glimmering night sky. She was a vaulted ray of stardust arching across the globe. And Susan was no longer there. (Was he ever?) Susan had vanished again as Joel collapsed on top of Francine – a definite intimacy between the two of them, deny it as she may. For she felt the need to play with his spiky hair, yes, caress it, which was also Joel's post-coital frown bronzed in dust.

They held each other for a long moment as juice evacuated her boiling canal, mingling with Gran Canarian rock.

104

They would combine for centuries, Francine thought, wistful in a fickle after-sex loveliness. Joel pulled out with a pop. Stuff gushed. Everything was back to normal.

14

THERE WAS SOME truth in the notion that, as adults, we longed for the seeming purity of the decade we were born in, or were children in. This could perhaps be called nostalgia, if nostalgia was a yearning for things past – emotions, say, or happy past events. But what we felt for those distant days often became a standard in a kind of Utopian life opposed to how horrible the adult world had become for us. Little Johnny Coy had been experiencing this – this longing for the 1940s when everything, for him, was just fine. They'd been driving in the mountains, in the wistful air, and Johnny's nose had been aching from when he'd previously banged it, drunk – although he had no memory of banging it. He was feeling both miserable and sore, money and a 300-year life-span apart. No. The sweet 1940s was where he was at then – all his aunts and uncles alive and well, and happy. His mum and dad. Him as a child. No big ideas bothering him. No big deals. Johnny got a lump in his throat as he saw his daughter's hand rubbing Joel's thigh. For a moment he had a perfect recollection of his mother doing that to him while still in short trousers. He was on a red 1940s London bus on a Sunday going to Lewisham...

Sulking, he then asked his daughter, who was driving the jeep in the hair-swish of warm wind, to stop touching Joel's leg, who was himself sitting in the passenger-seat to Stevie's Bernie's and Johnny's rear view of the world. She happily ignored him. For she'd been feeling unusually close to Joel, negotiating the perilous roads as she was which wound round everywhere and spiralled into sunlit abysses. She'd been feeling something close to love, touching his bare legs with definite loving gestures.

Johnny, holding his gouty shoulder, blew out air wildly.

106

Where was his mother? Where were all his aunts and uncles? His felt acutely lonely suddenly in the company of people much younger than himself. It was horrible. He could easily have cried. Francine turned to glance at him with a spoilt frown. She wanted to say, What is your problem! but couldn't because of the roads. Abstract shapes of ancient burial tracks, seemingly. Then. 'Where's the nearest boozer?' Johnny asked, head rocking left to right as the jeep twisted left and right.

'There isn't one, daddy.'

Wind in the hair. Stevie. Who then said, most sarcastically, 'You ex-rockers! I don't know…'

He gave a great big tut and a piss-taking shake of the head.

'Don't get too close to the edge,' Joel commented, glancing down a ravine.

Johnny gave an I'm-going-to-have-you-bumped-off gaze at Stevie, then turned back to his daughter's long and caressing hand. It bothered him greatly: he was jealous of it. He was jealous of it because he secretly wanted his daughter, and had always wanted her. But it bothered him more because of how he was feeling. And how he was feeling was this: he wanted the past but ultimately he knew he was a fucked-up paedophile who had the money and contacts to cover his tracks. But no one knew about that then. Johnny's dirty little secrets were still buried in the future. They weren't due for release for another ten years. Francine's apparent care for Joel was actually causing him a wave of depression, and Johnny didn't get depressed. It was like a foreboding. A black sensation. Whatever rubbery smile he had, was lost. And then, strangest of all, Johnny glanced behind to see if they were being followed! He looked out from the back of the open jeep: he sensed they were. He sensed they were being followed.

107

It was a definite flood of paranoia, sharp in his bent bones. They weren't being followed, but he thought they were. He thought a vehicle was not far behind them.

Oh, mum? he thought. Where are you? Where's dad?

Bernie watched him look behind, clearly appearing concerned. Was he? Was Johnny concerned? The little man tried to mask his emotions – or at least the semblance of them. For inside his paranoia was fairly acute. He'd been followed before in a chauffeur-driven Bentley. It was the same feeling. It was the desire to look behind at the weaving-away road. This time a van was tailing him. He told the chauffeur, an employee of EMI, the record company The Wallbeats had signed with, to lose it. The Bentley roared off. The van was never seen again. Just to make sure, though, Johnny – this was 1972 – had a guy he'd been concerned about, a certain Mal Oldam who had told Johnny on more than one occasion that he was just lucky and not talented, assassinated. That seemed to do the trick. For Johnny was never followed again. He wasn't the kind of guy to make real enemies, he believed. Coincidence? Someone as important and as valuable as Johnny Coy couldn't take that chance. So Mal Oldam, bad-egg and ponce, Johnny reasoned, as well as nobody, was silenced forever. Johnny was in Cannes when the hit was done. No worries. He'd be simply carrying out a service to humanity, he told himself. He employed the *dark forces* of England. No worries. No problem. No nothing. The following week Johnny was balls-deep in a squealing 10-year-old who'd been abducted for the purpose in a (coincidence?) white van by, it could be said, the same *dark forces*. No worries. You're a king, mate. The girl, though, was not then murdered – as was the usual (skint) paedophile's wont. (Murdered? just to keep some old hairy prick out of prison?) Johnny had always been rich enough to cover his

108

tracks. Yes. Rich was where it was at if bad deeds were your bag. Rich had you innocent every time. Money made you holy, in fact. People always believed you.

'We're here!' Francine then declared as she threw on the brakes.

Fuck! Johnny was thrown forwards and he hit his already-sore nose on the jeep's roll-bar. He gritted his yellow capped-teeth and shook his loose growling head. He was sure, oh he was sure, that this arse-birth yank was for the chop. Yeah, he was sure. Fucking ball-bag helmet-sucker.

'I wanted to show you this,' said Francine, switching the engine off and pointing up at the blue-brown ridge of mountain above them, glimmering in the steely light like some kind of iceberg. 'See! See that! Isn't it incredible!' They all looked up except Johnny, who knew about it already.

The air was much cooler at the height they were at. It was more reasonable, to Bernie's body. It was nice. And then, gazing aloft, they saw that thin clouds would come quickly up from sea-level, become stunned, turn a corner of the mountain ridge, then simply vanish in a vapour just as quickly. It was a very remarkable sight. It almost looked like a trick. Most dramatic. It was something you could watch for ages. The cloudy side of the island met the sunny side right above them. They merged directly on this line, this Maginot Line. It was like a strip of heat drawn on the mountain-face. Up the clouds came only to meet their destiny, their death. It was cloud vanishing-point.

'What causes it?' asked Bernie in gay awe.

'It's got to be cold meeting warmth, dear,' suggested Stevie, climbing out from the rear of the jeep awkwardly. He then stood at the side of the road with his hands on his hips, stretching his spine.

Francine, climbing out too, was wearing a very short tight

109

denim skirt with a baggy white billowy shirt tucked into it and zero underwear. Zilch. Her tanned brow was sweaty, her inner thighs, sticky. Yes. And her ass? Her ass was decidedly moist, so she without hesitation pulled the skirt from out of her crack where she stood. Johnny watched her obliviously do this, still in the rear of the jeep, leering. The ambience, however, largely because of the spectacle or phenomenon taking place up above, was definitely serene. The entire area was silent, except for silky wind. And even that surged over rocks quietly. Francine's white shirt seemed to add to this atmosphere as it gently flapped; it was a beautiful white kite in a deep blue dreamy sky. All were now standing, gazing upwards. It somehow seemed man-made, this cloud-disappearance on that tranquil mountain ridge. Then Johnny got his sense of foreboding again, and he began looking down the dusty road they'd just come up. Could he hear a vehicle climbing the hill? He listened carefully, half-deaf as he was. (Wasn't that the trade-mark of a good rocker?) Ah? Speak up! Yes, he could. He could hear a vehicle. But who knew he was here? Who'd be tailing him?

An old car came and went, breaking the atmosphere for a moment. Johnny froze as it clanked past.

The driver looked decidedly like fucking Marco, for God's sake, to Johnny, who, rubbing his eyes in the low Wild-West sun, opened his dry mouth as if about to yell. But it was gone, and the deep silence returned. Somewhat shocked, and while the others remained gazing up at the mountain ridge, fascinated in their standing-staring amazement, Johnny sent a text-message from his mobile to his hit-man in London. It read: *Coyote here, top job for you. Usual pay, plus 10% if job done well. Details to follow.* Coyote was Johnny Coy's codename whenever he wanted someone killing, which, yes, he'd done before. This time it was definitely to be Joel

Maize as soon as they got back home. Johnny had decided for certain there and then. He'd made his decision as they all stood in the road looking up at the cloud-show. Yeah. Fuck Joel fucking my daughter! Fuck him to death! Johnny stared at his victim as though the murderer himself, which in a sense he was...

Joel was doomed.

They drove on a bit further, stopping again to look down on the village of San Nicolas from up high, all spread out like a miniature garden, then turned round and drove back the way they came. Joel had his hand on the high-inside of Francine's thigh now, squeezing it and tickling it sexily. Johnny, in the back there, gazed at the (dead) hand in deadly wonderment – wondering whether to have him done at the fucking airport!

There were two different tracks Francine could have taken while driving down the mountain to the Port of Mogan. The jeep however chose the one that led to the village of Mogan, and Susan's place. Yeah. The jeep. That chose. It even (as though absent-mindedly) threw on the brakes outside the little lane which led up to Susan's front door, all by its self. The gang jolted forwards in the sudden dust-rise, in the sudden inertia. And there was the big man himself, sitting at a table in the garden with five bottles of cold beer already opened. He was clothed in his usual blue-black garb up to his neck.

'My friends!' he howled, swigging from a sixth bottle and seemingly cool beneath his great tent, his great sweltering cloak. 'It am too hot for am de driving! Come! Join the Susan! Have am de beer!' He beckoned. Four of the ten children were playing around the table, trying to catch a hen. Serena the youngest wife was sitting on the stone step to the front door mending a garment of some kind by

111

strenuously stitching it. She looked up and smiled, pulling cord. Her brown skin flexed across taut muscles and other womanly shapes.

That was good enough for Johnny, the slag. He cranked himself out from the rear by climbing behind over the rattling number-plate, then rubbed his leathery hands together in hearty anticipation as he creaked upright on his tiny creaking legs. 'Ooh, lovely! Give it 'ere, then! Lovely!' He walked resolutely towards Susan.

Only then did Bernie realize, watching Johnny's little ass in his tight and fetid leathers, that he'd seen Susan way up in the mountains about 30-minutes ago – or thought he had. He thought he'd seen him riding a donkey. But no. It couldn't have been. He said nothing. Did Susan ride a donkey? It couldn't have been. He shook his head to himself.

Presently they joined Susan around the wooden table, watching this swift hen evade its captors in the brown, colourless, rocky garden. Glug glug, went Johnny's meagre throat, cold beer flooding his frivolous stomach. He took two little mouthfuls. The mountains, as always, flooded the ambience with *their* ambience: they seemingly engulfed the tiny village on all sides with their vast and overwhelming shadows, with their enormous power. They also seemed to empower Susan. They seemed to have given him a greater strength somehow – made him even bigger than before. And Susan was big, bigger than Bernie remembered him from just a short time ago. Mountain-big. Susan guzzled a bottle of beer in one Hemingway mountainous gulp. Then he'd ask for another, and guzzle that too – mountainously. Unlike Johnny, who watched him agog, his throat muscles and oesophagus muscles seemed to not engage as the bubbly fluid ran down them. He just sucked at the bottle, and… *BURP!* Yeah. Real loud. As though from a deep well.

112

An earth belch. Susan cast a shadow over the table with his belches. Johnny attempted the same single gulp of an entire bottle of beer, but failed miserably. He nearly died. He nearly choked. Doomed Joel had to pat his back for him.

15

IT WAS BEAUTIFUL. It was all so beautiful. Francine Coy was going to exist for another 270-years or so. It was just… beautiful. She was so happy. It was sinking in. Yes, the rich shall inherit the Earth. No problem. It was theirs anyway. It was made for them, by their own kind. That's what the Earth was: a playground for the rich! It was so beautiful. The poor only got in the fucking way. They were always fucking it up, the poor. They had so many damn issues! Mostly, ah, about being poor. Yeah, the fucking poor. Francine would have to look into that, she thought. She'd have to look into the poor and their lowly ways. Yes. The poor would need to be rendered void somehow. (It should be said that what Francine meant by 'poor' was people who had to work for a living. The actual poor she had no concept of. None. People on the street? Where?)

'O my beautiful friends!' Susan declared as if toasting them. Then he said, 'So you went up to am de mountains so see am de cloud-vanish? Huh! It am good, eh? It am real good. My trick, dat. I perform it. I keep it am de going!' He glugged another bottle of beer in magical horror.

Francine gazed up into the mountains to where they'd just been, and thought about her 'poor' boyfriend beside her whom she'd only just fallen in love with. Would she make him rich altruistically, or just fuck him off? It was a hell of a dilemma, a hell of a question. She'd never been the altruistic kind, of course. Altruism and the notion of it had always pained her, had always puzzled her. But she did however love Joel, now. It had come upon her like a wind. 'You – make – that – work?' she then asked Susan very slowly, in a taken-aback gaze, pointing up behind her.

'Am. Am.' Nodding. 'It am de brilliant trick!'

114

'Oh, yes,' laughed Johnny. 'It am de brilliant trick all right!' He looked at Stevie as if to say, is this towelhead for real or what? But Stevie dropped his eyes.

'It's natural!' said Francine. 'No way are you doing that! No way!'

'Am. Am. I sometimes sleep up there! It am de good place to am de dream. I am de dreamer up there. Ci. I dream of am de flying up there. Clouds up there give this to head. Fly-clouds, like. Clouds up there give am de wings! I am de flyer when I sleep up there under de cloud-vanish. I am de dreamer!' And with that Susan swiftly clutched the darting-clucking hen between his bare feet as it flashed under the table for the tenth time. No boxer could do this, nor a dreamer. It was a lightning martial-art's reflex: the hen clucked badly, using an instant atonality in its recognition of death. Ba-*bah*-ba. For Susan gripped it so hard that he actually killed it, and the children eventually began to weep. *The hen am de dead*. Mallibenny the wolf came to see from behind Serena in the house.

'Don't you just dig his accent, man,' Joel commented, looking down at Susan's quaking ankles with floating feathers, shaking his head at the hen's demise. 'Shit…'

Francine held her mouth. 'O my God! O my God! It's dead! O my God!'

'It was probably going to be eaten anyway,' said Stevie, smoking philosophically, and holding his bottle of beer like a fat pen with two fingers. He then said, while feeling mysteriously antagonistic, 'That's what someone should have done to John Lennon years before Mark whatever-his-name-was shot him!' He smoked on, glancing down at the crushed hen, sipping cold beer in between drags. It was a comment plucked from the ether, seemingly.

'What the hell are you talking about now?' asked Johnny

115

after a pause to take it on board. 'John Lennon was a great man. He was a thinker and a great artist! Don't say he needed to be murdered.' (Rich from Johnny). 'Don't start this shit. I'm warning you, don't fucking start.' Johnny pointed at the sky as he shook his conspiratorial hand.

'Debate is not allowed in your regime, is it,' said Stevie from a cloud of philosophical smoke. 'John Lennon was a pathetic whimp with the brain of a child! Ha! A thinker! Pull the other one! Him and that idiot Yoko were fools, total clowns. The only reason he was given the time of day was because of his fame and money, not because he had anything much to say-'

'Now look...' barked Johnny.

At that second Susan raised the table by magic.

It reminded Bernie of how people flew with anti-gravity belts in 2270. *Back to the future*. It silenced the gang almost like the hen. Mallibenny now whined in the background. Cervantes the parrot began squawking in the house. Pigs in an old stone pen started to squeal. Then the older wives, Moon and Moya, appeared, wait for it, on the magic carpet – low (waist-height) carrying two bunches of flowers each. They had drifted in from the back of the house. The carpet, a kind of big Chinese deal in greens and blues, hovered by the raised table to relinquish (that seemed to be the word for it) the two wives. It just hung silently as they hopped off. It gave them up. They placed the flowers on the table, which in turn lowered back down to the floor.

Joel watched it all with his arms held out. Do what? He swigged his bottle of Dorada like someone seeing aliens, which he reckoned he'd done in the past. Big fuckers, man. Bad mothers. Stevie too had been rendered dumb, for the beers had eased any possible agitation or concerns which were, needless to say, ample. Well, obviously. But the beers

116

eased them. They eased consternation.

'Ahh! Flowers from am de sky!' Susan bawled, all cosmic and weirdly awesome. Moon said something softly to him in Spanish; then Moya knelt before the big man, tiny in the intense sunshine, as though before her king. The younger Serena was nowhere to be seen.

'Hey,' whispered Joel to Francine, 'Like, check out your dad! He's gone, man. The moment has seized him. Dig those eyes, brother! He – is – out – of – it.'

Francine glanced at Johnny, who, it was true, had been seized by the moment. He was utterly spellbound. A trans-fixed child. She'd never seen that expression on his face before. It was one of painless fascination at watching your torturer finally de-bowel you with a beautiful blade. He was just looking, like a flower. 'Daddy, get your act together! Get a hold.' She snapped a finger at him.

Johnny's jockey's body jauntily jolted. 'O my good God!' he yelped.

'How did you – are you – doing that?' asked Stevie of Susan, nervous.

Two locals then appeared at the garden-gate, and everything swiftly stopped. In the following second Susan beckoned them forward, and, afraid like unsure men in Saddam Hussein's entourage, entered the domain. They spoke secretly in Spanish. Susan bowed a head to listen. The wives returned to the house. The magic carpet lay motionless on the hot ground, seemingly benign.

'What is it?' Francine asked, sensing the change of atmos-phere and seeing Susan's expression alter to the bloom of concern. Or close to it. He looked to the road, as if trying to peer further.

'Bloody foreigners…' Johnny grumbled.

Then Susan thanked the two men and gestured them to

117

leave. He turned back to the gang and sighed. The two locals walked away from the house most briskly. Then, in Spanish, he said to Francine, 'You are being followed. My friends don't know who they are, but whoever it is they've been shadowing you since you've been on the island. They've parked just down the lane from here. Would you like me to go and kill them?' He gazed at her for a serious answer.

'What?' She spoke in the same language. 'By whom, Susan? I mean, why? Oh, hang on a minute. It could be our man with the injection, you know. What day is it-?'

'Saturday.'

'Saturday? Are you sure?'

'Yes. It's Saturday. I'm sure.'

'Are you sure you're sure?' Francine now appeared worried. 'Christ. I thought we'd been here for weeks! We've only been here for a few days...?'

'What's going on?' Johnny asked in English.

'Daddy, shut up. We've got trouble. Did you know it was Saturday? Why haven't we heard from our scientist? Why didn't you tell me it was Saturday? I thought we were to rendezvous with him today. Are you being secretive?'

'Saturday?' gasped Johnny. 'Is it? Well I never...'

Francine reverted back to Spanish. 'I think it may be all right. I think it may be our scientist. He's very nervous apparently. Susan, no. Don't kill him. I think it's all right.'

'Hey,' snorted Johnny, 'did them blokes fancy you? Is that what this is all about? Did them two fucking dagos have the hots for you, my sweetheart!'

'Daddy, for God's sake...'

'Hey?' snorted Stevie in response, 'it's *those*, old boy. Say, those. Yes. That's it. Those dagos. Why can't you people ever say *those*? Why do you always say *them*? I don't get it.'

'You're fucking dead you are!' Johnny snarled at him.

118

'Hear me? Dead! Dead!'

'There is only one,' Susan then said in Spanish rather mysteriously. 'Only one will live for the 300. The other four will die like everybody else. There is only one.'

16

'WE'RE BEING FOLLOWED,' said Bernie, who vaguely had some Spanish, and had been slowly working out what it was that Susan and Francine had been saying.

'How did you know that?' Francine then asked of him, not knowing that he understood a little. She lit a cigarette and pulled on the thing while frowning. *The wrinkles! Aigh! The Wrinkles!*

Joel wanted to go see. I don't got it, he wanted to say as a joke to Stevie's remonstration with Johnny, but he didn't. Instead he now wanted to kick ass. Yeah. Fight Club and shit. Stevie, on the other hand, was now concerned, and had forgotten about Johnny, who didn't give a fuck anyway. *He* now wanted Stevie whacked for (a) speaking detrimentally about John Lennon (b) for picking him up on his fucking grammar. These were good enough reasons, Johnny reasoned. Fucking fruit. (Privately, though, Johnny thought it was *them* and not *those*. Well, he didn't really know). Then again he was more interested in the notion that Susan's two friends had come to gaze upon his gorgeous daughter. Pricks. Spiks. Shits. *THEM DAGOS!* Johnny swallowed on his own bile. Bloody Spaniards. He couldn't stand them. (Who could he stand?) They were always rambling on – in, well, Spanish. Spiks. Cunts. (He couldn't stand anyone outside of white London, really – a concept becoming extinct before his own horrified eyes). *White City!* He took a cowboy slug of moody beer and contemplated the dog races. Trap-2, he thought. Trap-2 always wins! He wanted his own kind, whoever they were, wherever they were. (Was there a kind?) He wanted his own people...

'He's good people,' said Joel lightly about Susan.

'They came to tell us that they thought we were being

120

followed,' said Francine. 'I've told Susan that it's probably our man with the nano-injections. There's no problem. Destiny awaits, people. It's sorted.' She sucked in more smoke in the optimistic knowledge that all smoking-related problems would be ironed out by her nano-robots anyway once in her body. She visualized a steaming iron running over cancer cells and flattening them. 'Daddy, let's go and get him. Why is he hiding from us? Daddy...?' She blew smoke at an inattentive Johnny...

...Who knew the answer. He knew that the rogue scientist (rogue scientist?) wasn't there, because he hadn't told him to be there. Instead, as they sat there swigging, he sent another text-message to his hit-man in London, Sly-1. Sly-1 was the codename to Johnny's top hired-killer. Johnny had used a Sly-2 a Sly-3 and once a Sly-4, but the latter made such a balls of the hit that the person was left alive and in a terrible, permanently-disabled condition, still able to describe his attacker to the police – who knew it was a professional job botched. Consequently Sly-4 was then done by Sly-1 – under Johnny's well-paying orders, and the body was disposed of. Not because Johnny felt sorry for his victim. No. Sly-4 was done because Sly-4 fucked up. That's all. And Sly-4 *became* fucked-up himself, big-time. Sly-4 was vanished from the planet by his own 'kind' – whoever, wherever, whatever they were. (How many kinds were there?)

It's no secret that most, if not all, hired-killers are ex-army personnel. They have the training, the knowledge, the balls, the desperation: they always need the money once in boring civvie-street. The army are trained killers, of course, trained *to kill*. They are of a kind. And that's what kind they are: killers. Some people are doctors, others, IT merchants. The army, no. They are trained to take life – usually efficiently – preferably without emotion. This is

121

great news for anyone in the business of wanting to get rid of someone if you could pay and, most importantly, weren't prepared to do it yourself. For you didn't want any drunken hang-ups afterwards, any 4 a.m. tearful phonecalls. Johnny's Mr Sly-1, an unusually ruthless, cold, calm smiling man in his early 40s, with a frightening scar on the side of his neck and an unnervingly slow blink-rate, had actually served with Sly-4 in Bosnia, Sly-2 as well, but not Sly-3. But he knew of him, he knew about him: *they were the same kind.* Sly-1 also knew how much money would be involved with each covert hit, and, although he didn't actually know who he was working for – Johnny never, ever met him – he knew that his employer was both generous and prompt with the payment – a king's ransom to Sly-1...

Coyote here. It's now 20% more if hit done good. There might be another. I'll let you know in time. If yes, I want it doing slow. It's a pig's ear.

A hot poker up the arse! Johnny pondered as he finished his bottle of beer in, how many, 40 swigs? then text that message off. Evil? Perhaps. The car covertly turned around and sped away down the rugged mountain road towards the Port of Mogan. It would never be seen again. And it was forgotten just as quickly. Money did that. It gave one a lesser concern for things which might be of relevance. It also prevented one from visualizing the consequence of one's words or actions. For it simply engendered a shrug. Francine had always spoken or acted on simple (was it simple?) impulse, and the consequences could go hang. If you don't like it, you know what you can do! she would bawl – but there was a terrible ignorance attached to this, of course. It made her quite grotesque, really.

'Why would anyone want to follow us?' asked Stevie reasonably.

Bernie, sitting back rather *existentially* and looking up at the blue sky as Sartre might watch women in Paris, said, 'Because they're dagos, dear,' very quietly, very sarcastically.

Johnny now stashed his mobile away in a tight rear leather pocket, arching his minuscule bum up as he did, that jockey thing again. The mobile burnt him with its dastardly efficiency. Glancing around most innocently, he then seriously suggested this. 'They could be old fans of mine stalking me, you know. That has happened before. Mind you, it was 1974. Huh. Back in them days I had fans on every corner!' He glanced at his empty beer bottle as though coughing feathers.

I just don't get it, Stevie painfully thought, not daring this time to speak. Why? Why? I just don't get it. Why was *those* such a difficult word for a working-class person to say? I just don't fucking get it. Perhaps it wasn't part of their parents' vocabulary. Yeah. That was it. It was an unknown word to them. And, while he was at it, this moralizing he was good at, did money change your class or background, he pondered watching Johnny, sheepishly? Truly? Ah, he couldn't have been fucked any more. He waved his own mind away from him, making Joel watch him in a puzzled manner.

Then Susan suddenly stood – his usual gust of accompanying wind – and gave a massive white-teethed grin. 'My friends,' he declared back in his own brand of English, 'we have de party! Have lots of am de food! Have good time. Wives have ready! Come! De party!' He pointed.

De party? Well, yes. Kind of. De-bauchery, more like. And wasn't it a funny thing in the English language how two very disparate words could be so close to each other! Example (a) has already been covered: *knighted, benighted*.

123

Example (b) is as follows: depraved, deprived. Maybe they're not, after all, that far apart. It could have been argued that Susan's wives were deprived, while the big man himself? Well, yes. What follows here possibly touches on it. For depravity comes in many guises, as Stevie knew only too well. COME TO MY HOUSE! Susan had yelled, wild-eyed. The pigs squealed in a knowing terror. The children now, from crying over the dead hen, whose ability to procreate had clearly waned, (procrastinate, procreate? Maybe not) began dashing around everywhere like an army of confused ants attending a fat and depraved baby-eating queen. It was as though they were on automatic drive-pilot…

And yes, the children too, just like their mothers, worshipped Susan. Perhaps that's where all the energy and power came from. Looking back now, it seems plausible. It's well documented elsewhere that the worshipper gave all the power to the worshipped, and not the reverse. The figure of worship was powerless, really – in some senses vampiric. Stevie, for example, sucked everything from Bernie, who, in a type of love-awe, not only allowed it to transpire but actually needed it to simply subsist. Hence Stevie's brazen power over his lover. Susan however was on a larger scale. An almost Christ or Allah one. Unlike Christ or Allah, though, (who were they, by the way?) Susan also had power *without* his worshippers. Christ and Allah could only move mountains because the people who believed in them firmly projected that potential: the belief moved the mountains. The initial spirituality a living person might display soon takes a nose-dive into magic, once familiarity sets in. It slopes towards occultism or wizardry, as, perhaps, happened to Susan. Being alive probably did this, it probably helped him slide. (One needed to be dead to be worshipped properly). Susan still had his huge sorcerer's living body. But

124

the unseen power, this knack he had with things of the night, did for the most part come from the people who believed in him, or were afraid of him. For Susan was a *loner-icon*, in the sense that he would act bereft of an audience, and sometimes even unconsciously. And low, inside that house, cold from an external heat-haze, a strange calmness came over our gang. It was a cathedral-calm, a veneration tranquillity…

Johnny pulled out his mobile in this calm and, although nervous about it, held it up. Hee-hee. He gave a dumb smirk. 'I've just received a text-message from our man,' he lied, shaking a little. 'Huh! You'll never guess what the dickhead's gone and done. Huh! He's gone to Lanzarote instead of here! What a dickhead, huh! I told him Gran Canaria. But no. Being a dickhead-scientist he's got the wrong island! Look!' Johnny held his mobile up again which showed an illegible tiny bunch of words on a mini-screen, which was illuminated softly by a pale lime glow. No one really looked. 'He's staying in a hotel in Arrecife, or somewhere. Huh! What a dickhead! Oh well. No nano-injections today, then…' And with that Johnny flicked his mobile off and tucked it away again in his arse-pocket like a person with bad thoughts on his mind. Shady, didn't cover it.

Madcap Francine then broke the strange quietude. 'Susan, darling, do you know what my ambition is for the next 300-years? I'm going to spent 10-years in every major city of the world! Doesn't that sound terrific! 10-years in every major city! Wow! Oh, I can't wait!' She kind of squeezed her arms together and emitted a tight little yelp.

'… And me with you, sweetheart…' Johnny put in.

But Susan didn't respond. Instead the same routine happened as before. The wives arrived in the dining-room with great jugs of sangria bloomed with orange-peel. The parrot began squawking. Some flamenco guitar music

125

echoed from a crackling stereo, flamenco great. The sixteen-seater oak table had been polished for the occasion. *You're all fucked! You're all fucked!* Cerevantes the parrot croaked in Spanish. One of the wives hit him on the way out to the kitchen. Then, and as before, Susan stood at the head of the table and de-cloaked. Gasp! All gazed upon his donkey's swinging penis in a disconcerted silence. It seemed to be turning darker and looking up at everybody in the induced cloaked-dropped draught. Stevie, tight-throated, now felt a desire to sexually experience the big man – in whichever way possible. It came over him as a salty wave. (How little we know of other people's lives, when it came down to it. Even the one's we *think* we know about: how little we know). For Bernie too, nuclear and aflame, went red-faced with whatever notions had been placed in his mind. He just didn't care any more: he was going to take that pecker on board this very evening!

The parrot was also given sangria, and the parrot drank it. Come what may.

Screna threw him a slice of orange peel as well, which had been hanging copiously from the fat jugs. It was then that Joel reckoned they'd be as drunk as parrots later, if later ever arrived. But what a nice thought: as *drunk as a parrot.* Minutes later – an earlier later – the three wives again came marching into the dining-room with great platters of food, dressed in their usual sacks and makeshift belts. They were harmonizing to a Spanish folk song, which clashed poly-tonally with the flamenco music – but it seemed somehow to work. No pig this time, just roasted vegetables and strange fruit. And yes, the murdered hen roasted in an oven…

Hands off. That was entirely for Susan.

The sangria had been laced with the magician's own LSD, and part of the vegetables was mandrake root.

126

Consequently the ensuing riot would be hallucinogenic, but Johnny nonetheless dropped a triangular Viagra tablet in the belief that yes, he'd been given the eye by Serena, and yes, he'd definitely be diving in there later. (Viagra took about an hour to kick in, he knew). That would be time enough for Johnny to work his charm and get that Spanish bitch upstairs! He leered at her long brown legs while Susan watched him. Was 59 too old for a one night's stand? Was it fuck. How about 259! Would that be too old as well? Johnny downed the spiked sangria as though it was going out of fashion. This guy could drink when he put his mind to it. Gulp! Down went the big V also, surreptitiously. And even if he didn't get into her knickers, he mused, he'd fucking go out to fucking Maspalomas or somewhere and fucking buy it! Yeah! Any amount, too!

There was a curious other-worldly atmosphere as the ten children were marched into the room and all lined up down one side of the table. Naked Susan said something quick in Spanish, and the three wives told them all to be quiet. They were. Susan then muttered a kind of grace, or an offering, and ordered the kids one chunk of steaming veg each, which had been roasted in olive oil. Taking it, each child was then told to take a sip of sangria on its way out, and each child did. Curiously enough none of this seemed in the least bit odd to the gang. Even as the children were being marched out of the room, fingers pointing at them in stern gestures, they were already ravenously snatching at wodges of food like hungry people – licking fingers, gulping liquid, big-eyed and competitive.

Susan the patriarch then sat. As the kids filed passed the parrot, it said, *Time for bed! Time for bed!* in manic Spanish. The wives followed as though programmed to taking the children upstairs.

127

'Hey, man, do you like eat this way all the time, huh?' Joel asked, thinking about a movie he could make on this Susan guy. He tore hungrily at roasted parsnips.

But Susan became cryptic. 'I do this in memory of myself!' he bawled, maybe getting the syntax wrong or the general idea. 'It am de eat-good-today-you-leave-de-king-dom-manyana ting.'

'No shit? Cool…' Joel didn't hear a word.

'I kill more chickens,' howled Susan. 'It am de ting to do! I kill more chickens!' He'd already eaten the cooked flesh from the hen's carcass, and was sucking at tiny bones as he spoke. Now he JCB'd whole swathes of vegetables up against his mouth and kind of absorbed them. Grease encircled his great lips. But the vision only inspired the *whole sick crew* to do something similar themselves. Even Francine began using her hands to eat with. For it had been hinted at (had it? had it really?) that one of the smallest children should be sacrificed for the feast. Yes, it had been hinted at, somewhere. The child should be roasted on a spit in aromatic oils. There was a special oil which Susan adored and which he'd used before. It was a product of Pakistan. Naurus Sundip Lasora oil, cordi latifolia. Oh, ci. That's what the flesh would be roasted in. Beautiful. But who'd engendered this idea? Which Iago placed the thought in the susceptible minds of our gang? Now Johnny was almost becoming delirious with the conceptualization of it. He was becoming unhinged. He twitched as he gorged as he nodded as he drank. To eat, ah, a child, ah, cooked, ah, on a spit! His right foot jumped rapidly up and down as the ankle danced with nerves. (The food would only serve as a dampener for his red-faced Viagra). But that seemed now not to matter. For Johnny had turned cannibal. He was going to eat a human. He was going to tear at a child!

128

Really? Who would kill the child first?

Moya, it seemed to Johnny. She was the eldest wife, the toughest. She'd suffocate the bastard. 'Any more parsnips?' Johnny then roared with a demon anger. He cared little for any ramifications: he was becoming possessed! But just then, as Johnny's eyes danced like his right foot, (that plumber's DNA surging around his system on a promise) the flamenco guitar music was turned up and the three wives came high-heel clacking back into the dining-room.

Shocked, Joel glanced up from his plate. He burped. Buuuuuurrrrrrrrrrpppppppp! saying Pardon me, all American. His life seemed to fade into a sweet oblivion at that very second. Or the memory of it. Again he couldn't remember anything about himself, like a person suffering from Alzheimer's. His brain was all snowy and frosted. But look at those legs! Wow! A mesmerized Joel...

Being shaken by his girlfriend. 'I thought you only had eyes for me!' said a jealous Francine, pondering too the notion of eating human flesh. She paused to wipe grease from her mouth.

'Wives good flamenco dancers!' Susan then declared. 'Am de best in whole of de Gran Canaria! Wait and see. You like. Wives am de brilliant!' He began clapping in time to the music, but soon gave it up in preference to eating with the same shovel-slabs. He nonetheless kept his big animal's eyes on the ladies, who were now dressed in immaculate tradi- tional Spanish costumes – black short fluffy skirts, red lined basques over them – black high-heels on bare brown fine legs. They kept twirling and swishing their long black hair, saying Rrrrrreeeeeeebah! all the time while clicking their fingers and giving lewd looks.

The spectacle enhanced the manner in which the crew ate. Mastication/masturbation? Serious shit. Yelping,

129

screeching. Susan began clapping again, this time while laughing with a wild expression on his face and yelling phrases in Spanish seemingly germane to the situation. He then picked up a jug of sangria and poured it all over his head. The delicious juice ran down his naked sweaty body, only to be licked off by Bernie. No. That didn't happen. Fiction, old boy. Fantasy. It simply ran onto the stone floor and the wives stamped on it: it splashed. Rrrrrreeeeeeeeeeeeebah! A bit got Johnny in the eye, but fuck him. Cerevantes the parrot made a riot out of it too, while Mallibenny the wolf howled in a possessed manner. The pigs outside (Drake's offsprings, presumably) snorted and squealed as though electrodes were being shoved up their arses: the parrot then gave a whistling sound to harmonize with this noise, as the dancing continued. It just went on. Sweat-soaked, the wives now, as did the whole sick crew from concentration, flew into a kind of fixated convergence of one isolated consciousness. They seemingly merged.

The parrot broke its thin chain during this swift coalescence, then glided into the dining-room only to perch itself on a window ledge.

Johnny threw chunks of food at it acting as a whole unit. It dodged them. You're fucked! You're fucked! His whistling became so high-pitched and shrill that it vibrated glasses. Then Joel made a dive at one of wives like a hyena, but was instantly knocked unconscious by a coat-hanger from Susan, whose swift and powerful arm no one saw raised. The wife in particular, Moon, simply flicked her black hair away from the dive and danced on, even more raucous than before. Twice now Susan had felt the need to assault Joel, which, although for good reason, was appearing to Bernie like a vendetta. But then Bernie was so fucked-up that he couldn't tell which way was down. Francine said or

130

did nothing. She was in an Eastern trance. She wasn't even sure that she'd seen Joel fall, squinting, as would be Joel himself… when he came to.

Say what? Aw, man. My face hurts!

No. Francine saw only big Susan speaking directly to her from across the merger-of-minds, quietly in all the mayhem. And what he was saying was this: 'Umdededediddlydiddly-yum', a number of times without either moving his mouth or appearing to look at Francine at all, whose model's body now writhed where it sat at the insane poem. She'd started to intoxicatedly swish her strawberry-blonde hair too – only not as wildly as the three wives/dancers. She was grinning, and going *Yah* all the time. But then, horror of horrors, and to the bewitched bliss of the hungry crew, the magic carpet came bloodthirstily drifting into the room, carrying a sacrificed child.

17

ALL STILL.

My God. Did it really happen? Looking back now I can't honestly say whether it did or didn't. Because all's I remember was that we were eating hot aromatic juicy chicken and slurping sangria like attack-dogs from one of Francis Drake's aggrandizing ships, were they ever given sangria. The dancing had stopped, the music had stopped, the parrot had flown, the wolf was now silent. We never saw any of the children again. Not a glimpse. Six human beings were making noises like lions at a kill, that's all: tearing, chomping, snarling, burping. My God. Did it really happen?

All still.

There seemed to be a lot of chicken, a surplus even, and its white meat appeared to quiver in sweetness with every phantasmagorical mouthful. If we were to be the long-lived, then Allah preserve the planet. For we were scumbags from a very high-order at that moment. Francine ate well beyond her capacity like a starved caged animal. Oh yeah. We were beautiful…

Bernie suddenly glanced up from the feasting with a deranged frantic look in his eye. He looked at everybody else as though for an answer to his derangement. But then something compelled him to resume the devouring. Something told him not to stop it. And the eating was awful. The silence only echoed our glutonous tearing. It was an echoing of the noise from hell.

And no one had a sense of danger.

Bernie, oddly inanimate in his big-eyed slaggishness, from wiping his mouth and feeling finally full, had then slid beneath the table and, still with a full mouth chewing, began administering the most vile fellatio to Susan

132

– seemingly intoxicated also. The big man just seemed to take it in his stride while he continued to gorge. In fact he carried on eating while being blown as though not even feeling the sensation. And even now, as that monstrous, ugly, deformed pecker of his rose in the molten air – that dash of salt in its cheesy hum – with little Bernie's gob arching and bobbing all over it, not a flicker shone from his big black face. Oh, Bernie gagged a little and even groaned as he tried his best; but everybody had begun talking again after feasting, and no one noticed what Bernie was even doing. Yet Bernie's fellatio was, to him, totally outlandish and fucking disgraceful. He *knew* everybody would be watching, because it was well-bad. Then when the wives were directed to come back in – clacking and hair-swishing as they were – Bernie only sucked more heavily on the knob and attempted to make it sing with his tongue, then deep-throat it, which was something that normally choked him.

'Yeah!' yelled Johnny, entertained. 'The women! Yeah! Get 'em back in 'ere! Slags! Fucking slags! Fucking Spanish cunting slags!' He cupped his hands round his mouth, 'Fucking cunting twatting slags!' as he screamed that last bit. 'Get 'em back in 'ere!' Johnny's base views in life when required always helped him augment things like this, he knew. And he was proud of it, too.

Francine then let out a shriek to accompany her father's scream. 'Daddy,' she gasped, swaying on her seat with terrible rolling eyes, 'take me home! O, I'm drunk! Take me home! O my God!' She clasped the sides of her head in a dishevelled, inaccurate manner.

'Bitches!' howled Johnny further. 'Bitches!' He shook a royalist fist.

'Gobbler the father,' Susan then prayed. 'Gobbler the mother. Gobbler the son and am de holy ghost!

133

Gobble-de-gobble-de-gobble-do!' He gazed down as he said this with huge bulging eyes beneath the table to look upon kneeling Bernie, who, in turn, gazed up in quiet disgust with himself.

Then Stevie sussed. 'Hey, fuck! Hey. Fucking look! What?'

But Bernie ceased not. Could not, in fact. His little head, with his short well-cut hair, swooped all over the vast black penis in a similar motion to Cervantes ducking left to right on the perch. Bernie's brain now held the firm image of a slab of white cheese with a flickering lightbulb fitted in it, connected to the mains. It was a bizarre image. But that was the moment Francine passed out into her own arms. She just flopped her head flat onto the table. Stevie stood, and, swaying backwards, dived down to join his lover at this other feast – this desert. For two heads were better than one. And the two heads almost fought over it. Stevie used a hand, too. Up and down. Up... down. Susan's penis was as thick as a slim adult arm. No question. Stevie was in awe. Joel, now rubbing Francine's unconscious back, just laughed his dick off at the two gays dining so avidly without invitation. He thought it was hysterical, even though he'd been whacked by the big guy and had witnessed gays giving head before. Then Bernie began blinking in a flickering manner, and declared that, 'There's is a light in the cheese!' which he could clearly see – itself winking on and off.

Winking/wanking? Wanking and winking, Bernie had taken over the up-and-downs of Susan's slab and was also rubbing the thing on his cheeks, which, it has to be said, was now very wet. It has to be said because the wetness was part of the magic, and the magic was all a show. It was theatre. The whole world was a stage. But the magic, in the form of sticky wetness, was now all over Bernie's

134

face, and, uncharacteristically, Bernie adored it. Stevie then jumped from the penis and cracked his head on the underneath of the booming table, to which Bernie didn't even acknowledge. Stevie didn't see stars. He saw a flashing lightbulb stuck in a slab of pulsating white cheese, which caused him to frown from the nonsense of it as well as an instant aching skull. He stared into space for a moment watching this lightbulb. Uncharacteristically too, Francine began snoring like a farting pig where she sat. She was a fat gorged pig. This caused Joel laughter also; he then left his lover to try his hand once more with one of the wives, now that the big guy was otherwise engaged…

Cervantes the parrot had fallen ill from sangria and orange peel. Thankfully he was silenced – his head held low. But then everything changed. Susan, after being blown on a double-headed bobby-horse, now became seized with madness and sex. He suddenly bent down to grasp little Bernie from under the table and, with one large arm, raised him skywards from the gap between the table and the chair to kiss him on the mouth. Bernie went all limp as he was gripped, all moist as Susan's camel's tongue entered his quivering throat. And, as the big man stood, crazed Stevie still had *his* lips stuck to the helmet, and was brought upwards, banging his head again, as though attached to a rising rope. Within seconds the threesome abandoned the room.

Susan whisked them away to the pigsty for hell.

That's when Bernie for the first time experienced a cock up between his lungs. Drunk as a parrot, he could do nothing but allow his floppy body to be thrown from side to side as a ragdoll in the soiled surroundings. He put his hands out in a useless attempt at protecting himself from the dirty stone walls: his eyes rolling in his head, a flamenco tune he'd heard before somehow made itself relevant to his plight. It was an old popular song from the early 1600s, he somehow knew. The tune stuck, as did Susan's submarine. And yes, they don't make them like that any more! Popular songs from the 1600s were much better than the ones from the 20th Century, Bernie bizarrely thought while being fucked. More structure. More relevance. Hmmm. Not as pretentious. Aeeemgh! But then Stevie made a powerful attempt at mounting Susan himself, and succeeded. Whump! He entered him like slipping on a sock, and the big black man was then sandwiched in between slight sliced white. What a sight. Susan's mass equalled that of Bernie's and Stevie's combined. No question. It was a mass well and truly squared, too. For in physics if mass determined the acceleration produced in a body by a given force acting upon it, namely, in this experiment, Stevie, then how fast did Susan's acceleration pump? Well, very fast is the answer – and that will have to do. Because poor Bernie gasped for life in this friction-hammered transgression, his bewildered love-pocket squirming in the agitation…

Back in the dining-room Joel had come on heavily to Serena, who was by no means rejecting his offers. And Johnny, checking that Francine was definitely unconscious – he recalled checking his first wife in a similar manner at an award's ceremony in 1975 for best song-writer of the year: she was also unconscious, a depressed Tina, at the opulent table – propositioned the two older wives with much money in gesticulating English. A wad of pesetas, a flapping tongue. They frowned at not comprehending. *No comprehendo!* He wanted to rim them at a grand a piece, he was trying to say. It might even have transpired. For back in the pigsty Bernie was now in a genuine, if not intoxicated, state of gagging shock. He kept gazing towards the egress with wide terrified bouncing eyes – his face pointing down

136

– his hands in reverse trying to meekly stop the thrust, while two men were on top of him. Well, three really. He couldn't catch his breath, apart from anything else. He'd never known fucking like it. It was fucking awful. Yet it was also fucking fantastic – the cutting-pain cutting right up to his sloshing brain: Bernie was being taken by a Jumbo Jet!

Blood had drained to Stevie's feet and cold tremors were arising in his gut.

He was going to empty into Susan's black hole. He could scarcely believe his own senses. But then, wouldn't you know it, alcohol did its dastardly trick and slipped in unnoticed. Yes, Stevie was losing his erection. Bastard. He tried to pound harder to compensate. Nothing doing. It only made it softer. It only made matters worse. Booze and erections? It's well documented elsewhere. So-close. So damn close to orgasm! Bastard. Stevie was now so flaccid that he slipped out – wanting to stay in – slumping downwards in an angry curse. Fucking booze! He gazed down at his glistening cock. Fucking hard-ons. Even the sight of Susan's enormous buttocks thrashing away on top of mortified Bernie didn't bring Stevie's blood-rush back. He just fell back onto the soiled ground and shook his soiled head in resignation, as though drunk – which indeed he was…

Bernie was being hammered.

137

18

FRANCINE HAD BEEN dreaming at Susan's banqueting table. She'd been dreaming of dust. Lots of dust. No, not cocaine. A different type of dust. Something finer. She'd been dreaming of a fine powder covering the entire surface of the globe, including the oceans. Worse, it was a living powder. Well, living as in nano-probes. Or Nanobots, as they would come to be known. Silicon Valley had been eaten away by its own creation. Whole civilizations had vanished. Everywhere had been eaten away. There was only grey powder. Blue skies, but grey powder. Yes, the miniature machines, which, in the dream, Francine already had surging around her body, had eventually somehow become conscious and had been assembling complex alloys, atom by tedious atom, to go beyond simply repairing human beings: they had learned how to create their own kind!

The Nanobots had discovered how to reproduce themselves, and their offspring could now subsist away from the fuelling blood of their host. Indeed they had acted like artificial viruses on the planet. In short they'd gone on the rampage; time to take over, boys; powder remaining where streams and forests once bloomed. And the powder was itself alive: the powder was simply more Nanobots reproducing themselves. *Grey Goo?* Yes indeed. Just like Francine's brain. No, sorry. If one was to live for 300-years then the first 70 hardly counted, it could be argued. The first 70 would be a grey goo. (The entire 300 would hardly count in Francine's case). But this powder, this dust, had now, in this dream, brought the age of 70 back down to earth just where nature, now in the form of robotic powder, had always wanted it! Nature had us by the balls again. No longer did human beings live for 300-years. Not only that, but 70-years,

138

the old biblical deal, seemed like a big life-span: 70-years was for the lucky! Help was at hand, though. The process was about to be reversed...

Francine Coy became the cleaner of the planet Earth.

She became a scrubber. Mankind was to be wiped out by creatures of its own making, yes. But Francine Coy knew the remedy. She could reverse this terrible calamity of robotic reproducing powder. She was going to create a superbug that would destroy the Nanobots, as they built themselves. The bug would be made of similar alloys, of course, only it would be designed to feast off nano-powder! Oh, fantastic. She would become queen of the world. She'd be remembered in history. She'd be-

Whoops! She fell off the chair and banged her head on the leg of the table. It woke her.

'Where am I?' Was it her father's severed head on the pillow next to her? She'd forgotten the dream already – or it was fading fast. Who? *How...?*

She felt for a second however as though tiny things were running all over her. What had she been thinking of, she thought, believing that she hadn't been asleep at all or even dreaming, but thinking? From the floor of the dining-room she gazed aloft. *Powder!* She rubbed a benign finger and thumb together, then made an attempt at clambering up the leg of a chair. The room was now empty. Her head was now empty. The surface of the table was like the surface of Ganymede: *craters of empty plates and glasses.* It was like the aftermath of a great party or something. Where was, what's his name, Joel? Yeah. That was it. She clicked the same fingers. Joel. ABCDEFGHI – J! She grinned and hiccuped at the same time. Don't panic. Drunk, yes, but don't panic. Hic. Not panicking, and not caring in the least where everybody was – though without the use of her

139

legs – Francine managed to pull herself back up onto the chair most painfully, only to spin as though freefalling with a tangled parachute. She grinned again as a moron grins, glanced around as walls raced by, looked back down at the floor as an ape might watch a spider, then literally fell back to sleep on her arms with a soft crash of the head. Again she dreamt, but not of powder coating the world… 'Don't panic, darling,' Stevie slurred to a moaning Bernie, who wasn't panicking, but was instead, well, haemorrhaging. Susan had torn him in two like a slaughterman splitting a cow. From that day on (Bernie would later reflect) he'd never again be either constipated or able to hold in a fart. To use a phrase Bernie's father might have used: he'd have an arsehole on him like a torn pocket. It would billow in the wind. But no matter. That was private. It was between Bernie and his underpants. Stevie then saw what he took to be faces all around the outdoor pigsty, as though a number of people were standing there just watching. He blinked up at them like he was astounded – alcohol naturally preventing the full-on emotion to transpire. Then, glancing back at the loving couple snorting and pulling on the ground, he looked back up to see the faces not there. They'd gone. He blinked again. Blinking and, coming to think about it, the faces, Stevie now reckoned, seemed to be, well, medieval-looking. As though, like, they were from another century or some-thing? 'I can't accept this…' he then whispered to himself, blinking again. And at Bernie, too, who now seemed to be actually experiencing a female orgasm: he said the same thing. He couldn't… accept… No! He somehow got to his feet and ran away. Well, stumbled away. Into the dark of the village. Into the night. A spare-of-the-moment flee, holding the brow with the back of the hand. *For-sooth!* But even in the silent dark he could still hear Susan's animal roars and

140

chomps. He visualized his great pumping penis squirting into his lover's shaken body. Ooh. Not nice. A shudder. Bernie! My Love! No. Not nice at all. It felt horrible to him in his confusion. It definitely hurt. So Stevie ran further away.

Then he was run over by a car.

It came out of the night like a bull. It was Marco. He was driving. He was going to see his sister on the other side of the island or something. (I've only had a few ales, officer). Stevie just ran out into the road at the wrong damn time. Smack! Over the bonnet. Crunch! Cracking the windshield. Whump! Right over the roof. Flop! Back down on the road again.

Marco screeched to a halt and came staggering back in the dark.

Stevie was dead. Marco didn't recognize him, though. It was just a white man's body on the road he'd hit. A tourist. He wasn't concerned, just bothered about being caught, that's all. So Marco, the great chef, the great spiker, (a respectful chef's bow) contemplated driving off. He glanced towards his clattering old wreck, contemplating. Oh, ci. I go. I out of here. Then he looked back down at dead Stevie. Shit. What to do, man? He rubbed his spikey chin. Susan instantly knew what had happened, but was finishing off where he'd already begun. That, seemingly, was more important. Bernie, half-dead himself now, but definitely fully-fucked, was certain he'd been ruptured in the process because he fancied he could feel semen, hot semen, not cool as it should be, flowing into his fluttering stomach. Yeah. He could feel it. It wasn't an unpleasant sensation, though. Which was just as well, because Bernie was about to be devastated, Satanic evening apart.

141

19

BERNIE LOVED STEVIE. No question. He adored him. Bernie could not live without Stevie. No question too. He cherished him. *Bernie needed Stevie.* And Bernie got to his feet in the hot pigsty and felt as though he'd left his bottom on the ground. He actually looked back to see. He didn't mean to hurt his lover, he just… couldn't help himself: Susan took him over! The big man had placed his own supernatural libido inside him, as well as that awesome penis. God, it had been like a living animal in his bum, squirming. Inside the house Johnny and Joel were now clubbing it with the wives. Metaphorically, they were also inside Susan somehow. But Bernie, outside in the night, had been made pure. He'd been kind of reborn under the stars, lovemaking. And love makes things new again. It has that power. For Bernie saw, amid all his gasping and panting, that he truly loved Stevie. He saw that now. Christ, never again would he let himself be fucked by another man. Never again. He made that vow with Susan's semen running from his split crack there and then. He even whispered it to himself: *Never again will I let another man fuck me.* He felt good about saying it.

Susan then rushed past him in the dark, twirling him in his prayer.

What had Bernie been thinking of? Never again. Never. He just couldn't. Seconds later Susan was carrying Stevie's limp body into the house. Though Bernie couldn't quite see, he knew that it was Stevie and he knew that it wasn't good. It was bad. He went cold. No, he went dead. What was it, he thought? Marco had indeed fucked off, but Susan knew. Now Bernie knew. Now a cloud of depression edged over his glinting horizon. Destination desolation. In the dark Bernie's face had turned to grey. It had turned the same

142

colour as the powder in Francine's mad dream, who'd been dreaming again, and yelling *No more pork!* in her sleep. Susan placed Stevie on the great table. He then gave Francine a shake. She woke, but said, *Leave me alone!* all girl-like and puerile. And as Bernie entered the house and before he'd even seen Stevie he began to sob. Not the dunce-sob of the panicked soap-opera ruined imbecile – the terrible wailing and the quaking, the hammed-up shuddering and pointing – but a quiet, slow, awful, resigned sob. To make matters somewhat worse Joel was having *his* dick sucked by Moon upstairs. Yeah, she'd gone for it. She'd fallen. She could handle it, in her sexy Spanish way: Joel saw stars. Bernie, knowing this too, entered the dining-room. He wanted to die himself. He knew he could no longer go on. Bernie saw his reflection in a big mirror…

I can't go on. I'll go on.

But Bernie *would* go on. He'd continue living, continue to live. Because, and no one would ever know whether or not Susan had anything to do with it, Stevie came to. He wasn't dead after all. He was only stunned. He'd been knocked out by the heavy blow. Shaken, not stirred. Probably because of the alcohol in his body, his relaxed muscles simply flopped over Marco's car and prevented even a rib or a bone from breaking – he just banged his head and suffered concussion. 'Oh, Christ,' he groaned, back from the dead. Bernie dived down on him and cried his little heart out. He held him and kissed him and wept over him. Moments before he'd wanted to die; now, at this moment in time, which, to the horror of all common-sensical people, had past even before you had time to grasp it, (so shut the fuck up about *at the end of the day*) Bernie wanted to live again. He wanted to live. And he did. He lived. He would be the *long-lived*. He knew that. Along

143

with Stevie, too. He also wanted to live – now that he'd tasted death. He said YES to life! So he sat up on the table, holding himself, (his head hurt – he'd been a cadaver after all) and half-gazed at snoring Francine, who, dreaming of devouring more pork, was oblivious to it all.

Susan, now smiling, nodded slowly, then left the room. He was still naked, but like an undertaker. He was met in the hallway by Marco, who'd come back with a very guilty Catholic conscience. Oh, ci. Jesus Mary and, er, Joseph. (Joseph who, by the way?) He entered Susan's house with his arms held out and a great Spanish babble concerning a tourist he thought he'd hit on the roadside, but was no longer there. Susan put him in the picture, which calmed him. Yes, he came back, but he shouldn't have driven away like that. That was wrong. "Oh, ci, Susan, my friend. It was very wrong." Nodding, he glanced through at Stevie, who had sensed eternity. Peace away from all human emotions and desires. It was, he thought, quite beautiful. It was magical. And still. Very still. He never really made it clear. Because magically he climbed off the table and gave little Bernie a hug and a kiss without a word. Floods of liquid were still pouring from the latter, floods of salty liquid. But more was now going on upstairs. It sounded as though furniture was being moved around. And then, listening to this sound, and gazing up at the ceiling in some puzzlement, it struck Stevie that those faces watching him on the floor in the pigsty might have been Susan's children. He wasn't certain – being the good philosopher – but they might have been. They just might have been the ten children. No. Hang on a minute. Stevie reckoned there were only nine faces watching him on the ground in the pigsty…

Nine. Yes. There was a space at the end for a tenth, he recalled.

But then it all started up again before he could double-check.

Cervantes the parrot had seemingly recovered. Mallibenny the wolf now was wagging his tail somewhere. Susan and Marco were drinking on the porch – the big man in a fresh robe – Marco the chef now off-duty and totally relaxed. And the wives, most astonishingly, came dancing back down the stairs to flamenco guitar music once more, but did not this time appear pristine. A satiated Joel was to follow. Jesus, man, he'd moan! And Johnny? Where was he. Well, being the old rocker, he'd gone in search of the children. He just couldn't help himself. He'd gone *to see*. Not finding them anywhere in the house, he would then vacate the premises and actually hitch a ride back into town – Puerto Rico, not Mogan – with the old Viagra in his system burning away like the soldering iron his father would use in his life-long career as plumber. "You've got a leak, Mrs Hancock. Your shithouse is too old, you deaf old bat!" In hc'd dive. Yuk. Thinking of his father, all that shit, all that piss, all that going-nowhere except to someone else's toilet, Johnny knew that Viagra only lasted for four hours: he needed to get *his* shit together if he was going to buy box. If he was going to purchase pussy. Then the wives, in Johnny's empty absence, seemed to dance in a heat engendered by their husband's buggery. Indeed, as they circled, standing Stevie and aghast Bernie, who appeared to be encapsulated in their lair like daft Custer at Little Big Horn to an overpowering Sitting Bull's warriors, they clicked their fingers and screeched more loudly, and seemed to go ultrafrantic with every twirl. What on earth had Susan done to them? Rrrrhhhhhheeeeeeeemmmiiha! Bernie's traumatized tears somehow dried on his distressed face with the unsettling madness of it all. They just froze and attached

145

themselves to his skin. It was a swift kind of loss of purity, had Bernie wished to put a tag on it. For that was how he felt. The dancing was like some sort of provocation. Add to that, later, Joel would tell of fantastic head and a wonderful orgasm in between Serena's teeth. Man, he coated those peckers like paint! And she swallowed, too. Oh yes. Right down. No messing. Two big fuck-off gulps. This information only served to heighten Bernie's notion of disturbance. Of suffering. Of his loss of innocence.

And the flamenco music, too. That seemed to be more crazed, more wild. Consequently, Stevie now needed to get home. He wanted to be in cosy, safe London again, he felt. (Huh, safe?) But that's how he felt. For hadn't this Susan bloke just melted the pussy off his little lover and reached an orgasm so spectacular that the moon actually shuddered in orbit? Indeed. And Bernie's sullied hole now appeared to create an echo as he moved his ass-cheeks to (squeak squeak) walk. The echo, it further seemed, was that of Susan's prodigious roar as he came. (It was the animal in the man). Yes, Susan's cum-roar had somehow remained alive inside Bernie's arsehole. It was a bellow that even Marco heard back down in his restaurant as he contemplated driving up the mountain to knock Stevie down at the exact right moment (the chosen moment?) – a deed which Susan may or may not have engendered. But how did a roar remain somewhere when the 'roarer' had long since ceased his noise?

Stevie would need all his philosophical training, all his philosophical understanding, which wasn't that great anyway, for that one. Berkeley would need to be called in. *To exist is to be perceived?* Oh yeah? Then how did Susan's growl remain as an echo in his lover's not-perceived chasm? Well, because it was perceived as such afterwards.

146

Stevie, desperate to get home, reckoned that Susan had engendered the perception of his cum-howl directly in the mind in ways which a tree, whether it was there or not, simply could not do. That is to say he'd given it *real* substaniality as he'd formed it out of the real world – the world of the mind, that is. Stevie was aghast. It was totally fucking amazing…

Totally fucking amazed, Stevie and Bernie then edged past the dancing girls in a haze or daze of possible tangibilities, and moved towards the hallway for a taste of freedom.

It tasted good, this taste of freedom. It tasted very sweet. But it was brief. For as they got to the hallway the wives suddenly stopped dancing and the music stopped on the stereo. A veil of silence fell in the house that could only be perceived as…rain? What were these crackpots on! The silence they created was, well, to Stevie, unreal. That is it had no substantiality, if silence ever could. It too had an echo. An echo of silence. The echo was that of a coquettish continuation of high-heels clacking on stone floors. And it was daunting in its mammoth vibration. Cervantes, in this silence, in this boom, said *The master's had his fill, the master's had his fill!* in Spanish, but for everyone's ears. It made Bernie blush. Bernie had been had. O yes. The master had had him all right. The air around seemed to sing it.

'Let's go,' Stevie then said in the echo of silence. 'I don't like it here any more. Come on. Let's fuck off.' As he spoke Joel had already been trying to wake Francine. She spluttered to life, and was okay. No way was she driving, though. No way. Marco watched Stevie leave most sheepishly, who told them that Susan wasn't really called Susan. It was a nickname in Spanish that translated into English as that. Bernie only later discovered this.

147

20

STEVIE AND BERNIE were in the rear of the jeep. They were holding each other in the great starry Gran Canarian night. But all was not at an end. For inside the house Cervantes fell from his perch and was dead. He dropped with a little flop. This disconcerted Susan so much that the big man began weeping over the tiny body. Marco watched him weep with either concern or consternation: he didn't seem to know what to do. Joel, helping a staggering, moaning Francine, equally couldn't believe his eyes, if indeed that was what Marco was doing. (Were eyes to be believed?) For Susan cried loudly and with immense gusto. Great big sucking sobs. The parrot, just lying there, had had a heart attack, it would transpire. It had eaten too much pork, drunk too much sangria. Ugh! It had keeled over like a fat smoker at a daughter's wedding reception. Poor Cervantes. Gone to parrot-heaven. Susan then stroked him on the floor. Mallibenny the wolf now did a special kind of howl outside in the night, which only served to freak Stevie out more, just around the corner from him. It was a kind of tribute-howl: Cervantes, Mallibenny's friend and confidante, had flipped over on the floor before finally giving up the ghost. Mallibenny had seen this, with his pale blue eyes, then scampered outside to get it out of his system, to get it out of his wolf's blood. *HYYYYYOOOOOH!*

Stevie now had a headache like Jupiter being hit by Shoemaker-Levi-9.

The size of Susan's dick! he kept thinking, holding his head, marvelling at Jupiter's absorption, which was nothing like his. Accidentally, Francine kicked the dead parrot as she reeled, the late parrot, as she lurched towards the doorway under Joel's thin arm. It did not go down well with Susan.

148

Crying, he dropped his garment very theatrically (boy, did he like doing that – nudity once again), to give her a terrible magical kind of glare, and finally picked Cervantes up. (*Was he just pining for the fjords?*) The wives had now moved outside as well, and were sitting on a wall, smoking. It was as though they were the cast of a show or something, just taking a break. Bernie, cuddling into Stevie, did not like the way they smoked. He did not like the way they looked. It was all so phoney, he felt, so put-on.

Think theatre. Outside in the dark Francine's crazed glazed eyes gazed across the surface of the landscape in gash gold-vermilion. She was shining as a blue-bleak ember all right. And she'd fall and gall herself. No question. For she was, it was true, in the brute-beauty and valour of alcohol, a windhover! She had caught the morning morning's minion kingdom!

Give it a rest. Her father, no windhover, down in the bright lights of Puerto Rico, had bought two 19-year-old slags from Reading at a high price. He intended to boast about it the following evening – but he'd be dead before then. For now, though, the effort was to get Francine in the jeep and somehow drive back down the mountain. Bernie had begun to moan at the pain in his arse. No metaphor. It was literal. It was a hot and stinging pain. Hot and burning. His colon had been slapped around. But then there was the sweet smell of pot in the air and the wives had started to giggle where they sat. They passed the joint to each other in turn. Bernie was wrong. They weren't just smoking. They were potheads! He watched terrified as they each blew him a lewd kiss in the dark, laughing. He buried his head into Stevie's armpit, who was himself much too concerned about the large lump rising above his ear like earthrise seen from the moon. (Had anyone ever truly walked on the surface of

149

the moon? Stevie reckoned not. But that was for another story. That was for the story of the con-firm NASA). Here, Bernie's penis now spoke for his brain. Astonishingly, head buried in his lover's protection, it started to rise as well, saying Pull me, all slag-like. It was being dragged upwards by the arrant sexiness of the three wives. Gulp, went Bernie's subconscious. For he'd believed that he only had eyes for his own sex. Gulp, again. After all these years! Had he been deluding himself? Surely not. Surely one's sexuality wasn't *that* fickle, was it?

Er, well. Bernie pushed his little head further into Stevie's well-perfumed armpit, only to pause and gaze out from it like a meerkat on guard. His cock was now very hard. This caused him a great deal of consternation, of private trauma: it frankly shouldn't have been happening. *He was gay!* What to do? Sex with three women, at the same time, one in one! No. Good God. Dog. God. Dog. God. Sex/perplexed? Ola, a wife teased in the darkness. Bernie had a hard-on for you, Bernie thought! There was a fuzzy kind of haze-hum now going on in his brain, which had been tenanted by his dick. Stevie, feeling Bernie bury himself into the side of his body even more, which itself was sore all over from the car-blow, as well as hearing this fuzzy haze-hum, thought of how narrow the gap was between artistic refinement and cruelty, being Stevie. It was... so big? He visualized a finger and thumb pressed together. Was Susan artistically refined? Stevie didn't know. He couldn't say. His hair's breadth between the aforesaid two had constant electricity passing over it anyway. Whatever Susan was, then, he was a cunt for Stevie now. A big cunt. Indeed the two were almost identical. Artistic refinement and cruelty? Susan and Stevie?

A cunt and a dick? Peas, mate.

JS Bach's music had a precision to it that Stevie had often

150

admired and even contemplated during sex. It was steely, spot-on, accurate – sharp. Quite wonderful. Quite ruthless. He also liked Samuel Barber's music, Michael Tippett's, and James MacMillan's for similar reasons. But all that now felt dirty. All Stevie's myriad fucking now seemed vile to him, via his art music. He'd been taught a lesson, seemingly. He'd been given a musical tutoring. And it hurt. Like learning the violin, it fucking hurt. He was Alex in A Clockwork Orange. That's who he was. Sick with pain. Nauseous with suffering. Art didn't really do this to you, in the final analysis. No, not really. Art didn't actually *hurt* you like a punch could. Well, it could, it could make you suffer, a bit, but not actually. (Yeah? Define what ART is, then?) Long live the Philistine! Stevie was desperately confused. He physically felt it. It was a definite feeling in his body: *confusion*. He actually felt physically confused, he thought. It seemed to surge around him in electrical pulses, going, *Which way, man? Which way?* all mad and stupid. And then when he watched Joel, this New York Jew whom he'd only recently met, stuff Francine into the jeep like a large cabbage then return to the three wives on the wall to begin kissing the one who'd blown him upstairs, well, Stevie freaked in the sheer horror of, as he deemed it, promiscuity. He flipped. He pushed Bernie away from him and jumped out from the rear. He then kind of shook himself down on the road or perhaps took a St Vitus's dance. It was difficult to say. But whatever it was it felt to Stevie like something to escape from, from within. Something to get out of yourself by jumping up and down. So he did. He jumped up and down. He'd once read of a guy in the Middle Ages who was in bed suffering from the Black Death in his wattle-and-daub house on the Thames. One day this guy couldn't take any more. So, in a mighty plagued effort, he jumped out of bed, flung himself out of the window, and crashed onto the Thames below, from where he swam across to what was known as the Isle of Dogs, only to clamber ashore there in a crazed effort, and ran around until he dropped. He then fell unconscious. When he awoke he was cured. All the sores and lumps had gone. Stevie was suffering from the Black Death. He needed to swim the Thames then run around until he dropped. It just shows you what the body is capable of, he thought, jumping.

Was sex a private thing, or was it there to be watched? Watching, Bernie was now overwhelmed at the vision of both Stevie taking a St Vitus's dance and Joel feeling the tits off all three wives, seemingly simultaneously. Indeed the insides of Bernie's hole felt like a whirlpool as he watched. A whirlpool spiralling upwards. A watched whirlpool. So, was it a tornado snorkelling Bernie's ring? And while he was at it, watching that is, he imagined the tornados on Jupiter, whose head hurt like Stevie's, though that could have been the other way around.

Whichever way round it was Bernie felt like he'd spent a week on Jupiter, whose liquids and gases no one could really visualize, in their flashes and crashes. Yet Bernie flashed and crashed. He flashed and crashed.

Susan, observing Bernie glow, also watched Joel actually insert his little penis into two of his wives, (almost simultaneously) as he stood at the door smoking a clay pipe in the dark. To a watching flashing and crashing Bernie he was monstrously phlegmatic behind that small glow of fire. Marco had now seemingly departed. It wasn't clear whether he saw Joel or not, and it probably didn't matter. For Stevie would never know that it was Marco who knocked him over anyway. No one felt the need to inform him. But it probably didn't matter. Reality was, after all, in the mind. Every mind

152

saw reality differently. Ergo *the penis* knew nothing of rationality – being a crazed organ believing that its reality was the only reality. And yes, it probably didn't matter. Joel's reality was different to Francine's, whose reality was different to Susan's, and so on. For Bernie then, unrequited love was the killer; that was the reality; but it appeared now to alter, and *did* matter. For Stevie, still crazy after all these minutes, was suddenly in love with him! Stevie was suddenly loyal! Bernie's reality now seemed brighter…

…When Francine kind of came to.

Watch it. Oi! She'd already pissed herself on the seat. A hot wet patch now clotted her fazed sensations. Yuck. 'Let's go!' she gasped, gesturing for the jeep to move her soaking arse.

'I've already gone,' sighed Bernie from behind her.

Remarkably, Francine had somehow stirred from her coma. She was no longer a flat-liner. Feeling like shit, however, or a pan of fried shite might have been more accurate, and spinning, she very annoyingly began honking the horn to the jeep, whose Herbie mentality, in her reality, wanted to protect her. (Remember Herbie?) Beep beep. Oh, that terrible drink! That terrible booze! Beeeeeeeeeeeep! You fucking bitch! The noise ceased Stevie's jumping, who, wouldn't you know it, was cured just like that bloke with the Black Death. He stopped jumping, felt himself as though amazed, was amazed, stood with his hands on his hips and a thumping heart, then said, It worked, very quietly, like a cured person. (If you're ever diagnosed with the Black Death?) Yeah. Speaking of which Francine wouldn't stop beeping the horn. A sorrowful withdrawn Joel had to come and see. Sorrowful, but also murderous. He was going to ring her neck! He'd had his dick in, and-

'What the fuck are you doing? Hey? Hey? Quit honking

that fucking horn! Hey? Enough already! Quit it. I said…
quit it, you stupid bitch! Right now!' He snatched her hands
off it then actually made to slap her across the face.

She turned her head away with a drunken hair-flick, then
put her hands back on. 'Don't you call me names. Daddy!
Joel is calling me, hic, names. I want to go to bed! Hic. Come
…….on! Oh look! Now you've made me all wet. Hic. Did
you throw water over me? Joel? Did you? I'm soaked!'

'Yeah, right. You pissed yourself, you goddamn rich
whore! Aw, man.' Joel rubbed his hair as though (a) trying
to decide whether or not to fist this cow or (b) which
trajectory in life to follow: her, or them? He glanced behind
to gaze upon the shuddering wives, then glared back to gape
at Francine. Hesitating, he chose the money. He went with
the green. Money, after all, could get him three chicks like
that anyplace. Yeah, fuck it, man. Currency wins. Back the
bread, the winner. 'Hey, psycho-babe, we're going home.
Okay? We're going home. Jesus. The things I do. The things
I fucking do…'

'Where's, hic, daddy…?'

'Daddy who, babe? Daddy who?' Joel started the engine
angrily.

'I'm, hic, soaked, Joel. I'm all… sticky…'

Joel recalled seeing his mother piss herself once. She'd
been unwell, on medication. It was Christmas time. She'd
had a few drinks: the medication needed to come out. So it
did. It came out like piss. All over the kitchen floor. His dad
beat her for it. His dad beat her for everything. That's what
Joel's dad did: beat people he knew could never beat him
back. The piss-stain was on the tiles for a long time after.
Joel was now touched to think about it. But he also recalled
big Susan arm the wives inside the house as he tore away,

154

then seeing a full moon hang eternally in that black fuck-off sky like some kind of grinning supernatural face.

Oh, shit. Thinking about his mom, within no time he'd rolled the jeep and Stevie and Bernie were flung clear from the rear. It landed back on its wide wheels with a thud, but Stevie and Bernie were cut and bruised, on the ground there, screaming. "Why have we stopped?" asked a stupefied Francine strapped in in the front and shaken to her hair-roots.

Even at noon the next day, beneath the brown mountains, with the big moon still in the sky, Stevie had a headache that could actually be heard. And that swelling? It looked bad, to Bernie, who'd only just come to and had woken everybody else by screaming loudly in his sleep. *This farce.* Yes, Joel had rolled the damn jeep last night, and Bernie had been dreaming about it. *You've killed us, you fucking idiot!* Joel had been driving with a terrible hard-on, you see. An absolute distracting woody. It was painful, to say nothing of frustrating. Hence the instant erratic night-time driving and eventual rolling. He'd then, after the crash, taken a wrong turning. There's a very sharp left-hander on the approach to the Port of Mogan from the village which takes you down onto the coast road. Joel had taken this, then remembered that he shouldn't have. He braked violently, did a two-pointer, thundered back. Now, in the brilliant sunshine of tomorrow, seemingly stuck in a crazy episode which just could not progress no matter what, Bernie, who'd soon be acquiring a lazy bowel, decided there and then that it simply wasn't worth putting up with this any more just for longevity. It just wasn't. *The Long Lived?* No thank you, for him. Not with these monsters he wouldn't. And that was the moment the bold Johnny came strolling back in. He had *I bought it last night* printed on his brown brow. Yes, the

155

leathers had been off. But he looked grey. He looked bad.

Smirking, Johnny then frantically entered the outdoor space of the terrace with a mad sense of depravity about him, a mad sense of himself. He was, after all, madly depraved. No, he hadn't slept; but being somewhat disorientated after plating two 'tarts' in their apartment he'd walked most of the way home, the dickhead. Was he all right? Yes, as far as Johnny ever could be all right. He was okay. Very well, thank you. He was very well all right. But he didn't look it. He looked like shit.

'Joel rolled the jeep last night,' Stevie informed him as he sipped orange juice and gazed at scrambled eggs as though they might move. 'He nearly fucking killed us! Have you seen my head?' He presented his lump to Johnny, which was acquired of course from being knocked over by Marco – but Stevie was…no longer sure how he got it.

'Mad bastard yank!' Johnny then robotically declared. 'He needs to be fucked off pronto! Was my daughter hurt? Has anything happened to Francine?' Johnny now looked to Stevie as earnestly as he possibly could, which wasn't very earnest at all.

Francine, naturally, was still in bed – hungover. Or she would be when she got up. No dawn-rising today! Stevie shook his head. 'No. She's all right. She was strapped in. Clunk click every trip! Bernie and I were flung into the fucking air, though. Look at this lump!' Stevie presented it again. But Johnny didn't give a shit about his fucking lump or his fucking poncey views, and made this perfectly clear by ignoring them both and walking into the house in search of Francine. On creaking up the stairs, he contemplated simply crashing into her bedroom like a distraught father and holding her in bed. But on arrival of the landing this ideal vanished, as he distantly heard Francine's bed rasping

156

up and down. It was a familiar sound: *the sound of bedroom sex.* Pausing there, and not to make a balls of it, as Beckett might have said of him, Johnny's mind flashed into overdrive. He just… had to… have a look… *secretly.* And so he crept into the room with the spyhole and uncovered its lovelorn horror. Taking a breath and holding it, one large gaping eye saw another. No, it wasn't someone gazing back, it was Joel's anus winking at him as it bounded up and down on Francine's rippling backside. Oh… my… God. But hang on a minute, Johnny peered upwards to tremulously view the entirety of his daughter's naked quivering body, his daughter's shaken nudity, only to see that she wasn't taking part. That is, she was unconscious, and Joel was raping her. He was sodomizing her!

Now Johnny had a sweat-stained dilemma: does he burst in and burst Joel, thereby disclosing his obvious voyeurism, or does he keep stum and leave it all to Sly-1? *Do that bastard slow!* He felt his heart beat in his brain. Veins on his temples bulged. Alas, he wasn't rational enough to think clearly. And besides, he probably couldn't burst Joel anyway. Joel would probably stab him through the heart. Eight seconds later Johnny was standing before a buggering Joel Maize on the bed, who looked up at him like a puffer fish only without the puff. Joel instantly yanked his dick clear of Francine's wet sphincter, who was so comatosed that she didn't even moan, and went to cuddle her by the way as though not noticing Johnny. But Johnny… was just about to… he was on the verge of…

…When Joel leapt to his feet. Being a genuine psycho, an American psycho, had its advantages: one didn't even need an excuse! He gripped Johnny around the throat with iron fingers and told him what he had to do from behind wild lips. Again Johnny's brain throbbed. Joel rightly guessed that he'd been spying, somewhere, though he hadn't yet been able to discover the hole. 'Look, you motherfucking scumbag, here's the deal. You say nothing, I say nothing. Deal? You say something, I say something. Okay? I'm raping, but you were watching. If you talk, I do too. Got that?'

Johnny would recall later taking one awful hell-crammed glimpse of his daughters a-hole, the only one he'd ever have, and would recall its contours: a brown ring encircling a red one encircling the abyss. The galaxy. Johnny saw directly into Francine's darkness, thanks to this wank fucked-up yank, who'd been fucking her up by opening her up! From that moment on, if he ever did, he would see his daughter differently. How could he not? How could he ever again look into her mouth? Back in his bedroom Johnny turned to pale lime as he stood contemplating by the window, gazing out. Yes, Francine would never know either way. But Johnny would. Did. Johnny knew. Would. Always. For 300-years! Did. Would. He watched a boat in the harbour glisten on silken water. Couldn't. No. Not with that, he thought. Couldn't live with that. Couldn't go on. Joel too had seen it, but he wasn't the first to enter hyperspace. No. His wasn't the first dick to walk on compressed air in the darkest matter. And besides, he *could* live with it.

A metallic crunch. That's what Johnny felt in his tiny head.

It was the same sound as the jeep being rolled last night. *Crun-ch*. It squeezed in on him, this sound. For he was sure his head was going to fall to pieces. So he held the head as he sat on the corner of his wooden bed in the white-painted room. He held his head to stop it falling apart. It was like holding an empty space encased in plastic. Like holding a ball. Johnny's brain very possibly had too much air. *All the*

158

drugs, man. All the booze? All the wanking? Yeah, too much wanking, too much goddamn air. Phew. It blew him away, his brain. (All that talent!) All the air drifted out from his ears and blew him away. It wasn't knowledge or intelligence that he was haemorrhaging. It was just air. Air on the brain. He'd known it a long time, this bleeding air-brain of his. Yes. A long time. Yet he also didn't know it. No. He didn't know Himmm. Funny how you think when a crisis suddenly stresses you. Funny how it gets you. Johnny reasoned that he didn't actually know himself, on his final morning. He wasn't quite sure who he was any more, if indeed he ever did. He needed to find himself, he thought, if indeed he ever could. For he didn't have a fucking clue…

A metallic crunch. Ooh. Johnny had noticed the stars last night for the first time in his life. It could have been because he wasn't able to fuck the two tarts he'd handsomely bought. He wasn't sure. (He just couldn't get it up, man – Viagra and all). Oh, he'd seen them before, the stars, millions of times. But he'd never actually noticed them. This wasn't good, as it signalled, to him, a weakness. (After all these years?) It meant that he was becoming mummsy. *Noticing stars!* Fuck off. But perhaps it was a start. Perhaps it was the beginning of the new Johnny Coy – the well-travelled experienced mind. Noticing stars? It shouldn't be a bad thing, he told himself. But then, aigh. Yes. Just when he was starting to come round to the new him, he sensed that all that food in his body now needed to vacate the premises. He now suddenly saw, from black eyes out of a pale lime face, seeing different stars, that maybe he might not even make it to the bathroom. He suddenly saw, from dancing eyes from a quickly-reddening gleam, that he was going to shit his leathers!

Outside on the terrace, under the glare of sunshine, Stevie

159

was in a subdued talkative mood, having already defecated his huge and stinking load. For what Susan had done to Bernie last night had done this to Stevie: made him faithful and devoted. He was now the one-man-one-guy kind of fella, coyly. A monogamous gay. That was it. All change. No more spreading it about. AIDS too, don't forget, he didn't forget. 'Love you,' he sweetly whispered, dropping his gaze. Then, for some reason, he said this. 'Did I ever tell you why I dropped out of uni as a mature student, dear?'

'Yes dear. Many times. Love you too…' A blown kiss.

'No, I mean properly?' Received. 'Did I ever tell you what really went wrong in my second year at Birkbeck, Bernie, with all those negative shits?' He looked to Bernie, who gently shrugged, as if to say, Must you? But Stevie must. Couldn't not. Would always. 'Our tutor,' he insisted, 'a certain Chris Smith, an unfortunate name if ever there was one, suggested that we did a mock dissertation in preparation for our final year. He asked us to pick a current British figure, oddly enough, and deconstruct them – as Birkbeck didn't really go along with that discipline. He wanted to show us how useless it was. Derrida had upset their composure. *Birk* is the first part of Birkbeck, after all. Anyway, I chose the violinist Nigel Kennedy, as that seemed right for me. I began by saying that it wasn't snobbery, it was self-respect, pride to comment on this, but the uncultured mind knows only one concept, which it applies to everything: it confuses flippancy with humour. As an opener I wasn't referring to Mr Kennedy, I was referring to what he'd done by bringing art music to the herd, if indeed he had. But it was a non-starter with Mr Smith, who, an ugly man, believed that government subsidies for so called elitist pursuits like classical music, as he called it, only protected symphony orchestras from a concept known as commercial reality – an elitist pursuit in

160

itself, I pointed out. Mr Smith believed that the public felt alienated by these minority interests and that the pretentious people involved in them regarded popularity as nothing but mediocrity. Too right, I said. It is. That's why it's popular! Great things don't necessarily pay their way, and why should they! Huh! Pretentious! *Moi?*'

'I argued with him that people who talk about elitist snobbery usually contradict themselves somewhere along the way. They're usually sports fans, needless to say, where they only want the *best* players for their team, naturally. Everyone who follows anything only wants the best for it. But if you don't find what they follow appealing, then they'll treat you with the utmost snobbery, with the utmost disdain. For they too are following elitist pursuits. They too think they're onto something special…'

'Nigel Kennedy, I continued, had wrongly believed that by bringing art music to the people he could do the same for the people without the people actually becoming cultured – that is, touching some form of beauty every day and being aware of it, and then of not being able to live without it – which, for some curious reason, he abhorred. It was desperately naive of him, I argued. It was the same as Pavarotti singing for the 1990 World Cup: he'd opened the gates of oblivion!'

Bernie gave a stifled laugh. But Stevie didn't want that. He was serious.

'All's Nigel Kennedy was doing,' Stevie then tiresomely continued, a little angrily, 'war-paint and the rest, was rebelling against the bourgeois lunacy, that surface value, which he himself could never surmount – being 'bad' and all, I wrote. Look, I pleaded to Chris Smith after he'd casti- gated and scorned me for what he now called inverted elitism, I was brought up in a mostly tabloid-run household.

161

My background was Coronation Street ridden: it was bleak. It was George Formby. Al Jolson. It didn't turn out nice. Somehow, though, I heard Debussy's piano music when I was 18. From then on I discovered things in a world that was totally superior to mine, and I wanted it to remain that way. It was a world I wished to aspire to…'

Bernie now sighed. 'You've told me this before, you know.'

'Have I? I'm Sorry. I thought I hadn't. But I'm compelled, darling. Look, I actually saw Nigel Kennedy play the Mendelssohn live back in 1979 was I was just 19 myself. He was absolutely wonderful. An incredible performer. He made the piece live. We could hear him snort with expression. Then, many years flew by before I heard of him again. But when I did, he'd gone mad, and was saying things like, "Monsters baby," as though biting into an apple. He was going to football matches and acting, well, rather strange. Was this what bringing "music" to the people meant, I asked Chris Smith? By bringing music to the people, I wrote, with your Classic FM and the like, what you've done is destroy the very thing you wanted the people to know about. I would never have risen out of the mire had I not striven to! You don't bring it down to them, you bring them up to it! Chris Smith said that my argument was totally unsubstantiated. He said that it was beliefs like mine which ideologically needed to be crushed as they'd bolstered-up the class-system in the first place and had kept classical music for the few. But I thought he was wrong, because art music was for the few, the few who knew how to listen to it, I said, which had nothing to do with either class or even money. The following weekend I left. I've never looked back.'

Bernie didn't really care either way, but he smiled in the

162

sunlight because he knew how much his re-found lover needed to say these things. He was content when Stevie was happy, and he wanted to be content then. He watched someone do breast-stroke in the harbour waters below.

But Stevie wasn't happy. 'This is why,' he concluded, agitated yet distant, 'I get angry with members of the herd: it's all been taken now, and they're delighted about that. That special world of magic which we could rise to has gone. It's been crushed, and those who brought about its demise by singing and dressing-up like fucking clowns can take the credit. They can now take over in the crass world they wished for – huh, the world of the tyrannical plebeian…'

PART 2

1

IT WAS A while before anyone found Johnny's body. Stevie had to break the bathroom door open in the end. For Johnny had died on the lavatory while defecating. He'd bought it in his own shit. It would transpire that he'd had a massive stroke on the throne. There he was, slumped back with his leathers around his ankles, eyes half open, white-faced and lifeless, the road to perdition at an end…

Like many a rock-star of the 20th century he did not get to witness the new millennium, for what it was worth. (All those lovely fireworks)…

His brain had burst and there was nothing anybody could have done for him. Death came a-looking. It came a-seeking. And then, a desperately hungover Francine flipped. The whole episode caused her to blink very heavily like some deranged yob. She almost didn't know where she was. *The mood came swiftly.* But the smell in there when they finally got the door open would forever remind Bernie of how *he* felt about the man while alive. It was the smell of a freshly-manured sweet and sour field: the odour of Johnny's soul. Nonetheless at the time it was a glum spectacle to behold – the poor little guy dead for all to see. Dead, yes. And gone. Gone forever. To? Nowhere. To nothing. To never walk this way again, that's where. That brief flash in the pan they talked about. When the ambulance arrived the police arrived with it. There would need to be an autopsy of course, there would need to be questions, before the body could be released and sent back to England. Would there be a build-up from Marco's sauces in his brain?

Johnny was gone, and there was nothing anybody could do about that cold fact. But then Francine, as the police began to silently look at Joel very suspiciously in the apartment,

166

got it into her panicky mind that nanobots could kind of revive him, could kind of bring him back to life. Yeah, Frankenstein's monster and all that. Francine's monster? So, as the impassive Spanish paramedics removed Johnny from the apartment in a black bag that matched his black leathers, and the two policemen who accompanied them now looked at everybody as though guilty of a murder, Francine frantically searched for her father's mobile in his room and the rogue scientist's number. It took her some time – all that shaky fiddling, all that dropping of sleek metal – but she eventually found it. She also discovered his text-messages to Sly-1, as she sat on her father's ex-bed – though she didn't know who Sly-1 was. She didn't care, either. She just wanted to fiddle with the mobile.

I can't go on. I'll go on.

Daddy, daddy. Tell me you're not dead. Tell me you're still alive! Outside on the terrace, under the glare of the same sun, Stevie, Bernie and Joel were very quiet, and not at all happy. Joel mostly because he was worried that he'd induced Johnny's death by that deranged strangle-hold he laid on him. He *did not* want to go to a Spanish prison! Aw, man. But it also bothered him just how freaked Francine was when she'd held her father's corpse. He couldn't get it out of his mind. She'd kissed it and hugged it and even spoken to it. Then she shook it. It bothered him to think that maybe he'd been the cause of this unattractive anxiety. It had been very unnerving to him, being as he was always on the edge of sanity anyway. Bernie and Stevie too had been upset by this, even though they only saw it from outside the bedroom. They were quiet for Francine's loss, for Francine's shock, the horror of it all. It was distressing to see her in a way they hadn't seen her before. And to witness her become uselessly manic in her craved sense of overwhelming sudden regret?

167

That evening, while still sobbing upstairs in her glowing room, a stargazing Francine slowly began to recover. The onset of the galaxy night-sky – the first one she'd ever behold without her only father on this little planet – kind of brought her out of the whirlpool she was in. It lifted her up onto dry land. For the sunset was magnificent – the onset of the unbearable lightness of being? Great red rays streaked towards beaming yellows, which arched across greens; horizon-blues, heartbreak-glimmer oranges. She'd rolled over on the bed to look at it in her mess. The bedroom window perfectly framed its stolen magic. It was spectacular, she could see. Oh, daddy. Where are you? A stargazing reverie. She'd arrived at some sort of point in her life, that was obvious. A sunset-point, she vaguely thought. But right then she wanted to sell the apartment and get off the island. She wanted to go back to London. She wanted to be part of the scene again quickly before they all forgot about her…

Red-faced, she sat up on the end of the bed. Think distance. In just a pair of loose-fitting shorts and a vest, she felt her legs with the soft palms of her hands. She rubbed them gently across the light white hairs. Her thighs were now very brown – yet there was no sensation on the surface of her skin. Odd, as Francine had always been, she believed, a sensuous, touchy-feely person. Her bones too were numb, and kind of attached to something else. Then her head felt light. In this plight she felt desperate that she was in Gran Canaria and not London. Desperate. It was a very tetchy sensation. A spot of erethism. Then she vomited in the corner of the room. She just twisted round from the bed and allowed it to fire out from her mouth and onto the floorboards. *Splosh!* No problem. She'd been shaking for some time; she'd been nauseous for some time; it was as though she'd witnessed an accident or something. She recalled an impotent boyfriend of hers being threatened with violence by a previous potent one: the guy just shook and looked deeply vacant. That was her then.

Splosh! Oh, God, again.

What was driving her system? Was grief really like this? No. She hadn't even entered that stage. Grief didn't kick in for a while. It took some time for grief to take its ebony hold.

She would have a broken heart, sure. But not yet. Her heart hadn't heard the news, yet. Her brain was still at the printers getting the type-set sorted. But when the news would get out? Oh. Then. Yes. Then. When the news hit the shops in paper form. Snap, etc.

Francine was still also hungover from the previous evening's bizarre, if not occultish, tumult. She therefore had even less of a grip on what was happening. The impact, like that of the jeep rolling, hadn't impacted, as it were. But then, as a kind of opener to grief, she actually began to feel embarrassed in her own company. Odd, certainly. Embarrassed at what? She had no idea. Just embarrassed, that's all. A desire not to see anyone for fear of feeling worse? Perhaps. Embarrassed, for the first time in her life, actually, but only briefly, at being incredibly wealthy. Yes. That was it. That was the one. Wealth without having to firstly acquire it. That's what was kicking in. (Things were altering). *Born* into money. Money for blood. Money for bones. So much money that one could say, *I want that person killed tonight! Or, I'd like to fly first-class to LA and stay in the best hotel for three months with ten of my friends!* It suddenly, and for reasons she'd never ever comprehend, felt embarrassing not to be the same as either Joel, Stevie or Bernie, whom she actually needed right then. It felt wrong to her – but only

169

briefly. The embarrassment would pass. It would lift. Like all superficials, an unnatural bashfulness would rise up into the glazed sky…

Feeling wrong, though, and now beginning to understand that perhaps daddy had in fact departed for good – although she would become obsessed with resurrecting him – Francine felt the sweltering need to be outdoors on her own. She needed some air, even though it'd be hot. So she slipped out of the front and ambled along the long-lived marina in the desert sunshine. Dazed. Fazed. Ghosted. The boats and Spanish-style townhouses looked exactly the same as they did yesterday when her father was still alive. That is, they glinted and shone in the sun and the boats bobbed in the salt haze with their masts rattling in the soft breeze. Indeed, Francine could see that nothing of the world had changed. Nothing of the world, except her. Nothing of the world ever did change when somebody died: it was only the departed who no longer sat amongst it all. Strange that we go…

Feeling strange, and brooding outlandishly on the notion of complete negation, she sensed that she couldn't walk properly. It was a *strange* sensation, this notion, this sense. To feel strange and not be able to walk properly as well? It was… strange. In fact her long legs were now strangely wobbly. So, instead of walking to a quiet point along the marina, she wobbled to it… strangely. Like a 90-year-old. A weak wobble. A geriatric tremble. She could have done with a hand, she thought. Or a zimmer. But no one knew she was there. Joel was out on the terrace, contemplating Spanish jails. Stevie and Bernie were pondering on how eerie the countryside at night was to a cityperson, but not on zimmers. It was very eerie, they simultaneously concurred. She was alone. But that's what she wanted. She wanted to

170

be alone. That's what she got. Being alone, albeit briefly, she got on with it. She got on with edging along alone, wobbling, quaking. Then she recalled that dream she had the other day which woke her. The one with her father's severed head on the pillow next to her. That grim grin he was wearing, that small smirk, it was exactly the same one as… it was the same grin as… yes, the one he had on the damn toilet! It was the same ghoulish sneer! Had that dream been an omen? she then pondered, now quivering on the inside as well as feeling strange all over with wobbling legs and great wonderings on negation. Her brain was making sounds like an atonal piece, although she didn't know what that was. It was just a noise to her. An insane noise. Her brain was playing passages from a shimmering piece by Ligeti, though she didn't know who Ligeti was. (It could have been his Concerto for Cello, 1966. *Brilliant*). Squinting, she now felt unsafe for once in her blissfully safe life. A brand new sensation was descending in her mind: that of acute vulnerability. For Francine didn't know much, when it came down to it. As Nabokov might have said, she was not as intelligent as her IQ might suggest. As her brain buzzed, her emotions felt assailable. She was all exposed. Ignorance was being highlighted in humiliating neons.

She sat quietly with her arms wrapped around her knees, gazing at sunlight on seawater. A new type of contemplation now introduced itself to her – a deep and frightening one. It wouldn't be around for long, but its newness seemed mortifying yet at the same time just what she needed.

She was glimpsing the untouched fire of a vibrant immortality.

171

2

BUT WHAT WAS such an obscure thing?

Sitting still, on rock, at the water's edge, in the blue day, Francine only knew that she was now very afraid. Whether from glimpsing whatever it was, or the fact that Johnny's body was being sliced open somewhere, pulled back, emptied out, made into hell, just like that, she didn't know; because there, at the end of the marina in *Puerto Mogan*, Francine Coy, watching timeless mountain-ridges cutting into the big sky beyond, was trembling like a helpless little girl. It was as though she was sensing what was actually befalling (enthralling?) her father, step by step. *Afraid* didn't really do the emotion justice. Fear was a large concept. Simply saying the word '*fear*' only seemed to shrink the actual sensation into, well, a word. A little word. But *fear* wasn't a word. Fear was conceptual, as big as the world. Fear was just about as real as it gets for us human beings. For it moved mountains. It was atonal, it was shattering.

Fear was the unknown.

A word in your shell-like. Yes, even Johnny's ears were sliced off to be inspected under the icy microscope. One never knew. Au injection mark? A wee pin-prick? Poison. Spanish was the language used in the dissection of the body. *Spanish!* (What was that about turning over in your grave?) His poor little jockey's body had been by this stage completely mutilated, and its horror spoken about in Spanish! The eyes out, the tongue out, and then the floppy brain. Yes. That blood-coated fiend. That was the culprit. It was a congealed mess. Nanobots couldn't have saved him. Nothing could save him. He was beyond all help. Johnny Coy had returned to the void from whence he came: he no longer existed. And this notion, this concept, was beginning

172

to take a hold of Francine. It was a difficult concept to behold, this idea of a person no longer existing anywhere. Especially one's father. But once its rottenness had been absorbed it seemed difficult to imagine a life without it. For life was never without death: death gave life its zeal. But what a set-up! And Francine wanted to live, then, in the shadow of that new death. She wanted the zeal part of it. She wanted the opposite of death, forever. So she shuddered, never wanting to die, never wanting to experience what her father had just gone through. She never wanted not-to-be, or her sweet face to wear that terrible smirk, that ghoulish sneer? *The glare of not-being?* Atonality bashed its way round her skull.

Stealing herself, she rang the nanoguy.

On the edge of the marina, there in that intense blue day, she finally spoke to Dr Dunant, who resided in Vermont, New England, USA. He answered immediately, and he knew who Francine was. In a shaking voice she explained that her father had just, ah, died, and that, ah, if it was all right with him, there would now only be four injections required instead of five. Of course, in Dr Dunant's mind there were only ever two – Johnny had already put him in the picture – so he simply agreed to Francine's four, though at a slightly higher price, to which Francine didn't even comprehend…

'Is there any way,' she ranted on, 'any way that you could bring my daddy back to life! Is it at all possible!' And with that she burst into tears right into daddy's mobile, which still had his fingerprints all over it…

Echoing all the way to America. The voice at the other end was clipped. An emotionless tone. A mind used to calmly experimenting no matter what the cause or what the case. 'I'm afraid not.' All the way from New England. 'Nanotechnology isn't quite that advanced. It will prolong

173

life for many centuries, but it cannot bring life back. I'm afraid you're just going to have to come to terms with your loss in your own way. It's tough, I know. But life is. Can you hear me? Miss Coy? Are you still there? Good. Don't be afraid to cry. That's healthy. Let it all out. You'll feel brighter tomorrow. There is always tomorrow, remember. Now then, back to business. I told your father that I'd meet him where you are now – on Gran Canaria. We'd arranged it for next Saturday, but I may have to go to Lanzarote first. Is that still all right with you? Miss Coy? Are you still there Miss Coy…?'

Still there? Miss Coy wasn't anywhere, really. She'd have to get back to him. She'd have to get back to him and let him know. The following day the police wanted to question everybody individually about the old guy's demise. Yes, there were bruise-marks on Johnny's neck all right where Joel had gripped him. Questions needed to be answered, even though they had the real cause of death. They used an interpreter, and Susan (my name is Sue, how do you do?) showed up to give support to Francine, who sobbed a lot and wore no make-up.

Joel caused the police the most concern, naturally. This guy looked guilty – no matter what – whatever guilty was. Joel was guilty, most of the time. He was guilty of another murder, of course, which he'd only just recalled then. Huh? I'd, er, forgotten about that. Is he dead? Really? Fortunately, as was said at the start, no one looked into the lost heart of the bum in New York. Joel dumped the organ in another alley, where it was promptly eaten by dogs. Then he washed his hands in his own piss. The body was just carted off and destroyed in bum-incineration. No. A killer was not sought. No one in New York was looking for the heart-eater of a bum. Joel had got away with it. Johnny's case was

174

different, however, in that he had money. Even though he wasn't actually murdered, questions needed to be asked and *would* be asked because of his seeming position. Johnny was important. He wasn't a bum – well, on paper at least. 'No, man,' Joel protested in the kitchen. 'Hey, the old guy went out that night and like got into a deal with two sluts! They must've like bit him on the neck or something. Sluts are into shit like that, man. Fucking vampires and all. Me, strangle him? No way, bro…'

He had a pat terminology. Round about this time Francine began to confide in Bernie, or at least talk more honestly to him. The police were satisfied that no foul play had taken place, (Susan had somewhere along the way intervened) and Johnny's body, after being put back together in a kind of ghoulish compressed pancake, was allowed release for the UK. But things needed to be sorted. Johnny's estate was very large. Francine would become sole-beneficiary of the will, naturally, even though people would come out of the woodwork – there'd be blood-brothers and blood-sisters she never knew she had – but the very idea only served to heighten her creative distress. It was time. That's what it was. That's what would heal her. *Time.* Terrible time. Yet how awful time was to a human being. (Einstein's theory of what?) It healed, but it sure took away. It removed whole episodes, whole lives and memories. It crumbled eras, broke up buildings. Time rocked the epicentre of what a lifetime thought it was about. For time changed everything, in time. It changed the way we saw, the way we were, the way we might become had time not got in the way and messed it all up. Worse, it changed the way we looked. Terrible time made a really old person, who was once a really young person, seem silly to other really young people, who would themselves become really old people, in time. So imagine living

175

for 300-years? Francine had imagined it. She'd been there. All that experience, all that seeing things go and change? Could someone of 275 relate to someone of 28, and vice versa? No, she hadn't thought of that one. The sheer mass of memories and emotion, of knowledge and hopeful understanding? The gaps, the spans would be too great! This was how Bernie was beginning to see it, anyway, while comforting Francine in her first genuine need. But what she really needed was this time thing. She needed its vile rape, its healing bullying, its distant placing. She needed a whole chunk of the stuff behind her in order to get on with, yes, life, which was never far away from death. Yet time, when new to us, *did* make death appear remote. A future spectacle. Something for older people to worry about. Terrible time conned us in that way – being ultimately circular in its falsity.

(A play about time). Hi. I'm 290-years-old. I've been here, done that, did that with people who were 200 when I was just 98. I attended things which were abolished or demolished 140-years before you were born, magical things. Nice to meet you. What was that? You've got nothing to say? Piss off, then. Sorry. Was I being intolerant? Dear me. Time, you see. It must be my age. (The end).

It just wouldn't work. The gaps would be far too great…

And too much. So Much. So few would know of so much. Consequently, the few would burn out all alone. They would perish. But imagine the memories? Visualize the prodigious understanding! Nano-probes would know nothing of that, would know nothing of the understanding. Dark-matter would take on form and react with its surroundings. It would be up there at the level of worst horrors. Dark-matter would descend from space and eat ancient human flesh violently.

176

Comically, Susan had been telling Francine in the interim that the ceiling to his living-room had come crashing down while he and the wives slept soundly in their kingsized bed. (Was it dark-matter's prank?) They woke suddenly to a drop, a smash, broken bits of wood, dust, a terrfying stillness. He spoke in Spanish to her. He spoke matter-of-factly. "It must have been dry-rot," he concluded. There was a hell of a weight focused on the legs of that bed. Susan explained that, as the bed hit the ground below, he instantly leapt from it and began charging around the house like a crazed rhinoceros. *CRASH!* He became a bull chasing people in the street. The stereo was destroyed. Mallibenny was almost crushed as he'd been sleeping in the house. He was going to get Marco to help him with the repairs, but that piss-head had been on a fucking bender and was fucking pissed out of his fucking twatting brains somewhere, the prick.

Francine didn't hear him. She told him instead that she'd dreamt of horrible men in her apartment and they had horrible horny faces and had come looking for her father. It was a terrible dream, she told him. It was so... real. Then she fell asleep in his arms in the space of 5-seconds.

177

3

IT WAS A new beginning. That's what was now seemingly transpiring. A new beginning that she never ever wanted to happen. She never ever wanted this beginning to begin in her life, no matter when it began. She just didn't want it. It was too tough for her, I know, because she told me. She began to lose what little reason she had. She began to go mad. It was very possibly a nervous-breakdown. Difficult to say. There she was, running over the sand dunes of Maspalomas, pulling tongues at nude-bathers. Or, dashing through the blooming gardens at the Port of Mogan – the bougainvillea bursting with life, unlike her father – and, yes, screaming. Screaming. People looked. She'd hold her head. Marco hid his big brown face in his newly named *Restaurante Cofradia*. (It was becoming a popular place, his restaurant. Also, one of his myriad brothers would later acquire the *Restaurante Calipso* further inland, which local people would eventually use more than tourists. They were doing well). What was happening to poor Francine meanwhile was that she wasn't. Susan, unfortunately, had seemingly vanished. It was said that he'd gone to Tenerife on business. Though *what* business one could only speculate. Magic business perhaps? Child-eating business? No one really knew…

One extremely hot day Francine had been told by the authorities that it was time (she could no longer delay it) to accompany her father's remains back to London. *Accompany? How did one accompany remains?* They'd all been sunbathing at Maspalomas Beach, and were now very brown. Francine had calmed a little. Stevie however was still unwell from being knocked over: he kept feeling sick, and his bones ached a lot right down in the marrow, even in the sunshine. Francine also was unwell, but in a different way, of course.

178

She'd just stay in the sun all day wearing only factor 6 oil with no hat and no sunglasses. If anybody tried to advise her to the contrary, she'd bawl abuse at them. And when an official called round to tell her (politely – a polite notice) that she had to get Johnny's rotting body the hell off the island she pulled tongues at him and immediately went swimming in the harbour, naked. The man simply watched her slip out of her bikini through aghast bulging bloodshot eyes, and looked depressed. Shaking his head, he politely left the premises, forever recalling that little bulb of bliss between those two brown cheeks of crimson joy. Oh, ci. Okay, fine. No problem. Time to go? Time to leave? (*Time* crops up everywhere, doesn't it), Swimming in the nude, she asked Stevie to arrange it. She asked Stevie to do it. She couldn't do it herself. She wasn't up for it. Glug glug. She went under. Then she came up again. Glug Glug. "Stevie, darling, I want you to arrange it all. I want you to do it. Will you? Will you do it for me? Oh, say you will. Say you'll do it for little Fran. Say you will." Glug glug. No. She wasn't up for it. She didn't know how. He did. He said he'd do it. He'd go to the airport and actually do it, as well as saying he would. There wouldn't be a problem. There never was, as far as Francine was concerned with Stevie, except sexually of course. Never. It was also dawning on him just how good it all was now that Johnny was no longer alive, was no longer in the world. A shadow had been taken away, seemingly. Yes, it was dawning on him, in the sun. It suddenly began to feel very good. *Johnny Coy was dead!* It suddenly began to sink in that that little disgusting fascist bastard was out of it. (There was a God, after all), Good. Gone. God. No more. To sleep no more? Ho-hum. What a loss! Such a fucking tragedy! No, it was brilliant. The world was suddenly an infinitely better place for Stevie because Johnny was no

179

longer in it, and this concept was taking a hold of him. For Stevie truly hated Johnny, he could now behold. He hated him as only total opposites can hate: with a passion. Johnny hated Stevie, sure. But Stevie *hated* Johnny. O yes. He fucking loathed him. It was one cunt less. That's what it was. One *big* cunt. Like some prat politician gone. Well, not that bad. But the world was a better place without them both. A much nicer place. A smiling Stevie.

A frowning Francine. Her bowel had been affected. She'd had the shits. She was suffering from a reactionary-depression. A very powerful, a very frightening emotion. The feelings were real, yet they were outlandish. For they'd never been felt before. They were big, destructive feelings. There was a numbness, but combined with this was a wild recklessness. Reactionary-depression affected the appetite, too: Francine simply could not eat. She wanted to shake her body off itself, if that was possible. She wanted to get out of herself. Her chest was tight and her guts blazed with tremors. Also her brain throbbed right at the front. Right there. At the front. She would, if she could, have killed herself. She would, if she could, have never woken up again...

Every time she saw her father's dead face in her mind she would get these waves of abject gripping anxiety rippling right along her spine and into her flesh, causing her long legs to want to shake and then to walk far, if she could. But she could not. These waves seemed to grip her every hour or so, and made her shake. It was a definite physical sensation, well beyond anything she had experienced before in her life. She had absolutely no control over it. It was a sadness too she'd never known, this anxiety. A deep-seated sensation moving through her seemingly swollen body. Materialistically rich, Francine tried to ponder on her life within the superficial London scene in an attempt at alleviating the feeling. It helped – for a bit. For she then saw for the first time exactly what the London scene was all about. (We're talking early 21st Century scene, of course, not the scene today). It was an entire rag-tag of almost pathological falseness and bizarre un-called-for hatred. A milieu of elevating things which did not deserve elevation, did not deserve merit – the London scene. But that was okay. That was fine... or had been. It was no longer fine, Francine could now see. But it had been fine. It was her. It *had* been okay. But pondering the London scene helped no more...

No more miss Nice Girl. Here's what helped instead. It was a reality that her money – now combined with her father's money – earned her thousands a week in interest simply by sitting in the bank. Materialistically rich, in the past (that is every moment up until this particular moment for her) the idea that her money earned her a small fortune every *day* always brought a broad smile to her face, even when she was defecating on the loo, and had zero problems in her life. For it was a very powerful, a very reassuring notion, money just out of having money. Fantastic. It was great. And it was this, sunlight into the darkest caverns of the soul and all that, illuminations in the canals of the clouded brain, that did it. Once, some time ago, Francine was with friends in the old Hardrock Cafe opposite Hyde Park which she used to frequent in the early 1990s. Suddenly, after a couple of glasses of white wine, amid loud sounds of contrived rock-music of course, she gave out a girly shriek as – for the first time that day – the old money deal dawned on her once again. Her friends thought she'd been doing coke, and just laughed at her dumb laddishness. But it wasn't that. It was the deep-seated recognition that she would never ever have to worry about money – huh, no probs – and also that no matter what she did or where she went or what she bought she would never ever have to worry about money. Ever. Never. It would always be there. And it wasn't just the money: it was the fact that she could do whatever she pleased and where she pleased, and there would still always be… the fucking money. The money. It had a lovely sound, *the money*. Well done, daddy. I'm in the money – forever! Okay. So, the money. Yes. It was this concept, this money-concept, finally, that lifted her briefly out of that deep-black haze she was in. The familiar always-there notion which, smiling warmly, rescued her from certain madness, from certain bewilderment. *The money*. It was still there, some-where, hiding as a benevolent god. As money did. For it had been vast wealth in the past that had given her the confidence, nay, the arrogance, to burn as many bridges as she wished to burn – even when it wasn't required that she burnt them: it was simply entertainment. Now, though, it was her wealth she was calling on for genuine psychological help. And it came through, her wealth. It emerged with its golden hands held out. (The old adage of money can't buy you happiness, but it can make you comfortable in your misery?) Yep. Francine began to suddenly feel a lot better, comfortable in her misery. She started to recall her opulent life back in Chelsea. It was all coming through for her.

Indeed she even did a bit more sunbathing – using a more sensible factor and her cap. Deleterious comments even entered her mind once again in the piss-taking sun. Giggly comments. Comments she would usually make about her not-as-rich-as-her girlfriends. All those bitches she'd had to tolerate over the years? Only a minute ago she felt she needed them to exist, these bitches. No way now, though. No way. They were ridiculous. They weren't worth a frig. She could move on from them. They were, yes, bitches.

182

Useless slags past their sell-buy date. Or at least that was the way Francine saw them then, these girlfriends of hers back in London. For if her father had believed that he was someone with mafioso connections, then Francine believed that she was someone always in charge, especially of her alleged friends. And she was now in charge of her life again, she felt. It was all going to change. She was back on top. But things needed to be clarified, she thought, pulling the peak of her baseball cap lower quite firmly, looking down at her little round belly in the oily sun. Because it had all been a joke, her life. Well, kind of. A pleasant joke perhaps. But it was going to change. She'd wanted people's attention since she was a small girl, that much was true. She still did, only in a different way. Different strokes. So things needed to be clarified now in order that her life was no longer a joke. Like, say, who was for her politically and who was against her? She wanted to be taken seriously. She wanted to be treated as a grown-up. And those who weren't for her would be, by definition, against her. They would. Francine now saw, perhaps for the first time in her 32-years, that yes, she did indeed have enemies. It was a reality. There were those, in London, who hated her, because they had never taken her seriously. That's where their hatred manifested. It lived in the long-standing notion that Francine, ultimately, wasn't actually worth that much… spiritually. Consequently, they had treated her as some kind of shithead. That's how she was now viewing it. But then she began smiling to herself at this: *she was going to fuck them off.* And then she gave out a little laugh. A German couple who happened to be sailing passed her patio in a tiny boat glanced up to see what was so funny. All's they saw was a beautiful English lady baking in the hot sun.

4

BERNIE'S BURST SPHINCTER had been giving him trouble on the flight home. It had been, well, leaking. He now had a permanently-wet one, he was horrified to discover. He hadn't really noticed it up until then: he'd been cooling off in the ocean most of the time. But now he had, on the flight home, and it bothered him. For it was terrible. That damn monster Susan! Johnny's mutilated remains lay in a refrigerated hell just below Bernie's permanently-wet hole. (Odd how quickly things can alter in life. Johnny had left this life, with all its tribulations, all its joys and melancholic boredoms). The nano-injections? The rendezvous was now London – close to The Serpentine in Hyde Park, Francine had somewhat hysterically arranged. That's where they'd now meet him. From there they could slip back to Francine's place and it'd all be over. Four quick pricks. That'd be it. Longevity! Dunant would go wherever the money was, of course. He knew what he doing. (Or did he, as will transpire?) After this little sale he too would be a multi-millionaire. That'd be it for him. Sorted!

To Francine it would be worth every cunting penny. In charge, she was. In control. She was the cool TV newscaster attempting to appear unflustered on screen. Not a problem. (She'd seen one recently and believed that that was the way to act when one was *in control* – somewhat cocky and super-cilious). But while attempting to appear cool and unflus-tered when one is anything but, the face gives it all away. Especially the eyes. (It was the journalist's agenda to search the land for glib stories that would give them the credibility they constantly desired, wasn't it? Hence the eyes: they danced. But you couldn't kid all of the people all of the time – except perhaps Francine – people saw through it in

184

the end). Though Francine didn't give a shit about crime or unemployment or nuclear weapons or over-population or, except perhaps sexually, the birch. (And what a sexual concept it was). She just wanted to be in control again and to superficially display this quality like, she believed, the newscaster – all the pouting, all the grimacing, all the smirking in the depths of that long-lived agenda. Consequently, she was awfully rude to an air-stewardess who brought a portion of smoked salmon that had a very small grey mark on it. She swore very quietly but with intense teeth-gritting malice to her. That was how Francine feigned control. Yeah, and like it merited a response like that! That was how Francine believed the newscaster would have responded, and she may have even been right...

And it was during this interlude, this aggressive time-rendezvous, that Bernie had been thinking about, well, time. Yes, the clock and all its ramifications. Well no, not the clock as such. Bernie had been thinking about time in a stellar sense, as far as Bernie could conceive of such a thing. He was becoming quite a little thinker, was Bernie. He fancied himself as being a witness to the appearance of dreams. Especially, ah, with a broken hole. It somehow made it – no, don't laugh – easier for him to dwell. And dwell he did, in his own little broken-hole way. There he'd be, gazing out of the porthole high above the planet Earth – confirming the illusion of height – pondering time. He began to believe that everything had already happened and that that was why lots of people believed in fate: it had all been done before, it had all happened already. Bernie believed this. Everything. Before and after, as well as in between. Everything that was going to happen had already happened, and everything that had happened somehow remained, somewhere, yet it was also unfolding together backwards, to Bernie, who then

185

unfolded forwards on his seat to the soft chime of a cabin bell. That's what was going on in his head. (The soft chime, as well as time's arrows). This was the condition known as *The Unfolding Theory*. It was the condition of his mental health as they flew home from Gran Canaria. (Unfolding) Bernie mused on his theory, musing on an aircraft in 1999. But how did he get these feelings? How did he know that everything that was going to happen had already happened and that everything remained, if indeed it did?

He gave a great big other-worldly shudder in his magical insight. No one could know the future, he thought, not knowing his own reality or that Francine was definitely turning away from them. *Time?* No. It wasn't humanly possible. And if time really did exist then who was to say which way it should run? Huh? Huh? He recalled the lagoon next to the town of Maspalomas for a minute, as he tentatively ate (in time) his highly-salted airline meal. He thought of even more time unfolding, if time allowed. Those palm trees in the low evening light had freaked him. Beautiful, yes, but spooky. Bernie then camply recalled Susan. Most, ah, painful. A time-oasis man, perhaps? Both Bernie and Stevie were bone-burningly tanned, he could now see in the aeroplane's spongy light. Almost black, in fact. He could easily have been taken for a local, as he tried to pop his ears and move his jaw. Why, he was almost as black as Susan! But no. He wasn't Spanish. So he couldn't have been taken for a local. Yet in the cab from Heathrow back to Chelsea, still not with his ears popped, gazing at his bare arms in mild wonderment, the wise-guy taxi-driver made a glib comment about looking like one of them, but Bernie wasn't exactly sure who 'them' was.

Time ran backwards. Johnny was still alive.

No. It ran forwards, oddly. Time ran into its own oblivion,

which was what time ultimately did – being what time ultimately was. *An oblivion*. And Francine? How was she coping with time? In time? Well, it was making her harder, time was. Did. Would. That is, even harder than she was. Had been. Could become. Time was turning her into pure granite. It was making her timeless…

She had champagne in her apartment at Chelsea Harbour, she knew, as time then switched to its regular slot. That is, in its slow overkill of everything it was conning you that it didn't really exist and that it didn't really give a shit as it had a pull on your body.

On the approach to The Tower where Francine resided when in England, (she regarded it as "home") possibly somewhere along the King's Road in the steaming, brisk but slow-moving taxi, Francine declared to Joel Stevie and Bernie that the bubbly had been awaiting them in anticipation of longevity ever since she'd placed it in the fridge. It awaited! (It waited). Waiting, it just stood there, shivering in the dark cold vacuum. To her it felt good to be back – even though they hadn't been away for all that long. 'It feels good to be back amongst the endless traffic, the endless people of London. Great big steaming fizzing sweating rotating London!' she said. All the fumes, all the anger, all the loving. In short, all the life. It was true, London *was* life, unlike many other major cities of the world. Everything in the human world had happened in London, and would continue to happen there, almost simultaneously. For it was a *happening* place, man. (Bernie gasped at the antiquated phrase). A what? Yet how apt. It happened there, ergo it was a happening place, and that didn't only apply to the 1960s. The 1960s, via Stevie's father as well as Francine's, had run a large influence over the growing-up of all who were children in that decade – albeit subliminally. Johnny Coy, as Francine

187

was born in 1967, had turned away from it all in his latter, more responsible, seemingly intelligent years, being, it could be argued, working-class, and therefore ultimately conservative – even if at election time the opposite might take the vote. As Stevie once said, to the annoyance of Johnny, the 60s professed to give a voice to the "common man" but was actually too intellectual in its ideals to grab him fully by the short and curlies. That's why the common man of the 1960s, once he had children, definitely reverted right back to the ways and woes of his father's brigade, whom he initially rebelled against! And if Johnny Coy had been anything, well… exactly. Hence the priming of his daughter, and her recent rise above it. Johnny had been (now deceased) the archetypal common man, really, and proud of it. Then he became a has-been common man. What a concept!

World-weary. That's how they were. What with all that time and everything? No wonder.

The gang-minus-one entered the cool hallway to Francine's apartment to smells of lush carpet and faint hints of oils. Bodies had not been through this space for some time; the ambience was of dead stillness, of wilting flowers in a summer haze and of the timelessness of outer space. Francine told Joel to dump the cases on the massive bed, indicating in the process to Stevie and Bernie that they would be staying in the other bedroom as the holiday wasn't yet over. "It's not over, yet! I mean, come on!" Joel did as he was told. Like a butler. He was feeling unusually passive.

Time. It moved in mysterious ways. And yes, once opened, the time-still fizz of gas inside sweet liquid surged nicely around the gut and veins.

It was a nice surging – surge/surgeon? Francine decided for everyone that she'd send out for a Chinese banquet, yah,

188

from like, yah, the best London has to offer, okay. 'I fancy soup and crispy duck and loads of different main courses with fried rice!' In her madness she was now constantly starving, constantly empty, wanting to seemingly grow on all sides.

She'd been salivating with the thought of food. Of Chinese food especially. Salivating with it!

She'd wanted to bathe in cooled-off hot and sour soup, to rub chicken and ginger all over her face. She'd wanted to stand in a deep well of crispy seaweed, eventually consuming the lot over a period of days.

Surging traffic could be heard rumbling in the churning distance, along with her rumbling distant-churning tummy in the flat. Although it was happening, London was a place where the mobility didn't quite match that of desire, it had seemed to many people who had suddenly desired there. Only the bikes got through – either motor or push. Four wheels or two legs just didn't get you all that far, didn't get you any nearer.

It really was too far to walk, London – too far to drive at a snail's pace.

Knowing this, Francine hinted that the Chinese banquet had better be delivered by motorbike, or there'd be fucking hell to pay! Play? How close were they? Insanely close. By now the champagne had played *hell* with Francine's stern madness, making it even madder. She was madder than the maddest March hair. Wheei! Crazier than the most deranged Hatter. Hee-hee-hee. Lunier than the most fucked-up little Hitler. She pulled faces, blew air-bubbles, danced at nothing, then her and Joel had a shower together and sang with deep voices under sparkling rain. In there they blew air into each other's genitalia, too, wouldn't you know. Ho-ho-ho. Pay/ play? Way/say? Push and Blow, sorry, Stevie and Bernie, on

189

the other hand, as sane as anything, would never have sex together again. Ever. Stevie couldn't face it, he told himself in his ultra-private skull. And Bernie? Well, Bernie'd never really be up for it again anyway, if the truth be told. (The Stevie and Bernie Winter's show!) The sensation, or the desire of the sensation, had just gone. It had melted. Like snow. Neither fancied either any more. It was as simple as that. Neither fancied either. These things happened in life. One day you woke up, stole a morning glimpse at your partner, and, hey presto! It was all over. Who the hell are you? Aighhh! It's a terrible thing, the mind. It is the only true beast on this bestial planet of ours...

'I'd love a flat like this,' Bernie felt the urge to comment in Francine's mad absence.

'Absolutely.' Looking round. Stevie toasted himself his own good taste, though. It took a while to acquire, good taste. One wasn't born with it, naturally. Francine's apartment, for example, had none, even though it was spectacular. No, Stevie wouldn't like to live here in its present condition, even though he wouldn't mind owning the place. The original paintings were childish, to him. Puerile even. Although she did have an original by the actor Anthony Quinn of a man with wonderful eyes sitting on a donkey under a very blue sky which was quite good – bought for her by Johnny from the man himself.

Two glasses of icy champagne on an empty stomach did wonders for the perception.

A secretive person for the most part, (except when mediocrity forced itself upon him) Stevie now declared that he was 'Most hungry,' in this apartment that he thought had zero taste, but whose layout and location might've suited. And when Francine and Joel appeared again, naked, he felt the urge to tell her this. However, like his apparent hunger, in time he suppressed it because he was genuinely shocked at Francine and Joel's nudity. Yeah, shocked. They'd showered. Fine. But they were not going to get dressed again. Fuck it, man. A floppy-dicked Joel, lounging around. Stevie, in his private, silent, perfectly elite world, (and why shouldn't it be – it was a difficult concept to achieve) thought that Joel looked all right, actually. In fact he rather took a shine to him, now that he fancied Bernie no longer. Joel and Stevie? My God. But Stevie could suddenly see them as an item. Unlike Joel, of course, who saw only Francine, then, being, he believed, heterosexual. (Could Joel ever see himself balls-deep in Stevie, or vice versa? Well, it might not have been totally ruled out, as Joel actually wasn't all that sure if in fact he only fancied ladies – in a subliminal hum). Showing-off, Francine had to literally prevent him from mounting her on the sofa in front of the affronted guests!

Joel's hard-on was a bit embarrassing, though, being, as it were, small.

Even to Stevie, who, urbane, virtually never got embarrassed at anything, he found the little spectacle a little silly, a little tense. What on earth was Joel going to do with that tiny thing? He turned from it all in an appalled air. Good taste? Good God. But then Francine, now probably genuinely insane, probably genuinely deranged in her kicked-in reactionary-depression, flashed her bare arse to the world as she got up and waggled it, swigged from the cold bottle of Moet, burped, gripped her breasts, pulled tongues, then vanished into her bedroom where she did twirls like a little girl trying a ballet frock on. And then she did actually try a ballet frock on. Oh boy. All white and sparkley it was.

Poor kid.

Like the rest of us she would die in the future one day – or was that the past? Bernie couldn't say. There was one

191

single day allocated for all of us out there. But for her it would be in about 270-years time, he reckoned as he heard her singing to herself in the other room. (Would that be a Monday?) Did it matter which day of the week we died on? Deranged, her future was all behind her. Unhinged, her past lay all before her. What was happening now (whichever "now" that may be) would somehow remain forever-there, she was convinced as she swished around in front of a full-length mirror. It would always exist, somewhere, somehow... just, being-there. Had Francine had too much sun while abroad? Possibly. Joel presently joined her in the naked bedroom and dragged her to the big white bed most gruffly, being a part-time rapist. He then fucked the life out of her, briefly, with horrible gritted-teeth.

Ouf! Oi! Ow! The ballet frock helped. It did the trick. Rapists of course always needed some form of garment on to, as it were, take off. To remove. But by the time the Chinese arrived Francine was womb-sucking her lover like an octopus, so it really wasn't rape. They were both making terrible noises in there, too, in pleasure. Stevie shouted for the money to pay the delivery guy downstairs, as, naturally, he wasn't going to pay for the takeaway himself. (I beg your pardon? Me? Pay?) It was, ah, by the lamp, ah, on the shelf, ah, next to the phone, apparently...

Much squealing. Oh, for fuck's sake! He had to go downstairs to the security door to get the food, of course, (how tiresome) and fancied he could still hear the animalistic din from there, standing motionless on hand-painted solid tiles. He gazed wearily upwards to where it all came from, and, as in the jet on the way home, the gazing confirmed for Stevie the curvature of the earth – albeit the other way round. That is, from the ground up. But as we now know... that was Stevie.

192

Joel and Francine ate the Chinese in the nude, post-coitally. It seemed they were half crazed, and kind of hedge-dragged-ruffled. She hadn't once mentioned her father, Bernie noticed; Joel's DNA filtering into her bloodstream was obviously free to spill anywhere it now pleased. When Johnny was alive, though, yes, when Johnny was alive, Bernie surmised, Joel's DNA knew about it. Joel's DNA was worried about Johnny, because it was being watched. But now it knew that he wasn't alive, seemingly. Joel's DNA could party all it wanted. And party it did. It ran amok in Francine's womb. It too drank champagne. It too feasted on Chinese food. It too kicked up a fuss. Perhaps that was why Francine never once mentioned her father: she wanted Joel's grey goo to party in her fallopian tubes and give her some fun! Yahoo. Let's go! But the Atlantic Ocean was also in there, and the Atlantic Ocean eventually blocked these tubes with its dried salt. But no biggy. There were too many people on the goddamn motherfucking planet anyway. Ooh. Easy there. (Not very PC). But there were. There were too many goddamn motherfucking people on the goddamn motherfucking planet!

The following day in goddamn London, and a grey goo now descended from the sky. Yes, unlike Gran Canaria, it was raining. Heavily. The heavens had opened. Splashes abounded. But rain was nice, surely. It was cool – huh, literally. It gave us 'many' the life we so clung to. (Rain had always had a bad press in Britain, though. Weather-girls had tut-tutted over it, using words like "unfortunately" and phrases like "can't promise" when they presumed we all desired permanent sunshine. Britain was an island in the north Atlantic Ocean. What could one expect? It rained there! Did it rain on purpose just to upset them?) With no interests outside of money, fashion, being-seen or watching

193

TV, (and of course nanotechnology: one 100,000th of the width of a human hair, that's what it was) Francine took her friends for lunch/breakfast to a trendy unnamed restaurant in named Chelsea, in this rain. But it was atmospheric, rain. It changed you. (Maybe that was why it had always had a bad press in the UK. Change?) Splashing puddles and warm wet smoky smells. The gorgeous blur of lights and traffic in the watery city. It was quite beautiful, really. Quite... yes, atmospheric.

The owner of the restaurant, naturally, knew Francine – though a man quite unlike Marco. He was camp and thin, clean, 50-something and put-upon – though with kindness – well-groomed. Yet he kept a shy, low profile. Soaked, the gang of four now entered the tree-coated vestibule. It smelt good. It smelt of cleverly-cooked food and civilization in there, as well as rain-coated clothes. However, minutes later and Francine was crying at the table. Yes, sobbing. She was suddenly missing her father, missing daddy. It was starting to sink in, just like the London sky-water on her back. Grief was beginning to take a hold of her, the slob. Grief the pig, the prick... ultimately. Even though it began the healing-process – grief was a twat, when it came down to it. (Who wanted it to call!) And grief had sunk its yellow claws into Francine's delicate bones, quite delicately...

Without embarrassment, Bernie rubbed her back and said nice things to her, while Joel gazed around on the lookout for pussy. Tweak! His antennae craned his neck to another table. Oh, lovely. There it was. English. Posh. Lightly tanned. Shallow as fuck. A spectacular, fabulous lay! And her friend, too. Yum-yum. Yum-bums! But Stevie moralistically frowned at Joel's promiscuous glare, the hypocrite, and Joel momentarily ceased it. Resuming the gaze, he himself frowned at Francine's dumb antics, as he saw

194

it, when Bernie, himself morally observing Joel's gloomy frowning, offered her a silk handkerchief, saying, "There, there," as though consoling her, which indeed he was, when the shy maitre d' arrived to see if everything was okay.

It wasn't; but hey, who could do anything for Francine! Ever! Who ever anywhere could make Francine Coy "okay" when she bloody wasn't okay? Yeah? Well, perhaps this helped. Minutes later a type of fight actually broke out by the lavatories between three overweight, soft-looking businessmen in very tight suits. It was quite an hysterical thing to behold, quite astonishing. There were sudden raised intoxicated voices, (the grim shout of violence) one or two hearty pushes, then a kind of six-arm embrace combined with dragging movements and table-crashes. Women screamed, standing. Glasses smashed. Waiters rushed in to separate them. Joel, from glaring at walking-sex, laughed his head off at it. (Violent people always laughed at violence themselves). Then, in a perplexed instant, the moralistic owner telephoned for the police, as one of the puffed businessmen threw a misplaced punch. It caught a waiter on the ear, who went down crying, holding his pain. He was Italian. With that the other two waiters gripped the punching-man around the writhing arms and wrestled with him until they held him still, which wasn't easy. The other two men continued to push and pull each other and yell out-of-control insults. Now everyone, except our gang, was standing holding their mouths in shock. Francine, now no longer weeping, just gazed in genuine consternation. For it was a fairly harrowing spectacle, actually. A fairly horrible thing.

But then, before the police could get there, (and boy were they trying in all that London traffic) the men became suddenly overly-exhausted and slumped down on the floor

195

like well-fucked walruses. So when the police *did* arrive, which wasn't long, and the two big well-armed short-haired radio-crackling insensitive black and white behemoths stormed into the building like gangsters in search of their lost money, the maitre d' rushed them to tell them that, quietly, "There is no need for any more violence. Everything is, ah, okay." He calmed them in gestures. But the police had been called, and the police would act. They somewhat brutally arrested the three affronted businessmen, pulling them out of the restaurant, sweating and gasping, telling the two waiters to "Mind aside." The maitre d' was up the wall. Oh, his lovely restaurant! For although the men couldn't fight – even remotely – it was an ugly scene nonetheless, not at all good for business. And then outside in the street, as a police van came screeching up to the premises in front of a perturbed but wet London audience, the men remonstrated in the rain but were gripped harder and pointed at by the arresting officers. So they shut up. Four further offices staggered from the van. It was soon all over.

And then, during this mild chaos, Francine noticed through wet eyes one of her female coke-dealers still standing at the back of the restaurant. She gesticulated to her that she'd like a gram or three – if poss. A long nod. Hmmm, nice to operate under the very nose of the law, she vaguely reasoned. She'd left the table before anyone even saw her stand, and was soon in a pleasant-smelling cubicle, quivering with a fistful of notes.

Sniff sniff. All done. Whush!

Yes, the rush was instant, the charge of power almost overwhelming. Wow. Time for Mrs Hyde to make her wild appearance. Time for a... Tiger?

Back at the table and only Joel really noticed what had transpired. Yeah. Mr Sniff-out-a-deal. Francine was then

196

momentarily in a kind of glossy suspense as she sat; but that quickly subsided to be replaced with a, a, definite glowing sensation in her bones with a calm sense racing through her heart that could have fired-up the Space Shuttle. She'd be able to jog across the USA in a single day, she felt, then run for President of the world in the evening! Jealous Joel watched her twitch, frowning enormously, asking for a line himself. Francine frowned back as if to say, What? Joel frowned again as if to say, Please. Francine frowned back as if to say, No. Joel frowned again as if to say, I beg you. Then Francine frowned another frown as if to say, Eat shit, sucker…

Eating shit, (and did it taste bad) frowning Joel was now only one week away from his fate. He should have only been one minute away from death. But things had changed. Fate had changed.

It would have been the classic hit. The text-book assassination. *The old Hit and Run deal?* Yes, Johnny had done more than anyone could have believed, than anyone could have imagined. (His plumber father would have been so proud). For Sly-1 was ready to go. He was hovering outside in a stolen car, just down the road – London-cruising at a snail's pace with false plates. (He needed the money, brother).

Sly-1 never messed-up. No. Never. Psychos rarely did. But the police van had altered things: that wasn't banked on. Sly-1 hadn't taken the notion into account that the police might have been called to the posh Chelsea restaurant to arrest some fat unfit fuckers, as perhaps he should have done!

Shit.

In the "safe" restaurant Francine denied Joel his final request for cocaine.

197

5

THE WRITER WAS the go-between.

In a posh club in the West End, amid competing bars and jostling lights, Joel Maize was still alive when Fate – in the guise of Johnny Coy's dark ghost – expected him to be dead. Yes, Fate expected a lot, when you came to dwell on it. Fate in the shape of the magnetism of the universe? It expected a lot. And Francine was as high as a freefall parachutist...

She tugged at Joel's sweat-soaked shirt in the sparkling mayhem-darkness. She wanted something, though she wasn't quite sure what. Well, she always did. She always wanted something. But usually she knew what it was. This time she didn't. She didn't know what she wanted. So she began to shake as she clung to moist fabric. It could've been a delayed-reaction to witnessing a kind of fight in the restaurant earlier on? Or something like that. (She *did not* want to get blood on her face). Again, though, Joel was busy watching pussy shake its ass. "Son-of-a-bitch..."

No, Francine was not happy. It was, more likely, the four or five grams of coke she'd done throughout the day and the evening that was giving her the shakes. *Zapp!* A terrible delusional vibration shot through her vibrating veins. Mistaken, she believed that, all to the tune of a perfunctory beat, her father's ghost was lurking at one of the bars. She was sure she'd just seen him... it. She tugged at Joel's shirt again, even harder. He looked at her in the illuminated darkness with an awful lot of disdain. 'What?' He did not wish to have his libido dwarfed by the rich bitch he'd had to put up with, as he was now viewing the situation. Yeah, man. Gees. The things I do for fucking money! 'Joel, it's daddy! Look! It is! It's daddy! There!' 'Yeah, right.' He

198

reverted to pussy-searching. And, again, there it was! No, it was everywhere! Life was hard when you had a dick. It was so distracting, to say nothing of frustrating, it had seemed to Joel. It was all there, but none of it was for you! None! Aw, man. These goddamn bitches…

Francine leapt from her seat in search of Johnny's ghost. Oh, she knew. She just knew. It would be the kind of thing daddy would do, she reasoned. He'd become a fucking ghost! A heavy daze of depression then flooded over her as she pulled men by the shoulder and knocked girlies out of the way. However, daddy, or daddy's ghost, was nowhere to be seen, alas. Even in the darkest corners of the club, he lurked not. But perhaps that was it. One couldn't see a ghost. One could only sense them. Yes. One had a definite sense of another ethereal being, a deceased being. This straw-clutching appeared to help her searching soul. It appeared to appease it. Francine was appeased, kind of.

Francine was delusional.

Again the London police were called (or tipped off) and the London police came a-crashing into spoil the party – as was their wont. Suddenly there was a full-scale raid on the premises – shouts and orders everywhere. WPCs held onto girlies, and big ugly blokish coppers gripped the boys. Ow. Oi. Careful. The floodlights were splashed on, and the whole thing seemed like an act not unlike Marco's patio with Susan. It was as though it was a kind of camp stage-show or something for the armed-forces. Some lad growled healthy abuse to two big scuffers who, in turn, sprayed something at him and he went down in a ball of writhing flesh, holding his eyes. Not nice. Not nice at all. (Was that legal? His girl-friend reckoned not). Then the senior copper yelled mono-syllables into a loud-hailer for people to start lining up for searching. "Everyone," he bawled, nodding at a couple of

199

strays who were skulking by the exit. Francine mentally ran a camera all over her body to see if she had anything stashed. Shaking, she even looked up her hole. Whoops! She had, did. She had stuff stashed on her person. Shit. And Joel too. Well, he always had stuff on his person, even when he didn't. What Francine was carrying however could only be read as Personal Use, surely. No way was she dealing. (She didn't need to fucking deal. She wouldn't have known how to deal anyway). No. She had never dealt. But Joel had, did, and would again for 300-years, had Fate given him the chance. Here, though, he only had enough on him to raise a volunteer horse up a hill. That's all. To float a horse up a hill.

But Fate, like Time, worked in mysterious ways too.

Looking suddenly suspicious in the alien bright lights, Francine saw that Joel was then told to "Stand still and shut up!" – not that he'd been saying anything. But that phrase, that un-called-for aggression, appeared to be the catalyst. He was now standing well apart from Francine Stevie and Bernie, who were standing close to the exit by the skulking strays, and as two coppers approached him in order to search him, snap, he went for them with a knife.

Naive, perhaps, even genuinely insane, but Joel in his crazed mind believed that he was doing the right thing. (Look at me, mom!) He believed he was protecting Francine, protecting her money, which would one day be his, he'd believed. He knifed one policeman in the throat in less than a second, and the other, as he dived at him in a reaction, right in the chest. He then went berserk with the blade and began stabbing both men about the body in a slobbering frenzy before all the other police rushed him and rendered him very unconscious. The club became instantly panicked. Most people made an escape in this surge, while the entire force was occupied with Joel, and then their colleagues.

There was a lot of blood; an ambulance was called; Joel by then had a fractured skull…

Outside in the glinting West End night around Soho Square Francine ran for her life. She was already forgetting about her lover in the dash: she felt him leave her mind as she ran. She'd been there only with two gay friends, she envisaged saying. What was Joel thinking of! Yes, she'd deny him if it came to it. Who? Sorry, who? No. Never heard of him.

But it wouldn't come to it. Other people in the club were arrested before Francine was even seen leaving. Bernie and Stevie were very distressed. Running, they each contemplated what sort of person they'd been on holiday with, (Francine, that is) what sort of person they were going to spend 300-years with! She was psychotic. No question.

Memories would be of leaving the place down some melting steps, of shouts and yes, of people being pushed and pulled, of terrible violence doled out by the police, of running through Soho en route to Chelsea as though catching a stolen moped, of terrible violence doled out by Joel.

All mixed up. It was 4 a.m. before there was a rendezvous back at Chelsea Harbour, and an opulent apparent safety. Francine had somehow teamed-up with two of her girl-friends from the London scene, who were naturally highly intoxicated. They had no idea she'd even been away, let alone knew who Joel was and that the great Johnny Coy was dead. They didn't care, either. "Your dad's dead? Gosh. We had a great party on Friday, hic. You missed out, darling."

What had transpired had done more than shock everybody. It had freaked them out into a conglomerate of shaking, with the exception of Joel, who, yes, was right there at their side. Francine had never seen anybody slashed

201

or stabbed before. Especially a policeman. It had been so grotesque. So gruesome. They would surely now be hunted. They would surely now be considered as part of the crime. They would surely now be on the club's CCTV and eventually turned in by someone who knew them. Shit, she thought, shaking. They would surely now be as fucked as Joel, who, beaten almost into unrecognition in Francine's vision, was slammed into a cell to be told that he would die shortly. A cop ran a slow finger across his own throat, even though Joel was out of it. For you did not do that to a cop and get away with it. No way. (Shouldn't Joel have been hospitalized?) As things would transpire in the vision the first policeman died that night anyway. He just didn't make it to hospital. The jugular had been cut: he'd lost too much blood – everywhere. The second would be placed in IC for days, only to suffer a collapsed lung and other complications. But he survived.

Doomed Joel had taken Fate into his own watery hands, it seemed.

Fate had it that Joel was going to be found *hanged in his cell*, as the terminology went. Joel was going to be done by a kind other than himself: the illiterate yob in authority kind. (Was there a more frightening kind? Yeah, and like all these hardened killers suddenly become suicidal? No way). Bernie would later contemplate this as he slowly developed the need to somehow document what he'd recently witnessed, as he saw it. No one ever could be found hanged in their cell without a little help. Without a little push. Or, more likely, a big push. No one. It was secret execution, Bernie would come to believe, becoming then, post Francine's episode, the go-between. Yes, the writer. What, Bernie? It was all worked out. Or would be, one day. Bernie would work it out – somewhere in the future. Francine had been contemplating

202

what was happening to Joel, even though Joel was there beside her, talking. By whom would he be executed? (She shook). At which time of the day? (She trembled). And why, for Christ's sake? (She quivered). It didn't matter which time of the day. Cover-ups were massive operations when done by the authorities, Francine reasoned. It was all worked out. It was all planned.

Back inside un-worked-out Francine's flat, as the London dawn grew brighter yet paler in its born-again grey groaning, the lady had finally gone genuinely, clinically, insane. It was all an episode – all hallucination. That was it. A powerful mind-experience. The two 'friends' had done one, not even coming up for coffee or whatever. Bernie and Stevie too were quaking as they sat in opulence watching Sky-news at dawn, afraid at Francine's antics at just running out of the club like that and trying to get home, jabbering on about a police-raid and Joel, who, yes, was still there beside her even though she clearly could not see him. They would surely be arrested that day! she insisted. They would surely be traced and imprisoned until they were 70! She watched Sky-news like a hawk to see if their faces came up from CCTV footage. It didn't. Nothing. The breaking news instead was about an attack on two (decent) officers in Manchester while doing their honest duty…

The suspense was killing her.

6

THE SUSPENCE KILLED her.

She never slept. She just stared. It was the following afternoon before the cocaine-episode that was, strictly speaking, begun in the Tite Street restaurant began to lift, and when she actually saw Joel she freaked again. "You. Your. Your. Here!" He hadn't been anywhere. And no one had been stabbed or killed. Nothing. There wasn't even a raid on the club! Furthermore as none of them had slept (the light looked grim) a heightened sense of paranoia filled the room too, like thick ink. No one knew what Francine had seen. It was all so cerebral. She attempted to tell them, but it was all garbled and rambling. "Joel, well, he, erm, oh, the police, yah, and like a raid and shit, and then like he killed one of them, yah, and like they all killed him, yah, and, well, erm, huh?'"

Then she screamed.

Then she kept screaming.

Stevie tried to calm her. Joel then muffled her.

No good. Tomorrow was Injection Day. Screaming now would somehow get her body's blood kind of all mixed up, Joel guessed. Also, naturally, someone might hear it and maybe even report it – thereby endangering the operation, as he saw it. No way could Francine cope with an injection, let alone even know what was transpiring! She'd just run. So what could they do?

'Stop screaming!' Joel screamed. 'Jesus, man. Quite it already! What's with you, huh?' He bawled all that with his hand pressed firmly to her mouth – she struggled to pull it away. She screamed into the sweaty palm. It was subliminally unpleasant for her. Sleep was required, yeah. But sleep was not what they could get with all this motherfucking screaming! But then Francine slept while standing up, but only for two seconds. She dreamt for two seconds on her feet. (It was the quickest power-nap ever). It helped. A wee catnap. A swift stork-sleep. And it was during these two seconds that Joel saw her in another light: his access to assured sex! Chill, bro. Francine was Joel's access to a lifetime free of masturbation to relieve that motherfucking erection he always got which made him think bad mother-fucking things: she was his assured female body: his sex play-thing. Francine was Joel's love, which could have been inter-preted as *access to sex without too much bother*. For if men, hence Joel, liked anything, it was the lack of bother where sex was concerned. So during these two seconds of standing-sleep he smiled at her as she ghostily came to then floated to the bathroom for a piss. He smiled his reassured-access-to-as-sured-sex smile, which was basically a sly leer, an evil grin. Joel recognized, even in his hatchet-man's dark depths, that there was an ethereal godliness in the golden heaven of his post-ejaculatory sensation into Francine. He never aw, man – wished to be without it. No. He never wanted to be back 'out there' looking for it again, looking for what he already had, what he already knew couldn't really be replaced. Not fully, anyway. Hence how he always, when it came down to it, appeased her. That, to Joel, was love. He appeased Francine because he didn't want to be without her body. Simple. True love: access to assured sex, for him.

Do what? Peeing, Francine needed neither love nor sex at that particular moment. Well, at least not Joel's kind of love. What she needed was to be somebody else, somewhere else, and in another time altogether. Was that possible? Standing to wipe, what she needed was to maybe get this damn injection over with then take off out of London. Right off, right out, right on? Back in the living-room Francine then

205

manically declared this:

'We're all going to live for 300-years! We're all going to Liverpool as well!'

Wha? Joel looked at her without any love whatsoever, that is, without any desire at all. 'We're all going to where?' Not to mention why? Francine's make-up had long-since smudged and run from the previous night's chaos, and she looked like a circus act. (She was a fucking circus act!) Acting, Joel glanced to the other two, who, not acting, just looked even more perplexed. Neither Stevie nor Bernie had ever been to Liverpool before, and neither Stevie nor Bernie had the desire to. (They'd heard very bad, very-very bad, stories about the place – beyond the mawkish facade). No. Not Liverpool. Anywhere but Liverpool. Joel looked back at standing Francine. 'Why, babe, huh?'

'I was conceived there,' Francine calmly informed them. 'Daddy was doing a UK-tour in 1966. They played Liverpool for three nights. Mummy was with him. They stayed at the Adelphi Hotel, apparently, where they made me. I was born the following year. I've got to go there. I've just got to. I've got to be close to where mummy and daddy made me. Do you understand? We'll get the train.'

'Train?' gasped Stevie, holding his chest.

'Yes, the train. You're coming with me, and I want to go by train. I've never been on one before. We're all going to Liverpool on the train!' She skipped to the kitchen for a mug of coffee. While there Joel fancied he heard gunshots outside in the Chelsea afternoon. But it couldn't have been. No. Not in Chelsea. It couldn't have been gunshots. Blam! Blam! Blam! He swaggered to the window to gaze down at London's posh end.

Joel saw, or thought he saw, big Susan standing staring up from the pavement below, cloaked in his great black cape

206

or whatever it was, holding a rifle. He looked again. 'Hey,' he then yelled, 'there's the big guy! Look! Down there! The big guy from the island! What was his name? Susan! Yeah! That's it! Gees, man! That's him! Look, guys!' Joel turned to see the others in the room, turned back, and Susan (if it was Susan) was gone. He wasn't down there any more. Nobody came to see.

Cool Joel then gazed out of the window in a distant frown.

That's when Francine declared that she was going to bed, and that they could all either fuck off or hang-out. It didn't seem to matter which, to her. Off she floated, semi-dreamlike, followed by the gazing Joel who, in turn, was asked if he was deaf. 'Didn't I just tell you to fuck off?'

'Yeah, but you also said that we could like hang-out and shit. Can I hang out of you, huh?' Ouch. It was a bad simile, and Joel knew it. Consequently, he received a slammed door in the face. But no biggy. He'd had doors smashed into his nose, his brain crashed into doors before. Doors, who? 'Man,' he then calmly whispered into this door, which was painted in the colour smock, 'if only I had a gun. Yup. A big fucking gun to fire up that bitch's ass! Oh yeah. She'd squeal. Real loud.'

A subdued Bernie and Stevie believed him, lounging around on the vast sofa there. Moving like a spider, Joel then said that it was time they all forced 'this bitch' to sort out this goddamn nano deal. Yes, forced. How, was never revealed; for he switched on the TV as he spoke, watching some guy in a movie run past a door at speed, the roar of an engine chasing him, tyres screeching, him jumping over a wall, someone else flattening himself against the wall in the shadow of a blazing sun with a cloud of exhaust-fumes filling his face, the scene ending in a puff of gunsmoke.

A mesmerized Joel then eased his words into a kind of spoken breath. 'Yeah, man, like we, ah, need to, ah, get it, sorted out, huh?' The TV movie had completely arrested him. It had taken his wanton attention. And then, to his genuine consternation, Susan actually appeared in the damn film. There he was, standing tall, in Johnny's type of leather trousers (much bigger of course) and a green waistcoat, smoking a cigarette. It was the next scene. Big Susan (I'm going get that son-of-a-bitch who called me Sue) moved in on the drug-dealer. Joel's expression altered to that of honest dismay. Was he going crazy? He scratched his head. Looking round for support, Bernie and Stevie were simply cuddling on the sofa, softly, clearly getting comfortable for some shut-eye. Turning back to the TV screen Joel watched in awe as Susan (was it Susan, really?) beat some jerk up who held a knife to his face.

'What the fuck is this, man…?' Joel checked his pulse.

'Hey,' said Bernie groggily, 'is that who I think it is?' He pointed to the screen but Stevie had already fallen asleep on his little chest, so Bernie too just closed his eyes and never thought about it again. Well, not for at least 180-years…

Joel, in 1999, watched as one guy was shot in the head, and the back of it opened like a split melon. Brains and skull spread out all over the floor. Joel momentarily recalled the bum he'd de-hearted back in New York. For the first time since that incident he felt bad about it, albeit vaguely. He felt bad because he now thought that maybe he'd get arrested… one day. That was all. Maybe he'd get life for taking out someone who was, truly speaking, taken out years ago. Yes, Joel was a killer. A murderer. Just like millions more throughout the ages: he had killed. (It killed him.) He saw his own reflection in the TV screen as a shadowy scene transpired. He stood tall amid buildings and dead bodies.

He'd've cried, had he the capacity. Joel Maize would've shed tears at his own reflection. But he didn't. He didn't have the capacity for tears. So he just stared. He stared at his own reflection in Francine's big TV screen like Narcissus gazing at himself as it stood in between tall buildings, and which was now showing Susan the actor act like The Hulk. Susan the actor strolled towards the camera, seemingly, and gazed out of it at Joel, gazing in at him. 'It am good, huh? It am very good.' He gave a wide smile; then, with a whistle, disappeared once more. Joel's expression altered to that of a child at a night-time fairground. He really did need to stop taking drugs.

7

AGAIN HER FATHER's severed head was on the pillow next to her. And that's what woke her. That's what freaked her. There it Was, staring up, all wretched and torn in a ghoulish smirk. She remembered being cold, at home in her flat at London's Chelsea Harbour. No, she was hot, but not at her apartment on Gran Canaria – she really was at home at Chelsea Harbour this time – under a silent, glossy, grey-gloomy English dawn…

Francine Coy, naked on her huge bed, became momentarily iridescent. This time, though, it was because of her psychotic state. Again Joel Maize was beside her in this light, dealing privately with the remains of his own ultra-bad dream. He didn't stir. Push and Blow were asleep in the other bedroom. (She called us that occasionally, the cow). Confused, Francine looked at Joel's body and didn't have a clue whose it was. It was as though he'd appeared to her, from her dreams, or, more frighteningly, from *his* dreams. Normally she would have screamed the place down then gone for a knife. But not here and now. Here and now she was standing over Joel, half-marvelling at his bloke's skin with all its hairs and seeming roughness. For if Joel was anything, he was a bloke… in her English perception of the concept. A dude? Francine didn't know about that, didn't know about anything, then.

She was utterly daunted.

A dawn-daunting.

Unlike Gran Canaria, London was as noisy at dawn as it was as dusk. It was a noisy city, London. Maybe the noisiest. Usually made noisier by Francine's vocal chords, too. And this morning was no exception. For she began to shriek again. A fairly quiet shriek, it has to be said, as if in fear more than anxiety, which it actually was. Her thought-pattern ran

210

like this: when a person dies they are not seen or heard of for more than a million years, which equals eternity! Never! Ever! A million years! Her father was in this category, she could now perceive. The great Johnny had gone into the great abyss to meet, God, who? It was true what Nietzsche said, if God loved us he would make it nice for us, forever. All would be well. He would also be in agony knowing that many of us rotted in Hell simply for doubting His existence. But of course God did not exist, and had never existed. Furthermore, He never would. Human beings simply invented Him, as many human beings know. And now Francine was becoming one of those human beings. She'd shrieked (Aiigghhhh!) in the certain a knowledge that God had never ever existed, and that God would never exist, and simply that twisted men across the centuries had brought Him into being to compensate for their own impotency. That was it was. And that's what also made her shriek. Nonetheless it felt good, this knowledge. It felt good in its terrible torment. Her father had returned to the void from whence he came, and Francine now knew this as a truth. She was now a genuine atheist, in other words. She'd never see her father again. Ever. That's what she knew. That's what being an atheist meant: you knew for certain when people died they existed no more, anywhere, ever. And that had sunk in. For Johnny now it was the same as before he was born. *Back to The void...* or so Francine believed.

With great courage came a degree of recklessness, however. They were hand in hand, really. Well, maybe not recklessness, but a sense of, in your bold courageousness, something could go wrong and you bloody well knew it. Francine suddenly felt fearless and resolute as her sounds woke Joel, and she knew right then that today she would for certain get that Nano-Injection in her blood, no matter

211

what it might do to her, no matter when. She'd just do it. That was it.

Joel naturally woke in shock.

Yes, it was his dreams. Man, they haunted him. (He looked haunted – or was that hunted?) He was haunted. Joel's dreams haunted him like a sick ghost. For if Francine's metaphysical pain had chilled her soul on that cool early London morning, then Joel's dreams had gripped his unconscious mind as a JCB picks up soil. Ow! Oi! 'What the…?' Coming to, he shook these dreams, these demons, off like a pro. Be gone! And they were gone. Their hauntings began to fade…

But Susan? He was on TV. He was in a motherfucking film!

Aw, man. No matter. Joel needed to focus. Yeah, knock yourself out, he thought. He needed to get Francine on track for the meet with this fucked-up injection guy, whoever he was. Because Joel goddamn knew that yes, he too wished to live for a long time. So he needed to focus Francine, somehow, in some way. A tall order. From experience he knew that she could start up and bite and take her revenge on everything that had escaped her unfocused brain. She did it all the time. So he scratched his tainted head and looked daunted. (Haunted?) But Francine was already focused. She was way ahead of him. There was nothing Joel could do to focus Francine any more, because she was now completely and utterly courageous. Francine was now courageous because she was reckless. Hence focused. But Joel didn't know that. He also didn't know – and neither did Francine – that by some foolish mishap on Dunant's part there was, in that metal briefcase of his which was sitting in a steaming hotel room in the big bad city, only one Nano-injection loaded with the tiny robots. For they already existed, these

212

nano-probes. They were a definite reality. Alas there would be only one of the fabulous four who would get a 300-year lifespan. Only one! But which, ah, one? Even Dunant didn't know this, being, ultimately, a boozer. Yes, the time-worn piss-head incompetent scientist! Dunant did not know that, as Johnny had requested just two shots of timeless fun for him and the lovely Francine, he'd only assembled one, the drunk. The inebriate.

Francine floated purposefully towards the door to her apartment.

Purposefully, almost stately like Buck Mulligan, she then strode through noise and people en route to Hyde Park via Sloane Street with her mini entourage trailing her like a pack of baby tigers. Boy, was she going to give this world hell for a couple of centuries for what it had done to her! (What had it done to her?) She'd teach it. Like her father before her – although without ever being famous for the anodyne drone of pop – she now knew where people were going wrong, where people had gone wrong, and, where people *would* go wrong. And fuck her, she'd put them right! Oh yes. Here's how it is – okay? Are you listening? Remember, remember, Johnny Coy! On Francine strode somewhere along Sloane Street in her own autocratic world. The fantastic and irregular world that was truly art had no place in her heart and was not for the world at large, Stevie knew, and might even have said so had he not been so exhausted at the pace. Because he could see that, in her eyes, daddy was right, pop-music was art! Pop-music was what the masses needed in order to give themselves a happy existence! Or at least the semblance of it…

It mattered little how Francine was ultimately thinking, as we'll see.

Joel was again being stalked by his assassin, who had no

213

idea, naturally, that they were about to go up to Liverpool. He'd have no problem striking in busy London, though. No problem at all. He'd done it before. He'd do it again. He'd left quivering heaps of dying flesh on the roadside as a myriad shocked eyes had looked on, abandoning the stolen vehicle in another street with no prints or even dabs of DNA, then walking away whistling. *Whistle While You Work,* was his favourite anodyne heap of shit, the shit. The Prick. The cool cold bastard. He watched them from close by as they strode along. Johnny Coy had made this evil cunt relatively rich over the years. That, more than the fucking Wallbeats, was *his* legacy. Yeah, you're a king, mate. You're great. No sweat, Johnny baby. We salute your memory. Wonderful. To make a trained killer rich? Oh, great. Johnny and Stalin. Johnny and Saddam. Yeah, no sweat.

Among the crowds of an overcast yet warm Hyde Park was Doctor Dunant. Even though he wasn't, he appeared to be lurking in the bushes. He appeared to lurk in between people. In between the crowds. What was it with scientists and lurking? Where did that come from? Lurking, Doctor Dunant was a man from a darkened world, clearly. Bernie took him to be about 50, with greyish bits of hair around a bald pate, glasses over eyes that had seen the worst, the very worst, things. He was sheepish, and very badly-dressed: baggy green trousers tucked into a sickly yellowy flowery shirt – arm obviously lowered from carrying the weight of his metal briefcase. It was like a blind date. Francine had arranged to meet him at a certain point between the Albert Gate and the Serpentine which only she knew about, and there he was, at this point, looking round, standing out wearing a pink carnation.

Both Bernie and Stevie found it all a little ludicrous, actually. In all honesty they did not believe that this guy even existed, let alone had such injections which could give someone a 300-year lifespan! If he did exist, then they didn't believe he'd show. But there, apparently, he was. Consider: who would let a complete stranger inject them with a liquid containing tiny robots? Think convinced longevity. Following behind Joel and Francine (it was a hell of a walk along Sloane Street from the Chelsea Embankment – it took them ages) sweaty Stevie and Bernie were now feeling slightly nervous at the prospect. It seemed clear that the mad Francine was not only going to let this guy inject her (and not a meat one) back at the flat but that she would also probably be very insistent that they should be injected too – with metal. And that's what was making them nervous. An injection, by some nutcase? Stevie and Bernie were now thinking very negative thoughts about the whole thing.

'Hi, Miss Coy?' The accent was, to Joel's ears, educated New England. Now Joel too was a little touchy. 'Hey, this is a great park!' Dunant insisted. 'All this space in the middle of London! Wow. Absolutely fantastic! Do you know what, I've never been here before. It really is amazing.' Looking round as though amazed, wanting to be everybody's friend, he smiled. A Jumbo Jet crossed close by for landing. It was lower than the low warm grey clouds. Lower than the roar of traffic. Dunant and Bernie looked up to watch it, wanting to run. 'Awesome,' Dunant gasped, his Americanism causing Joel a grimace.

'Yes. I am she.' All formal. Mad and formal. 'We'll take a cab back to my place. We can do the electronic transfer there. Is that all right with you? Doctor Dunant, is that okay?'

215

8

STEVIE HAD AN urge to stand at Speaker's Corner. He did not act on this urge, yet it was a difficult urge to nonetheless suppress, this speaking-urge. And as he looked across the glossy park towards Marble Arch where no one congregated, he suppressed it – even though he wanted people to hear what he had to say. For Stevie had a lot to say, he believed. The only problem was he just couldn't have been fucked saying it any more. Yeah, that was the problem. Well, not any more he couldn't. (Could people be fucked hearing it?) Hadn't he said all he wanted to say? he gloomily thought as, amid the constant hum and throb of London's traffic, they left by the Albert Gate, quickly catching a black cab back to Chelsea.

However, 'quickly' was not how the cab travelled. Francine, in the centre of the back seat there between Joel and Dunant, felt that she'd finally become a woman – taking charge of things, as it were, slowly. And how does a woman feel? (Brave, eh?) In a word, Experienced. One needed experience to become a woman, Francine deduced. Experience didn't soil, it purified. Experience illuminated. Francine was now an illuminated, purified, experienced woman! She felt that she was shedding the traits of her spoilt youth as so many used skins. And as the hours wore on experience got rid of the things which had made her cruel and obnoxious – or so she believed. (Why, even the taxi-driver said so!) Her childish traits which had only hampered her before were now floating away – she could see them drift. Yes, *used skins*, seemed to be the phrase which suited her.

Dunant, on the other hand, actually looked like a used skin. Experienced? Well. Think OTT experience. Joel wanted

216

to murder him just for the way he looked. For Dunant stank the taxi out with the odour of grease and sweat combined. But then so did Joel: it wasn't a good start. Joel wanted to take his consciousness out of time for the rest of time. He wanted to negate Dunant's consciousness from the whole of existence. That was how Joel thought when he thought of murder. He thought of a consciousness being plucked out of time like an old hoop-game.

Stevie, on the other hand, had the desire simply to hold a mirror up to the man's face and say, Look, this is you! But he didn't, because he didn't have one on his person. But he would've done, because that was Stevie. Francine, in her newfound maturity that was humming in her brain like the rattle of the black cab she sat in, only had the desire to remain silent. She had a silent desire. (Can one have a silent desire?) Francine did. Or rather she had the desire to remain silent, which was perhaps a different thing altogether. But nonetheless it was a silent thing, this desire to keep her mouth closed in a silent inclination.

The taxi-driver, in an antithesis to silence, knew not what silence was nor had the desire for it: he babbled from open-of-door to pay-at-destination – like an old woman. But that was the cabby. (*Cabbies*. It was possibly endemic. Who knew. Everyone fancied themselves as an intellectual at the change of the millennium, including cabbies – and yet everyone also believed that they were anti-elitist, if indeed intellectualism was elitist? Such a conundrum). Francine paid the gab-cab off at the Chelsea Embankment (peace at last) and they finally embarked up to her apartment for the Nano-Injection!

The door creaked open as she boldly unlocked it.

What awful slabs of horror Dunant's hands were, she noticed. What terrible implements. They had ended animal

217

life in their time, these slabs. These slobs. They had it printed all over them: *We have ended animal life in our time.* And Dunant's face, too. It also had coldness and oblivion printed all over it. For it just stared, like a donkey in a silent field stares. Francine, still changing, still altering, (though not staring) suddenly had an urge to fuck Dunant off, with his death-hands. Yes, the world was now a different place for her. No, she suddenly did not want to live forever. "Get out of my house!" she almost yelled at him, as she was soaring high in her reconstruction. So high that those who could not fly could hardly see her? (Again, thank you, Nietzsche). For she'd shed skins, thus she would not perish. Well, not yet, at least. But then again it would be nice to live for 300-years and be wealthy enough to indulge in whatever took your fancy, so maybe a long life might be… *In-flux*, her mind was. It was moving all over the place. And then, before she knew it, Dunant had placed his briefcase down on the table in the lounge and had opened it with a clonk. Five normal-sized hypodermics lay flat in grey foam. (The one for Johnny, alas, would no longer be required)…

'Oh, gosh,' gasped Bernie, 'I really do hate injections!' He turned away. 'Are they just simple syringes?' asked Joel inquisitively. Dunant nodded with a puckered mouth. He looked to Francine for the transfer. Yes? By telephone? He shrugged, then, attempting to recall with a big dumb frown which of the two had the robots in (although it was really only one) he plucked out one of the needles and held it up. A silence descended upon the room which could not even be penetrated by the injection that was held up into it. 'Er, money first, if you please,' Dunant coldly requested.

Francine already had her mobile out. She immediately phoned her Swiss bank, who already knew that a trans-action was to take place: it was a very large sum. Dunant

218

gave her his account number and sort-code with *his* bank in Boston as she held the line. Another second, and the deal was done. A large sum of money was transferred from Francine's account in Basel to Dunant's in the US. Just like that. He heard Francine speak the digits, and swallowed. Then he gulped as she hung up. Deal done? That was it. No problem. Good God. Wow. It clearly felt good to suddenly have a lot of money. It felt good to suddenly know that money would never again be an issue. It felt good. It felt very good. And Dunant, now looking and feeling good, even though he distantly stank of stale booze, gazed round for the first customer. All were in awe at the swift transaction. Was it really that easy? Francine, not doubting for a second that everyone was going to receive the nano-probes, and looking quite good herself even though she'd just spent an inordinate amount of money, held out a long arm to be first…

A flick, then a squeeze, then a squirt of clear liquid. Then, ouch, in it went! Francine's heart-rate increased. A pulse bulged on her neck. She imagined that she could sense the probes already surging around her bloodstream. But it felt good. Like money, it felt very good. It felt like *life!*

Bernie went next – to get it over with. Pale, he literally went limp as the needle approached his tanned skin. 'Christ,' he breathed as it slid deeply in under it. Whump. It was a rush. The fluid fizzed in, and Bernie, no drama-queen really, fancied that he could for certain sense those robots fuelling up on his blood, then getting to work on his body straight away. All done. It was a remarkable sensation. Couple that with all that money flashing across the Atlantic and it was a bit like having iron-filings filtering through the marrow in your bones then being ignited by an atomic flame! He could almost hear them clanging. But then he went light-headed

219

and slumped back into Stevie's arms, only to be eased down on the sofa.

Fuck-wit, thought Francine, rubbing her arm and kind of smiling. Then she wanted to sob. Daddy (another fuck-wit) should have been here. Daddy should have been getting the same. Daddy the great musical genius should have been living forever! But daddy had gone. Daddy was no more. Bravely, she fought the tears back. But they lodged in her throat. So she swallowed them. It was a big gulp, swallowing lodged tears. Watching Joel take the sting, she wondered truly if she'd done the right thing. You know? Joel, who? He was a stranger to her, really. Almost. A john. But when Stevie received the probes she felt all right again. Yeah, Stevie was cool. He was okay. A faint smile. He was good people, as Joel might have said at one stage. Her and Stevie could have a laugh for centuries. He'd keep her company during all that change, during all that moving from place to place in order to appear, well, at that age to those around you even though you might be... 201, 202? I mean, come on! We'd talked about it before. You're with people for a number of years, and you don't age, while they – even a little – do. Aren't they going to say something? You could be a great, great, great grandmother and still look 32 in the face! Wouldn't those you'd got to know ask what the hell you were doing to remain so young? But of course you couldn't have children. That would be one avenue you could not go down. Think about it. Unless they got the injection too, and you were going to create a long-living colony as indeed Francine visualized then no, a child growing older while you did not would be out of the question. Also, would you move with the times like a youngster, or would you be stuck in a mental time-warp? You'd just have to keep on moving in your own inimitable way which would be idiosyncratic like nothing

220

before. You couldn't stay anywhere for more than 10-years, we reckoned. Yeah, there were lots of things to think about. *We'd* have to keep moving on, and we knew it. *I knew it.* I'm sure Francine knew it, too. Or it perhaps dawned on her then. Maybe the scare of it hit her right where she lived, once she'd had the expensive jab. Ouch!

As I recall she never even looked at this Dunant character again. She retreated to the kitchen as he made his unceremonious, sheepish departure. We were all somewhat stunned, I think. We were all somewhat shocked. Was it now a reality? We didn't really know. It would be difficult to say for at least, well, 10-years. We didn't really know. For all we knew Dunant had conned Francine – but somehow we doubted it. I don't know why, but somehow we doubted that those injections did not contain what he said they contained. True, poor old Johnny had done some checking on him before he popped his clogs. As far as Johnny was concerned Dunant was legit. A legit booze-smelling rogue…

London, though, never looked better, to me – as it glistened below in the rain.

And then the train up to Liverpool…

Christ, the things we did for Francine, when I look back! It was the following day I think, or possibly the following week (hey, you try remembering things that happened two centuries ago!) and the sun was right out and burning the ground, as it did then. The sun, the big dim sun. (Yes, the planet was warming, but not for the reasons you've been told.) Totally convinced that we were all going to live for centuries, our first day as long-livers was not a particularly good one. First of all the train was packed – even in First Class. Secondly none of us wished to be going near to Liverpool. But then, as we four were filled with the notion

221

of a massive lifespan, we obliged Francine as one might wearily help cripple No. 999 into the healing font. I mean hey, we had time to kill!

There were delays on the line, as it did then. The lines delayed. How can lines delay? Huh, they could in the UK. Lines could delay. (They don't any more, I have to tell you, because there aren't any lines here). Our line delayed then, however. It delayed. Stevie and myself played cards at the table during this delay, while Joel and Francine just gazed out of alternating windows in silence: the rest of the carriage, I noticed, talked to itself. Fortunately there was AC, so it never got steamy. But just to sit on a motionless train on a sunny afternoon feeling the minutes of your life ticking away into nothing, even if it was going to be a *big* life, was no one's idea of fun. Yet it was in this time-waste that I observed Francine alter some more. It was one of the most peculiar things I've ever witnessed, I think. And brother, let me tell you, I've witnessed some things over the myriad decades! To say that she grew up in those handful of days would be an oversimplification. She did more than grow up. She transmogrified. Francine Coy transmogrified into something rich and strange. It was something close to beautiful, I think – on the inside. She kind of became what she should have become, what she never really knew how to become, yet what appeared to be somehow inevitable: she became, in those moments, no, don't laugh, a superior being. No messing. It was a bit like, while in her presence, that sensation all of us have no doubt experienced during our teenage years: the notion of being in the company of older young people who seem to know stuff. One is in a kind of coy awe at them. Some intelligent observers from the American Wild West days used to say the same of the Sioux and other tribes: *We were in the presence of superior beings.*

222

Others had also noted it of certain SS officers who were not simple thugs. Well, to me, Francine developed this same quality. There was something to her which seemed almost indefinable. She had transcended...

Even though she needed to go to Liverpool.

Lime Street Station wasn't so bad – we only had the one moron approach for money, then a vile comment from him as he was told to get lost. But as we walked from the station to the Adelphi Hotel down Lime Street itself – a matter of ten minutes or so – three more approached and Joel eventually pulled his knife out to the final one. Bad news. A bad beginning. There were bound to be CCTV cameras everywhere: silly boy! However, Joel was, as has been commented on, shit-hot with a blade when it came to it. And it came to it then, inside big bad Scouseland. Restrained, all's he did was to threaten, then deftly put the blade back before any lazy fat scumbag watching a street-monitor could see. The bum pulled back in shock – Joel moved quickly on, thus confirming to Stevie and I yet again that he was your genuine American Psycho. So, again shaken, not stirred, we were in the rich foyer to the Adelphi before anybody could say *dunce*...

'Lunch?' Francine asked for food to be sent up to our rooms. Last night I dreamt of being in a plane on a long flight and falling asleep. I saw a huge wasp, the size of a man, crawling along the aisle, flickering and probing with its monstrous antennae. The vision, as I recall, came back to me then, as we hung out in the rooms watching TV and chatting. I fancied I could hear this thing arching along the long corridor outside our adjoining suites, looking for me. It was chilling.

Stevie finally spoke, as we masticated stale sandwiches and slurped hot coffee. 'Did you see Joel move on that skint

223

bloke? Fuck me. The guy only asked for money. Did you see him go? Did you? It was most disturbing, I tell you. I wasn't happy about it, Bernie.' He sat back in leather-surround and shook his attractive head. I knew then that I still loved him. Part of him was part of me. That's what love eventually comes to. You are part of each other…

I still loved Stevie at that time. I probably still do, some-where ancient and deep inside. 'Amazing,' I commented. 'I wish I could have that sort of nerve. I know it's horrible and all that. But just to be able to react that way sometimes? Think of all the shit we've taken over the years, darling. Just once I'd've loved to've pulled a knife on one of those bastards and been capable of using it!'

'Bernard, I really do worry about you sometimes. I really do.' Shaking his head.

'Don't.' Francine and Joel appeared in our room as I said that, and we assumed they'd already eaten. But of course there is and never could be any literal meaning to anything, especially assuming and presupposing things. They both claimed to be suffering a reaction to the nano-probes. (I know now that that couldn't have been the case. But that's for later). Both said that they were kind of itching all over and feeling very agitated. Although Francine hardly spoke. Joel not only spoke but he danced his agitation quite mani-cally before us as a kind of demonstration. He looked insane in his crazed writhe, the cunt. Writhing, he squirmed a dance-flurry which could only have been brought on by drugs, I guessed. But it was also quite amusing. (Did you know that you could die of sexual-frustration? It has been clinically documented throughout my long life. That's why ugly fat blokes, who are still around even today, looked so gloomy. Not only were they not going to get laid, but they were going to die from it, too!) Francine told him to stop it,

224

as to her it could have been sexual-frustration, this madness of Joel's, of which she liked occasionally to dole out – sexual-frustration, that is.

'It's a very strange feeling we have,' she told us, standing in the middle of the large room and looking curiously perplexed. 'It's as though something alien and alive is trundling around our veins, itching them.' (Well said). She looked to Joel for a response other than a dance. She did not get one. So she looked at me as a cow in a field looking up from grazing to see who was walking past. It was that sort of curious simple perplexity.

Then, a second later, she insisted on finding the room she was conceived in – immediately. We were on the 8th floor. She reckoned she was conceived on the 5th. (Who knew how she knew? But she knew). So we (like berks) dropped down three floors in the lift/elevator and stepped out onto the 5th – a silent, kind of ghostly, unused floor…

This was the floor, Francine told us. 'I just know this is where my seed was sown,' she whispered wistfully in the ghostly still air. Mere silhouettes, that's what we were, on that quiet floor. London, then, seemed like a distant vast noise in a kind of poetical desolation to me. Its wonder was having an effect: I wanted to be there, to be home. 'I have been too long in the surge of the big city, guys,' she went on. 'I've had images of this place before: my golden hair flowing in these corridors as though liberated in the countryside somewhere! This is where I belong!'

Wha? Joel looked at her, then at us. He too was perplexed, though for different reasons to Francine. Stevie edged in and, quiet, gently pushed open a closed door that was not locked. It was room No. 507. Clearly it was the very room – or so Francine wanted to believe. She stepped towards it in the dim light and drew in a big expectant breath. Alien,

225

she moved inside. It was a very nice, a very cared-for yet well-used room. Thankfully, though, she'd been too long in the big city, which also meant intense cynicism. And it was this, finally, that made her see sense: after all that she simply turned and walked out of the room, saying, 'Well that's that, then, huh? Let's get drunk.' On seeing, or feeling, this hotel room, she kind of reverted in a single instant. Again it was one of the most peculiar things I've witnessed. Madness didn't really cover it.

'What have you seen?' asked Stevie, peering inside the room. 'Nothing. I've felt it. I haven't seen it.'

'You've felt what?' Joel said, glancing over Stevie's shoulder.

'I've come full circle, that's all. Now I can think clearly.'

Think clearly? Gosh. How rare was that! I remember thinking, wasn't it the recurrent dream of Western thought that consciousness could be present to itself in the cool light of reason? Whatever Francine saw or felt in that (imagined) room seemed to actually achieve this for her. Her consciousness was present to itself, I guessed, in itself, there in her head, outside of all textuality and other opaque snared repressions. Well, that seemed to be what she imagined, I imagined for her.

She'd acquired the motherfucking impossible!

Was that possible? To be your own consciousness beyond language? It seemed unlikely. And yet, from the worn-down sumptuousness of the Adelphi Hotel, we wandered lonely as grey clouds towards Central Station, in the rush and dirt of the modem city, (they no longer exist) in a late summer glinting and floated (or were sucked) into a tiny pub off the main drag called The Globe, I think. It was an uphill pub, this tiny squat. Uphill and quiet. That is one trod upwards from the downwards-pointing bar

226

across a strip of mosaic to the nearest seats, and there was a lot of woodwork and decoration in the place as well as old photographs of Liverpool. (Again, all these buildings have long-since departed the planet now). It harboured the usual strays and uglys of early evening city boozers – the big-eyed, the big-faced, the swollen-eared, the scarred, the scared, the undead – but, to me, and even Stevie, it had a certain atmosphere to it. It was cute. Kind of cosy.

'Fuck me,' rasped a Scouse voice in a sullen fanaticism to a fat barperson, 'here we go!' He was referring to us, because, instead of looking at us with his comments, he slyly smirked at the lady he'd made the comments to but clearly (if you know about these sort of things) for us. 'It's the Time-Bandits!' he then comically added, leaning on the ornate bar with his pint.

9

TIME-BANDITS? HA! HE didn't realize how accurate he was!

All these ancients are long-dead now…

Look, before I tell you what happened, let me tell you a bit about the 23rd Century. It's a very different world to the 21st, to the one I knew while I lived in that time. Just this one phrase should do it: *time-travel*. We have time-travel. We can move through time. It's a reality to us – happened upon almost accidentally by a 'scientist' who had been working on space-vacuums and spin-systems. He'd spun vacuums at enormous velocities, generating immense space-bending heat, to actually create transversible wormholes in time and space, only here on Earth.

He'd also developed a tracking-device which could be traced anywhere in the solar-system at any period in history, he claimed. He left this device, so the story goes, in one of the protective bubbles he began working on at the time, and placed it and the bubble in one of his engendered worm-holes. The next thing he knew he was receiving a signal from c.1690, somewhere on Earth. He then reversed the spin and brought the bubble back through the Wormhole, with the tracking-device safely inside.

The next step he used a mouse, then a chimp, then himself, naturally – being a scientist. He then developed properly this bubble-vehicle, which had controls inside to reverse the spin itself in the era one was at – stretching across time. It became a mass-market thing just like the motor car…

What we have now in this silvery transparent bubble-vehicle is something that, not so much places a human being back in time, but creates a kind of *time-bubble* in a given, time-slot for that human being to peer out of, as it were

228

– in that time. It's a bit like being in a car in your time. One trundles through towns and lanes without getting out, without getting wet, watching it all through a protective film. Our time-machines don't have glass as such; but the principle isn't all that different. The main difference is, I suppose, is that you can't actually get out of the vehicle. The time-bubbles are sealed, unbreakable bubbles: one remains in one's own time physically, but steps back.

It's not perfect, but it works for me.

We can't go forward, as the future – even though I'm speaking to you *from* the future – hasn't yet happened for you. Well, it has in a sense, but our time-bubbles aren't sophisticated enough to transgress that domain. They can only spin backwards, alas. It seems they can't be spun into an epoch of oncoming void, for some reason. Why I'm divulging this to you is to put you in the picture as to how I came to be writing about Francine Coy, who, incidentally, died of pneumonia at the age of just 72 back in 2039. I had all but forgotten about her, to be honest, (one has so much to remember) when I happened to be taking a trip back to that time for both pleasure and research. The research being a pleasure too, as it's for my own personal link with the era I'm originally from. (It's a hobby of mine. I like to write about things from past eras – like this book, for example. Yes, books. They still exist, only in different form!)

The bubble was set, the date fixed.

No one, I knew, could possibly see our silvery gossamer time-bubbles, as, not much bigger than a large chair, they come from, as I've just said, a period that hadn't yet happened to the people who were being visited. (The tenses get very weird here. There have been reports of people allegedly seeing ghosts and lights and other strange phenomena over the years, which we in our period reckon are time-bubbles

229

somehow becoming visible to them. Some people do have that capacity).

Anyway, I dropped down into the spinning void and emerged in 2039 in somebody's house in London as the satellite news was on. Nice and cosy, it was, even though I couldn't smell it or anything.

The world was still in flux as to the way it would ultimately alter. I'd gone back to witness (again) the near-collision with the asteroid – for entertainment purposes, naturally – which skimmed off the planet and could actually be seen doing so by millions of stunned people all over Europe. It was a great streaking fireball in the sky. I'd gone back to view it many times before. The authorities, naturally, denied the existence of this rock until days before a possible impact, which was also amusing to observe.

The residents of the household, of course, had no idea that I'd just emerged from the future in their living-room. For it is all done most silently, no fuss, no visual. We simply slip from the spinning-void with not a hair our of place and into another period of concrete reality in a matter of seconds. Splash! Hello. But I observed something on the local news this time concerning the demise of an old London sloane. It got my attention. The name Francine Coy was spoken, and I fell motionless in my own ancient body as I sat comfortably in my brand-new personal time-bubble.

They showed a still photograph of her funeral. I gulped, and stopped the bubble's floatation-trajectory right in front of the transparent slim-line TV, right in front of the family who were watching it through me. They showed earlier photographs of Francine in her 50s, and that was the very first time – as we'd gone our own separate ways years before – that I could see how she had not received the probes: she looked her age. She looked well, but she looked her age.

230

I was overwhelmed.

I still look 29 in the body. I had assumed, after all these years, and, the last time I could recall thinking about her, that she would still look 32ish: I never doubted that she didn't get the probes. I always thought Francine and I would meet up again somewhere, someplace. If you saw me – my hair, my skin, my bones, my organs – I'm still 29. I'm not, I'm 236! But I still look 29. Francine looked mid 50s. I was totally shocked. She'd been conned. I needed to find out how…

And I have all the time in the world…

40-years ago I was injected by super nano-probes which have increased my lifespan to an indeterminate number. (Many people now have them, in fact). I could live for 80,000 years for all I know! What happened was this, back in 2003, long after Stevie and I had split up, I won the National Lottery worth 11m. That's what made living for so long so magical. You perhaps cannot imagine what it's already been like for me indulging in my every whim for 200 long years! It is beyond heaven on earth. It is a concrete Utopia borne from the greatest concepts of the universe.

I live alone, and happy.

I get up every day after five hours sleep or so and just live-out all this time to myself, all these millions of hours I have to view this planet in – with millions in the bank simply growing by the year – and never getting ill. But even I can't imagine living for 80,000-years! It would be to live entirely without the notion of death, which is what I do now, only vaguely. Ah, if only Francine had known! If only Stevie had stuck with me!

My *whims* often come in the shape of time-travel detective-work. It's great. True, it's difficult to get a real feel for a period when one is confined to a bubble; but at least it places you there in that time-slot and you can see what's going on with your own big eyes.

Every time has its slot, it transpires.

It is, as I say, a concrete reality. It's like flipping through a file.

It's amazing how the history books of your time had got things completely wrong. In many cases – like Jesus Christ for example (whom I've actually seen) – the entire concept is not only wrong but completely misleading, too. But that's for another story. In our story I went to see how Francine Coy, one of my dearest friends, was conned. And that's how come I came to write this. From discovering in 2039 that she hadn't, unlike me, received the nanobots, (as I say, I expected to bump into her somewhere along the way, in some country, in some time-slot) I decided then to go a little further back to, yes, 1999, to when it all started – see what I'd missed.

I can go back and record what I'd witnessed while I was actually living in that period – which is always weird to do.

You can't imagine what it's like having 200-year-old memories!

Guess what? The brain can retain that much! Astonishing, but it can. Our brains have the capacity for so much more than we ever thought possible in, say, the late 1990s. Century's old memories feel not much different to 20-year-old ones, actually. (You know how a memory becomes kind of mythical after about 20-years?) My 200-year-old memories of the late 1990s are by now legendary to me, but they are also hyper-fresh. Consequently, I get back there a lot just to confirm what I can't quite place as a man of 236.

Documentaries too, as you can imagine, are transformed.

All the history records are now changed. We have reams of footage from every period in history, including the

232

dinosaurs, which were nothing like we imagined – but I'm not going to tell you about that.

Can you visualize sitting in a transparent bubble 1-metre away from your grandfather, who is playing somewhere as a 5-year-old?

The probes are wonderful at DNA repair. If I walked into a bar you would place me at 29/30, I guarantee – should you care to look. Only if you engaged me in conversation would you know otherwise – that is, if I didn't act. Then you'd hear things which would not quite suit my young apparent years. If I was acting at being a 29-year-old, which I've learnt to do well, in whichever decade it might be, then you wouldn't give me a second thought. But we have to keep a low profile, us nano-long-livers. We have to act when watched. All that bullshit back in the 20th century about under-educated berks with guitars and attitude speaking pearls of wisdom in their 'music' was true. They don't – didn't. But they acted as though they did. It's the same with us. We act. We are actors.

10

WHAT HAD HAPPENED was I discovered that by traversing into Doctor Dunant's study where he prepared the nano-injections in America, in his incompetence he'd only filled one phial with the probes instead of two, as dear old Johnny requested...

Guess who inadvertently had the one pumped into him?

Back to Liverpool, and 1999. It was some hours later when Joel was stabbed and arrested. Yes, he'd almost bought it again – though not by Johnny's hit-man. Recently I'd gone back in time to check out that so called Sly-1. Talk about weird. Think superiority-complex. Think *I'm not just in it for the money!* He was definitely ready to strike in London, too. However, he did not follow us up to Liverpool as I first believed. That particular evening we'd left the tiny Globe pub and sauntered down Church Street to, of course, the overly-famous Matthew Street. Funnily enough it was down below in the grotty John Lennon bar that a bloke from Glasgow was telling us how he thought The Beatles were overrated, as people occasionally did when we were out, and I thought for a moment he was Sly-1. (These names are mostly irrelevant to 23rd Century readers – except for minority-interest groups who go back to the 1960s for time-travel fun. Other eras appear to be much more interesting, statistics show). Music to Stevie's ears, as I recall, had Stevie been able to understand him...

'And another thing,' this Glaswegian snorted, 'them songs? I reckon Lennon and McCartney did ney write them! I reckon management or whatever employed song writers t' write 'em! Aye! Lennon and McCartney did ney have it in 'em, like. It's all a fucking con. Lennon even admitted as much hisself: fucking Yoko wrote most of Imagine!' He

234

waved us away.

'I can't understand a single word you're sayin', man,' Joel eventually remarked.

'And you can fuck off, too!'

'Did you understand that?' I asked him.

Joel didn't. Sorry, *did ney*. These conversation. But they're true. People used to say things like this to us. Whether we attracted it or not, it happened. Complete strangers would tell us that The Beatles (*The Who*? No. Not The Who) were not as great as everybody thought. Not everybody in those days was a Beatle fan. For one thing they didn't exist any more! And not everybody went along with the popular money-pumped mainstream – even those who didn't know of things beyond the popular mainstream! I'm just documenting the way it actually was for us here, which, you have to admit, has been entertainingly insane and interesting thus far: that's how it went down for us. Joel turned to an aloof Francine, who was staring at the brick walls, down in this shithole of a bar. 'Is this guy talking Norwegian or something?' He meant it, too.

'No,' she sighed, 'he's Scottish, you prat.'

'What the fuck does that mean?' Joel genuinely did not know.

'It means he's not Norwegian!' Francine retorted, swigging her bottle of coloured piss.

'Are you, er, Scottish?' Joel very Americanly asked. The guy turned his back to us – as was the lone drinker's wont. He then, well, drank alone, happy. Happy also with the deluded idea that he was going to live for centuries, Joel tapped the guy on the shoulder. 'Hey, buddy, I asked you a question!'

With that Stevie and Francine downed their drinks in one and literally left the premises to rap-music, simultaneously.

235

I looked to Joel, then to my friend and lover leaving, then back to Joel again. 'Leave it,' I suggested, making to pull his arm. 'Come on. We're going.'

Outside in the busy atmosphere of an illuminated Matthew Street, amid the night's jostling crowds and movements, I observed Francine finally disaffect from Joel, who eventually left the bar. This time it was total, I surmised. Sky-high naturally on his own special drug-concoctions, Joel then made like an aeroplane and glided towards The Cavern club. Well, not the original Cavern, but a club built next door to where that place was, and resembling, for the tourists, the original's design. Although it has to be said that back then most people went along with the notion that the new building was the original Cavern, for some reason. Anyway, Joel was doing his aeroplane-bit along the walkway, with a bronze statue of John Lennon opposite winking at him in aeroplane-gliding admiration, and looking, well, like John Lennon in bronze: that is, a feigned, skinny coolness, when he tripped and fell and went to blame somebody else.

All this was on CCTV footage, so it can be proven; but as Francine, Stevie and myself walked the other way, and Joel began ranting at this innocent guy, it blossomed into a street-fight. Huh, a Matthew Street-fight! No way could any CCTV link Joel to Francine and us that night. We were never really together in that sense on the street. Even the patrolling CCTV vans looked the other way while we were out. But as the shouting rose, and two more blokes came to indulge in the hurt, Joel pulled his blade. The three of us (the remaining three) then headed swiftly up towards Castle Street then down, I think, Water Street to the Albert Dock, leaving him to it. Call it cowardly if you like. Call it disloyal or whatever you want. But we'd just had enough, so we left him. We sensed that it was the end of Joel anyway

– if not literally, then certainly as part of the long-livers, as I'd named us. In no time the police were heavily on the scene; but apparently Joel had escaped the vicinity. The two fat blokes who had joined the fight were easily arrested as they'd been fighting in between themselves; but the guy whom Joel blamed for tripping him up had also escaped, vanishing with Joel's knife…

Joel would be stabbed by his own blade.

At this stage Francine told Stevie and I that, even though her ex-lover had the probes (as she believed) in his system, no way was she ever going to set any fund up for him or anything like that. 'He's on his own,' she coldly gasped as we smelt the River Mersey in the summer night. Joel, if he was to survive that night's violence, would have to fend for himself – for 300-years!

Motherfucker. 'Hey, beautiful,' someone called to Francine as we eventually slid into a blue bar on the Dock itself. (It may even have been called The Blue Bar, for all I knew). It had communal toilets, I noticed. Boys and girls pissed together. There was a big gay-scene, too, in Liverpool, which, actually, turned out to be not all that bad. The place wasn't as awful as we had been led to believe. Stevie, I saw, sensing that this might have been a kind of surreptitious gay-bar, had been eyeing one or two sweethearts. (He may even have returned to the place long after him and I split up). 'Come and sit here!' this guy called out.

Francine looked the other way. At the bar there was another lone-drinker. Alone, he drank. Or just watched. Who could say. Personally I've never really done the lone-scene. Five times in 200-years? This guy looked okay, though; he wasn't Glaswegian, anyway. It was Stevie who broke the ice as we ordered our drinks. I felt that he thought the loner might just have been…

'No. I'm not. Sorry. But hey, it's cool. My name's Terry. What's yours?'

'Stevie. This is Francine, and that's my, ah, partner, Bernie. We're up from London for a few days. This is a nice bar. It's got a good feel to it. Are you a local, then, Terry?'

'I am, but only geographically. I'm not a Scouser spiritually, if you see what I mean. There's more to Liverpool than football and soap-operas. I hate all that crap. Lots of people hate it. See this place? I remember when all this was derelict dockland. It wasn't all that long ago, either. As you can see it's full of students now. I'll bet not one of them could imagine what's gone on before here, with all the shipping and the amazing stories that must have been attached to that.' He sipped his pint of lager, the only pint sold on the premises, as far as I could tell. This guy liked to talk, clearly. It had probably been building up in him, what with drinking alone and all. I think Stevie was sorry he spoke, however. The guy looked about 40, with a good head of hair and strong features resembling something Germanic, I thought. There was a faint sadness in his eyes which I could only glimpse when he said certain words.

'What's it like being working-class?' Francine then astonishingly asked as a party-piece, not caring for anything really or anyone, at that moment.

Terry gave a wry snigger. 'How do you define working-class?'

That seemed to take Francine aback. 'Accent and money' she quickly said.

'What about them?' He frowned at her.

'Working-class people have one, but they don't have any.'

'Is that it?' this Terry gasped. 'That's how you define people? If you don't mind me asking, you haven't been around much, have you? I can see that you've got money

238

and all that, but you haven't been anywhere other than money-places, I'll bet! And besides, to my ears you have an accent. Are you working-class? Were your parents? Is that it? Hey, no need to get all pissed off! Take it easy. Oh. Okay. Goodbye, then. Nice to meet you, er, Francine was it? Yeah. Bye. See you later.' He drank again, then gave a laugh to himself, shaking his woolly head in the blue ambience of mingled chatter.

If Joel had've been with us he'd've no doubt either stabbed or butted this loner, and Francine would've expected him to. But he wasn't; neither Stevie nor myself were going to do anything. Besides, I thought the guy had a point: Francine *was* childish, when I look back. It was good to witness her squirm a little, for once. Oh, she was rightly whacked off as we found a table far away from him. But there was nothing she could do about it. She just had to sit and roast. She just had to sit there and contemplate all her money and all the long years ahead of her where she could spend it, glittering away there in the far distance.

Sullen, she then phoned Joel on her mobile. His phone was switched off.

11

IT TURNED OUT that Joel was under arrest in hospital, having being knifed, (and knifed back in return) and would, as it transpired, be imprisoned in Liverpool's Walton Prison for four years before being deported back to the US.

We never really got the full story, but it seems the guy he picked on caught up with him somewhere and basically set about him with the blade. Joel, being a numbed-out nutter impervious to most pain, retaliated. Both were left badly injured, unable to walk due to massive loss of blood, and were soon arrested on the pavement in the dead of night – which didn't truly apply to Liverpool as there was no dead of night there. The following day Francine hung around the hotel ghost-like, pondering her parents and how they must have been all those years ago when they stayed there: how everything was then. Or how she imagined everything was then. Stevie and I went out to lunch somewhere close by, though she never joined us. She appeared quite wistful to me. She'd lost all that inner-beauty I talked about before. She only ate biscuits and drank coffee, lots of it. That evening she hired a local chauffeur and a big Jaguar through the hotel and drove us back to London in style and comfort, with more biscuits, vowing never again to take a train…

Goodbye Liverpool. It was nice briefly knowing you!

I remember we met up again at the Hayward Gallery some time after Stevie and I had split up (he moved out, not me. I stayed in our little flat until I was 40 – still looking 29) and she was totally changed. It was only about a year later, but it was a different Francine altogether. She even looked different: her hair was short, her make-up more severe, her expressions a lot sterner, her body leaner. We had a coffee and she was telling me about how wonderful it all was that

240

we were going to live for centuries, but she didn't seem convinced. Or at least she didn't seem overjoyed. By then I thought that the injections were a con anyway, in my own mind, but I said nothing. Little did I know that only I would be doing the centuries-living. It didn't become clear to me for a number of years…

'Have you heard from him? Have you seen him since he left?' She meant Stevie.

'No. Not a word. I don't even know where he is. To be honest I wish he'd come back. I've had one or two flings, thinking they'd get me over him. But they haven't. It's never the same, you know. We were part of each other, Stevie and me. We had a past. You can't just get that with anyone you fancy. It takes time. I'm not prepared just now to put that in.' (I never was – even though I've had an awful lot of it. From then until now I've only ever had flings and fucks and silly dates – but they suit me. I've never needed to replace Stevie. Besides, we have lifelike androids here which one can either love or fuck or abuse. I've even killed two or three: they can be repaired. But it's not the same as loving or fucking another human being – or even killing one, for that matter. Not that I'd know about that).

'Stevie was a one-off,' Francine then commented as she sipped her 11th coffee that day. 'I'm sure we'll all get together again over the next few centuries. We could even go back to Gran Canaria! Huh, I might even give Joel a call! He should be getting out of prison in a year or two, then taken back to America where he always belonged, huh, born-again! Yeah. I might do that…'

I looked at her, and felt quite tearful. She was so lost, so alone. So trying-to-be-tough. I was alone, but I could cope with it in the long run, I felt, even though I wanted Stevie back then. To me Francine couldn't cope. She needed people, even though she totally abused them when she had them. But money did that to you when you'd always had it, I believed: it made you naive enough to think that you could fuck with people completely and all would be forgiven and forgotten. And perhaps you could. Perhaps people were ultimately that shallow. 'What, you'd get back with Joel! Are you crazy?'

She stared at me oddly, holding her brown brow.

'Oh, I'm sorry, Francine. I didn't mean that. Hey, let's go and look at-'

'Bernard, I still miss daddy! I can't bare it. I think about him all the time. I so wanted him to be alive forever! What will I do? What will I do? I just... can't stand it!' She left her coffee and stood up. People in the cafe watched her; mostly, I thought, because she looked so... different. Beautiful, yes, but different. Unusual. I stood with her but she bade me stay. She then swiftly left the building and I literally never saw her again. I lived in London for another 11-years, but I never saw Francine Coy again. I looked for her. I don't know where she went, or what she did. She rented out her Chelsea apartment, then just vanished. And it wasn't until all those decades later, all those years, while I was snooping in my time-bubble, that by chance I saw she'd died aged 72! I just never saw her again...

I wish I had. I really, really wish things had've been different. Okay. Forget about it. That's it. You've arrived. Thanks for coming. You came in a time-bubble! How was the trip? Quick, eh? I know you probably think I'm a lunatic writing to you from somewhere like an asylum and, in a sense, I might as well be, but I'm not. I'm really here – buried in the future: it will all unfold...

Every day. Picture that. Every single day for two centuries, watching things slowly transpire, slowly taking

242

place and changing. That's what I've done. I've watched – I've observed – from different places. For the last ten years now I've lived here in Toronto, Canada. It's my first Canadian city, and I love it. Toronto is a truly great city. You should see it in 2206. It sparkles like a diamond. We have electronic pleasure-domes where your imagination gets connected in and is acted upon. The CN Tower is still standing, though others are equally as tall. We have launch-pads for outer-space on the roofs of buildings. The ten before that, Chicago, and all *its* amazing new architecture. (I could write a book on Chicago). The ten before that, New York. The ten before that, LA. And so on, or, so back, all over America. I've done what Francine wanted to do: spent ten years in major (and not so major) cities. But even now, at my age, I've only lived in five different countries! Five! I would need to live for thousands of years to spend ten years in every city and in every country. There's so much. And so few know of it. But I'm not complaining. It's been marvellous. It's been wonderful. I've never even been ill. I was injured once in a fall and by the next day the probes had mended my body. The probes even fixed my anus within days of the injection! The Bernie I used to be when I really *was* 29 is not the Bernie I am at 239! I don't even use that old name any more. My name now is Berstay. That's the way we use names here. We still have the old ones, but we add an extra syllable to depict either what we're doing or the way we (or others) feel we are – as people aren't given their names until their 11th year. I introduced the 'stay' bit to kid people that I'd be 'staying' around in whichever town I'd set up in. It also deludes me, which I like, because it can be a hell of bind moving on every ten years or so. Especially when you're over 200! Not that I have aching joints or anything. And that's another

243

thing with living for centuries: you forget. I don't mean your memory goes, because it doesn't, but you forget how things came about – how they arrived, who was doing what, where, and when. For instance I often forget that I've got nanobots and now supernanobots in my bloodstream! You just live, (for an awful long time) and don't particularly dwell on how you come to be living for that long, never thinking of death. The *whys* and *whens* become very vague – over the enormous years.

Nanotechnology has mixed and matched to produce new materials, too. There are things in nature now which nanotechnology has brought about by altering atoms. Things like the catabros, which is a creature that can move in and out of light molecules to produce new colours in the room it's in. The catabros is the most curious, supernatural creature you could ever meet. A cross between nature and technology. Weird.

Canada is much hotter than it was in the early 21st Century. Lake Ontario is warm enough to swim in all year round, and we even get tornadoes here. Ha, tornadoes in Toronto! It sounds like a good title for a pop-song, if there were any. Movies and pop-music are now minority-interests. The thing now is time-travel fun, and most people are obsessed with it. We even have time-travel stars, for God's sake – people who film themselves on 3d digit-cone going back in time, dressed like jokers and plonkers, and doing silly things in their time-bubbles. We have international screenings of them waving and blowing kisses at the front of historical battles, say, or at the scene of great shipwrecks at the moment of submersion. It's a bit like – and I've been back there to witness it – the way people were in the 1930s when the motor car became available to them. People today use time-travel as people from the 1930s onwards used their cars.

So watch out. When you're next abusing yourself you're probably being viewed by someone at close-quarters drifting invisibly by from 2206 and beyond! But don't worry. We've seen it all before. We're seasoned. *God is watching you*? Well, he kind of is. *WE* are watching you! But no matter. Thanks to Stevie, I have a solace in books. Yes, that nice place. In books I can still find how good life outside of them can be. For they make it rich for me. Books today however are no longer made with paper as they used to be; they use a new synthetic material which feels like paper and you read a book in the same way, but it's virtually indestructible. Synthetic books, they are – books born again, if you like – and they last for a very long time. I adore them. I have hundreds. (A bind when one is moving house). Yes, books. Even the word gives me ancient primary-value solace. Two centuries ago Stevie introduced me to books – the old books: I've never really been without them. His favourite novelist as I recall was Anthony Burgess. I picked up on him after Stevie's departure. But there have been others, too. Many. The long-dead-and-forgotten critics would turn further over in their invisible graves if they knew how many novelists from their time are still in print, *new print* – where they continue to be born again for new readers! Yes, they'd rot even more…

To modern readers names from the 20th Century are now ancient. To me – because I was around when these novelists were alive – they're current. But get this. I'll be reading people who are children as I write but will one day be dead-yet-read! They'll be ancient to new readers of the future. How weird is that? They will grow up and become novelists before my inquiring eyes, write, grow old, become legendary…

245

It's a funny old life, you know. You wake up one morning and think, hmmm, when I reach that particular year I wonder what the world will be like then – what I'll be doing. Then, the year comes, the year goes, and you wake up one morning, many years after that year, and think, it was nice all those years ago – in the distant past! You then become nostalgic for the year which, at one stage, was well into the future for you! Yes, it's a funny old life on this rich and strange planet...

Anyway. I'll be moving on soon, to another Canadian city. I'll be living happily, here in the future. You can depend on it. I just go from place to place, human to human, and take it all in. Thankfully I have no illusions about myself any more, so I never really feel threatened by anything. Also, I can report that less people fly into murderous rages these days than they used to – and I emphasize *less*, not all. But that has to be a good thing, doesn't it? True, human beings are still deeply intoxicated with their own personal lives, and to hell with everything else, it seems to me. This intoxication I have always found oddly disconcerting, ever since I was about 90 or so. I had hoped, as the time-lines moved along, that selfishness might have been traversed, as opposed to individualism. Ultimately, though, my hopes and expectations were not that great.

Lightning Source UK Ltd.
Milton Keynes UK
UKHW012235271121
394693UK00001B/7